BULLET PROOF

A RANGER THRILLER

JOSHUA HARKIN

INKUBATOR
BOOKS

Published by Inkubator Books
www.inkubatorbooks.com

ISBN (eBook): 978-1-83756-523-8
ISBN (Paperback): 978-1-83756-524-5
ISBN (Hardback): 978-1-83756-525-2

CHAPTER 1
2013

The weight of Frank Ranger's shackles grew heavier with each mile the prison transport bus drove. The whine of the engine droned along a long stretch of highway as midnight drew nearer. In less than thirty minutes, he would be delivered to the maximum-security wing of Montana State Prison in Deer Lodge.

One of only two other inmates on board the small bus spun around in his seat. He homed in on Ranger for the third time during the journey. "I know I've seen you 'round the Lodge before," Trevor Milano said, referring to the prison. "You got one of them faces."

Ranger continued to stare out a narrow, darkened window that lined up with his seat, ignoring Milano. Through the scratched, murky gray glass, he couldn't see the crisp Montana night sky the way he once could.

"At least tell me your name," Milano continued, leaning over his seat. A chain that ran from his handcuffs to his ankle bracelets was secured through a loop affixed to the base of his chair. It was supposed to restrict his movements, but Milano had pushed the setup to its limit.

"Sit your ass down," yelled one of the two prison transport officers on board. Behind the safety of the main cage, Officer John Brewer was sitting in a chair that faced the inmates while his colleague, Henry Foster, drove. An escort police cruiser was tailing the bus and was manned by a pair of overweight officers who looked like they were ready for retirement.

Milano waved off Brewer's order and kept staring at Ranger with a sardonic grin. "I'm gonna call you Hush. You know, coz you never talk."

Ranger didn't react. He was in no mood to entertain Milano's interest.

"What's got you down, Hush? Let me guess. Things didn't go well at the courthouse today, did they?"

Ranger shifted closer to the window.

Milano chuckled. "I'm right, aren't I? I know that look. You just got handed a long sentence. What'd they give ya? A dime?"

Ranger sighed at the prison lingo for ten years but gave no answer.

"Longer? A double dime?" Milano squinted and studied Ranger's face as if the slightest twitch would tell him everything. "No way. Life?" he asked.

A scowl enveloped Ranger's features. He couldn't help it.

"Holy shit. My boy's a lifer. Serious, man? You're too clean looking for that shit. What'd you do, Hush?"

Ranger said nothing. He'd given away too much already without meaning to.

"Milano," Brewer yelled, "one more word out of you, and I swear to God I'll lock you in the box with Fraley."

Milano turned around at the mention of Fredrick Fraley's name. The beast of a man, whom Ranger estimated to be at least six feet seven, was locked inside a secondary cage within the small bus. He had a shaved head, and arms that were too thick for regular handcuffs. After a long day at the courthouse, Ranger had overheard guards gossiping that Fraley spent his days in solitary confinement at the prison. He didn't play well with others. Along with a laundry list of charges, he'd apparently snapped the neck of his last cellmate when the guy complained about his humming.

"That's what I thought," Brewer said. "Now, listen up, all three of you. We've got thirty-two miles left before you pieces of shit get tucked back in your cells where you belong. Let's not make this trip any more unbearable than it has to be. It's bad enough we got delayed by six goddamn hours thanks to you, Fraley."

"Bite me," Fraley spat.

Brewer ignored the big man and shifted his focus to Ranger. He gave Ranger a hard stare. Ranger hadn't said a word the entire trip. He'd followed every order without question and had stayed in his seat. The officer should have been happy with his attitude, but as Ranger knew all too well, it was the quiet ones you had to worry about the most.

A minute went by before Milano spun around again. He couldn't seem to help himself. "Come on. Tell me what you did. We might not see each other again once we get to the Lodge. Give me the deets, and I'll spread it around. It never hurts for people to hear what you did to land in the big house for life. Most of the time."

Ranger faced Milano and stared into the man's eyes. Milano retreated a touch. He seemed ready to turn around and leave Ranger be when something caught his eye.

"What do we have here?" Milano asked, pointing to Ranger's tattoo on his forearm. "Oh shit, I know this one. It's a Battlefield Cross, right?"

"Yeah," Ranger muttered, finally speaking. He stared down at the tattoo and was surprised Milano knew what it was. The three-inches of ink was of a US Army helmet sitting on top of an M4 rifle that was facing barrel down between a pair of combat boots. It was Ranger's way of paying respect to the fallen soldiers he'd served with in the 1st Marine Division in Afghanistan. Their sacrifice would never be forgotten.

"You served, Captain Hush?"

"Sergeant."

"Huh?" Milano asked.

"I was a sergeant."

"Sergeant, captain. Who cares? Where'd you fight?"

"Afghanistan."

"And?"

"And what?"

"Tell me what you did over there. Come on. This trip is boring as hell. Give me something."

Ranger exhaled. It went against his better judgment revealing anything more to Milano than he had, but the moron seemed to enjoy talking to him. After six months of incarceration, Ranger was beginning to understand the importance of not making enemies. God knows when he first was arrested and arraigned, things didn't go smoothly. "I served in the 1st Marine Division," Ranger said. "Completed five tours."

Milano whistled. "God damn. We got ourselves a Marine. A real killing machine. You blow some villages up or what?"

Ranger flared his nostrils and faced the window again.

"Oh, come on, Hush. Don't be like that. You probably loved every minute of it. I'll bet you lived for that shit."

Ranger's fists clenched as his jaw tightened. A fiery heat surged through him. He was seconds away from losing control, barely holding back the rage boiling inside, when Brewer came through the cage door. The officer made a beeline for Milano and grabbed the man by the shoulder. He spun him around and leaned down close. "I said shut the fuck up, Milano. I've been on duty for three long-ass days, hauling dirtbags like you some twelve hundred miles from shithole to shithole. We are almost at the Lodge, but I will gladly pull this bus over and put a gag on you."

Milano shrugged. "Hey, it's all good, boss man. No need to lose your shit. I've got this."

Brewer held his glare for a beat longer. Ranger was grateful for the interruption. At the same time, he felt himself questioning Brewer's decision to enter the holding compartment on his own in such a way. With only two inmates in the main pen and the third locked away in his own reinforced cage, it was probably safe enough.

Brewer stood tall and shifted his focus to Ranger. As he stared down, his lip curled, forcing up his mustache. "Anyway, Milano, what are you doing wasting your breath on a wife killer like this?"

Brewer stepped away and left the holding compartment, closing the self-locking gate behind him. Milano faced Ranger again with a wide smile and an open mouth. "Oh shit. Did you kill your wife, Hush?"

Ranger bared his teeth.

"No way. What happened? Did she send you one of them Dear John letters or something?"

Ranger's pulse raced and begged him to unleash. Not just at Milano, but at Brewer as well. The officer knew better than to reveal why Ranger had been given a life sentence in prison. The son of a bitch had let the piece of information slip just to make his life harder. There was no other explanation.

"Wait a second," Milano said, practically jumping out of his seat. "That's where I know you from. You're that Army dude who came home from the war and went crazy, right? Walked in the door and shot your woman with your own gun."

"Milano," Brewer yelled, as if the inmate's behavior wasn't his doing.

Milano barely took notice and continued, "This is wild. We need a new nickname for you. Hush just won't cut it." He chuckled to himself and twisted the right way around.

Ranger's breath flew in and out of his lungs. He closed his eyes and tried to calm himself down. If he didn't get his rage under control, he was going to strike down anyone dumb enough to come within swinging distance of his fists. "It's okay," he whispered to himself. "Don't let them win." Ranger opened his eyes and regained control.

Now that Milano knew all about his life sentence, the second the bus reached the prison, word would spread from one inmate to the next in record time. The murderers, rapists, and scum would all hear how he was a wife killer and nothing more.

But none of them knew the truth. None of them knew what had really happened to his wife, Kaitlyn.

"What the hell?" Brewer let out, not addressing Milano.

Ranger shifted his focus to the front of the bus. With a furrowed brow, Brewer tapped Foster on the shoulder. "We got a problem."

"What?" Foster asked.

"Looks like Escort 1 is dropping back. Better check in."

"Again?" Foster sighed as he snatched up the handheld microphone on the radio. "Escort 1, how's it looking back there? Over."

"Bravo 1, we got some engine issues. Losing power. Over."

"Dammit. Can you make it to the next checkpoint? Over."

"Negative. I think we need to stop. Engine light's on, and we've got a weird smell coming through the vents. Over."

Foster gave Brewer a look. "Roger. Pull over in the next clearing. We'll cover. Over."

Escort 1 acknowledged.

"Son of a bitch," Brewer muttered. "We're almost done."

"Protocol says we got to pull over," Foster stated.

"I know, dammit."

Ranger could see both officers were at the end of their ropes. The journey, as Brewer had put it, was supposed to be a milk run from Helena to Montana State Prison. But the job had been significantly delayed when Fraley had refused to play ball at the courthouse. It took six officers and a light sedative to get him into the bus and into his cage. The drugs didn't seem to make much of a difference.

"What if we keep going?" Brewer asked out loud.

"Don't even think about it," Foster responded, shaking his head.

"We're talking twenty-five miles with no traffic and only three inmates. I can't see anyone setting up an ambush for these losers. What could go wrong?"

"Fraley is what could go wrong."

Brewer huffed. "We'll get help with that sack of crap when we arrive. But if we stop with Escort 1, we could be out here for hours, waiting for a backup unit to arrive and take over."

Foster shrugged and slowed down the bus as a clearing appeared on the narrow dual-lane highway. "Hey, it's your call, Brewer. But I'm telling you now, I ain't taking any heat for it."

With his arms crossed over his chest, Brewer spat on the ground. "Screw it." He took the handheld microphone into his palm and squeezed the PTT button. "Escort 1, we are proceeding ahead to MSP. Over."

"Bravo 1. Say again? Over."

Brewer repeated his last words and told the driver of Escort 1 to call in for roadside assistance. After some back and forth debating, Escort 1 acknowledged. The bus picked up its speed again and continued down the highway toward the prison, leaving Escort 1 behind.

"Breaking the rules, huh?" Milano asked Brewer with a chuckle. "I won't tell anyone."

"You shut the fuck up," Brewer said, jamming a finger through the cage.

Milano shot to his feet. "Why don't you make me, asshole?"

Ranger blew out his breath. Milano never knew when to quit. And apparently, neither did Brewer. Ranger watched as he unlocked the cage again and barged through. He reached Milano and shoved the inmate back down into his seat. "You think I won't beat your ass?"

Milano stared up at the officer with the same leering smile he kept giving Ranger. "Why don't you take these cuffs off me and make it a fair fight?"

Brewer held his nerve and stood tall once more. "One day, prick. But not today. Not when we're this close to—"

"Oh, God," Foster yelled. Before Brewer could turn his head, the bus swerved hard. At the last second, Ranger spotted the blinding lights of a truck rushing out onto the road. It collided with the rear of the bus with a deafening crunch that overloaded Ranger's every sense. The bus lifted off the ground for a moment, then crashed down to spin counterclockwise. Metal folded with sheer violence as glass and debris spewed in every direction.

The bus tipped to its side and landed with a thud that cracked Ranger's head against the panel of the narrow window frame.

As he clung to consciousness, Kaitlyn appeared from the shadows of the broken bus and stared down at him. He reached out his cuffed and bleeding hands toward her, wishing he could feel her touch one last time. But she came to a stop just outside his reach.

"I'm sorry," he whispered. "I tried."

She said nothing and continued to stare.

As the vision of Kaitlyn faded, she left him with the same damning look she'd given Ranger the day everything changed. When Ranger had lost his wife and had been told he would never see his daughter, Cindy, again.

As he was passing out, Kaitlyn's face morphed. It shifted from his wife's beautiful, soft face to the hardened one of the man who had entered his home. The man who had come with two other armed thugs and executed his wife before his very eyes with Ranger's own gun. He would never forget that face for as long as he lived.

Unable to fight it any longer, Ranger passed out.

CHAPTER 2

ONE YEAR LATER - ARIZONA

A loose rock in the dusty road scuttled along from the tip of Frank Ranger's worn boot as he strolled into the edge of town. For the last twenty miles, he'd followed a small, single-lane highway that was nestled between the larger three-lane I-10 and a dual railway line that stretched all the way to Tucson. As a wanted man, Ranger felt more at home on the lesser of the three pathways.

Eighteen months ago, Ranger had been left at Kaitlyn's lifeless side with the murder weapon in his hand. When he came to after a bullet had grazed his head, he found himself surrounded by the Helena Police Department. A dozen officers yelled and screamed as they aimed their pistols and shotguns at him, each one ready to put him down. What came next was a blur.

Ranger was taken to the hospital and treated for a concussion and the graze shot that came within millimeters of killing him. During his stay, he had four officers standing guard over him day and night. Two detectives came to question him as soon as he was medically sound and grilled him repeatedly to confess to the crime he'd been accused of. No matter how many times he tried to tell them he was innocent, that other people had been in his home, the detectives refused to listen.

Ranger was released from the hospital and arraigned. The judge wouldn't grant him bail and deemed him to be a flight risk. He was remanded into custody and spent the next six months in Montana State Prison, painted as a soldier with PTSD. One who had come home from war and was unable to adapt to civilian life. One who'd snapped and shot his wife with his own gun. But Ranger wasn't that man.

No one listened to him, including his own attorney. No one believed he was innocent. He tried to reach out to friends and family, but they all assumed what they wanted.

With a baseball cap slung low over a pair of scratched aviator sunglasses, Ranger clawed at a beard he'd spent the last year growing. Wearing an old pair of jeans and a stained gray T-shirt that covered the top of his arms, he desperately needed a shower. A few days had passed since he'd enjoyed the simple pleasure of hot water on his back, and the Arizonian desert heat wasn't helping to ease the thought.

According to the fold-out map Ranger kept in his back pocket, the one that also held a photo of his wife and daughter, he had just crossed over an invisible line that marked the border of a town named Namrena. The farming municipality was home to an old Marine buddy—Donny Brown. Ranger also knew him as Hatchet, a nickname given to him by their CO back in Afghanistan. Donny and Ranger had fought alongside one another during the war. Donny hadn't been part of Ranger's squad, but he had been in the same platoon.

Ranger had spent the better part of a year out of contact with any of his Marine connections, along with his family and friends. Worst of all, though, he hadn't seen his six-year-old daughter the entire time. No one had allowed her to visit him before he escaped, and there was no way for him to see her while he was on the run.

The trial hadn't gone Ranger's way. There had been too much physical evidence to counter his claims. The life sentence had been handed down to him in only six months. He was supposed to be rotting in prison for the rest of his life, but fate had had other plans during the trip from the courthouse to the prison. He'd escaped and been on the run ever since, hiding away from the law for a crime he didn't commit.

A horn blared from the engine of a long freight train in the distance, pulling Ranger from his thoughts. Sudden noises put him on alert and made him wonder if the police had finally caught up with him. Sometimes he hoped they'd find him and lock him up for good. Other days, he just wanted to keep on running.

Ranger's purpose, his drive, and especially his fight, had all faded since he'd escaped. He was supposed to be out there finding the people who had killed Kaitlyn. But he was a broken man. All he did now was survive, moving from one town to the next, keeping as low a profile as possible as he headed south, far away from the life he knew. He took cash-paying jobs wherever he found them and only stayed in one location for a few weeks at most—long enough to make some money and move on before anyone became too familiar with him. He gave out fake names like they were sticks of gum and couldn't remember the last time he'd used his real one. It was getting to the point where he needed to remind himself who he was.

He'd made mistakes along the way and had gotten involved in situations that weren't his problem, garnering attention from the kinds of people you didn't want to notice you. And on more than one occasion, things had gotten violent, leaving Ranger with little choice but to fight and run,

all the while being hunted by the police and other more reso-
lute individuals.

One night, when watching a small-screen TV in a cheap
motel he was staying at, Ranger saw a news reporter talking
about his escape. He heard the usual details from the reporter
until a man came on and vowed he would find Frank Ranger
no matter the cost. Ranger wouldn't have been too concerned,
but the man happened to be a determined Deputy US
Marshal who was also Kaitlyn's older brother, Dane Briggs.

Life on the road was hard, and Ranger didn't know who
had framed him for the execution of his wife. Only what the
three murderers looked like.

The freight train rolled slowly by, one car at a time. Its
rhythmic rattle sounded peaceful in Ranger's ears, making
the journey in the blistering heat slightly more bearable as he
took another step into the town of Namrena. The bulk of the
town was still a ways away. No welcome sign greeted him or
gave out any indication that civilization lay ahead. All he
could see was the road.

Ranger kept up his pace, aiming to find somewhere to rest
sooner than later. He'd pushed himself too far in the heat and
was feeling its effects. Ahead, he spotted a thick Joshua tree.
It was larger than most around and would provide enough
shade for him to stop for a few minutes and drink the last of
his water.

As Ranger moved off the side of the road to get closer to
the tree, he noticed a bench seat from a pickup truck. It had
been torn out and left there to rot. Whatever reason a person
had to dump such an item didn't matter to him. To his weary
eyes, it would be better than sitting on the punishing ground.

Ranger came to a stop and slid his rucksack off his back.
He let it fall beside the bench seat and watched a puff of dust
kick up. A throbbing that had been tugging at his right knee

was getting worse with each mile. He needed to get into town and put his feet up for a day.

Before the chance to sit in the shade came, a dusty red Ram pickup drove a short distance past him and pulled over. Dirt and rocks continued to roll on by after the late-model truck came to a stop. Ranger never heard the truck coming and realized the sun was disturbing his senses. He'd experienced something similar in Afghanistan when the desert heat became unbearable.

The pickup idled on the side of the road, giving Ranger reason to pick up his rucksack. As he did, he sized up the vehicle and kept his eyes on the lone man inside the truck, who stared back at him via the rearview mirror. The man regarded the abandoned bench seat as if it were his private property. Knowing better than to attract any more curiosity than was needed, Ranger looped his thumbs through the straps of his rucksack and continued walking. He passed by the red vehicle as if it didn't exist, but the driver noticed him.

"Hi there," a voice called out from the pickup. "Need a lift into town?"

CHAPTER 3

Ranger stopped and turned back to face the man who had just offered him a lift into town. He appeared to be in his mid-sixties, wearing a worn John Deere hat and a plaid flannel shirt that was unbuttoned to a hairy chest. He was most likely a town local. The man squinted at Ranger with blotchy, sun-damaged skin while flashing a welcoming grin.

"No, thank you, sir. I can walk," Ranger said.

"Nonsense. It's hotter than hell out here. Best you ride with me, son."

Ranger had survived this long by taking the harder options. He never caught public transport during peak hours. He kept his interactions with strangers to a minimum, and he rarely accepted a free ride into town. "It's fine. I can walk. Have been for the last twenty miles."

The man's eyes opened wider. "Twenty miles? You must be exhausted. Please, I insist. Let me take you the rest of the way into town. There's a diner there with decent food and cold beers. You can grab yourself a bite to eat and something to drink."

"I don't want to be a bother."

"It's no bother. I'm headed that way."

Ranger let his shoulders drop. He was exhausted and low on water. The last stretch of road had been more draining than he'd anticipated. Accepting the offer would go against his own rules, but he doubted the local would recognize a wanted Montana man in Arizona.

"Okay," Ranger said, giving in. He strolled back to the pickup, toward the passenger side, and unloaded his rucksack into the truck bed, noticing it was empty. Ranger opened the door of what appeared to be a brand-new pickup and climbed in. He took in the sight of the stranger and noticed he had a .357 Colt Python holstered on his hip. It wasn't an uncommon sight in an open-carry state like Arizona, but it still gave him pause. Ranger settled into place and said, "Thank you, sir."

"Not a problem. Say, you got a name?"

Ranger drew one from nowhere. "George." He made sure to remember the name and would use it on anyone he came across in the town he would eventually pass through as soon as he'd spoken to Donny. Consistency was key. He kept his eyes forward as the man pulled out onto the road. Ranger didn't ask for a name in return.

"Pleasure to meet you, George. The name's Bill Wilkins of Wilkins Farms." The man offered a hand to shake. Ranger accepted and got the greeting over with as quickly as possible. The less conversation that was had between them, the better.

"So what brings you to Namrena?" Bill asked as he reached into his front shirt pocket and pulled out a packet of cigarettes. He shoved a stick in his mouth and offered one to Ranger.

"Just passing through," Ranger said, declining with a raised palm.

"Is that so? Where you headed in the long run?"

It was a question Ranger had asked himself a lot. Every day, he took another step in the opposite direction of the place where his wife met her undignified end. He'd been on the run for a year after escaping the prison transport. The entire time, he had wanted to stop, turn around, and charge home for his daughter. He wanted to tell her he was alive and that he was sorry for leaving, but he knew he couldn't step one foot back inside Montana without risking his freedom.

"Well?" Bill asked again.

Ranger shook his head. "Nowhere in particular. Following the road, I suppose."

Bill stared at him as he lit his cigarette and drew in a long drag on the stick. He pushed the smoke out in Ranger's direction and eyed him up and down. Ranger could feel the man assessing his very being and felt an instant wave of unease wash over his body. He shouldn't have accepted the ride.

"That right?" Bill replied as he returned his focus to the long, straight road ahead. He didn't ask any more questions and continued driving.

It took a few minutes, but partial elements of the town of Namrena appeared ahead at the first intersection Ranger had seen in hours.

"To your left, you've got the Namrena Estates. Basically, where your lazy suburbanites come to buy up their slice of the American dream. We get a few snowbirds staying there as well. You know, your retirees and tourists who like to move to Arizona during the winter months. Main town's to the right past the highway. Most people around here ain't too fond of the estate. Hell, it didn't exist a few years ago. But that's just the goddamn progress we have to put up with these days."

Ranger breathed in a thick, smoky breath and let out a quiet sigh at Bill's rant. He'd seen the same thing happen in his neck of the woods. Even before he left. He didn't like it much either, but there was little to be done to stop the wheels of progress.

Bill drove the pickup down a lengthy stretch of road for a minute or so. "And on your left, we have a damn McDonald's. Beats me how that thing ever got built. The diner I told you about is up ahead, though. They serve decent home-cooked meals. Not this fast-food crap. And you know what? You look like you could use a good feed."

"I could," Ranger admitted. The words slipped out of him. He hadn't eaten for at least a day.

"That's wonderful to hear because you won't find a better meal in town than Rosie's." Bill drove the pickup off the main road and onto a dirt-covered parking lot. Ranger took in the sight of an aging diner with the name Rosie's written across a sign on its flat roof. The lettering was all faded and scratched from the harsh Arizona conditions. The establishment looked about as set in as Bill was with his opinions on the way things should be.

Bill parked with a heavy foot on the brakes and turned to Ranger. "Come on. Let me take you inside."

"That's fine. You've done more than enough for me, thank you."

"No, I insist. I know these people. Come on, George." Bill stepped out of the truck and flicked his cigarette into the distance.

Once again, Ranger had little choice but to do as Bill asked if he wanted to avoid suspicion. Plus, this guy didn't seem like the kind of man who was used to hearing anyone say the word "no" to him.

Ranger climbed out of the pickup and closed the door before grabbing his rucksack from the vehicle's bed.

"This way, George. I promise you, heaven awaits." Bill ushered Ranger along with a grin and a wave of his hand. He didn't bother to lock his pickup as he strolled into the diner. A bell rang out above Ranger as they passed through the door. It was late afternoon—somewhere between lunchtime and dinner, rendering the restaurant almost empty apart from a few customers.

Ranger spied a woman in her late forties moving around behind the counter of the classically decorated diner. She was scrubbing and cleaning the central counter with a dirty cloth and a bottle of cheap cleaner. The woman swiveled her head toward the entrance and almost did a double take when she saw Bill. She stopped cleaning. Ranger couldn't help but notice the tension in her body at the mere sight of Bill.

"Oh hey, Bill. How are you? What do you need?"

Ranger took off his sunglasses to get a better read on the woman. He couldn't be sure, but she seemed to be almost afraid of Bill. He could see anxiety registering in her eyes as she put on a forced smile.

"Nothing for me, thanks, Rosie, but you can set my friend George here up with a decent meal. A burger and something cold to drink." Bill waved a hand to Ranger as if he couldn't speak for himself.

"Sure. No problem. Anything he wants, Bill," Rosie said. The businesswoman turned to Ranger. "What would you like, George? A burger and a soda?"

"You don't need to make me anything," Ranger said.

"It's no trouble."

Ranger spotted something in her gaze that said he should accept the meal, that it would be best for all parties. With a stiff voice, he said, "Okay, I'll have whatever Bill recommends."

"Good man," Bill said. "And make that cold soda a beer instead. Man's been out in the sun. My treat." Bill shoved his hand into his back pocket and pulled out his wallet. It seemed innocent enough for a stranger to offer to help someone who appeared to be down on their luck, but Bill had a giant wad of cash sitting inside his leather wallet. He peeled off more cash than was necessary and slapped the money down on the counter with a smile. Rosie took the payment, placed it in the register, and rushed away into what Ranger assumed was the kitchen.

"You don't have to do that," Ranger said, feigning gratitude to the man he realized had a powerful influence over the woman and possibly many others in town.

"It's my pleasure. And you know what? There's a nice motel across the street that would do you wonders to spend the night in. You can recuperate before you leave town. How about you stay the night? On me." Another unnecessary amount of cash hit the counter. Again, Ranger tried to decline the offer, but Bill continued to insist upon being the world's most generous man while keeping a strong eye on his every reaction. Ranger wanted to walk away, but again, he accepted the offer and took the money. It was the only choice.

Bill nodded with a half grin. "I'll see you 'round, George. Best I get back to the farm."

"Of course," Ranger said. He let his eyes follow Bill out the door and tracked him back to his pickup. He watched as Bill fired up the engine and sped out of the dusty parking lot. The vehicle bounced onto the solid road and left.

Ranger wasn't sure what he'd just witnessed, but there was no way in hell Bill Wilkins was a farmer.

CHAPTER 4

BILL

Bill Wilkins pulled over after a short distance of driving away from Rosie's diner. He kept the engine running and fixed his eyes on the rearview mirror. He was checking to see if this stranger in town, supposedly named George, would take off the first chance he got. If the man was smart, he'd eat the free meal and go across to the motel straight away. Then, after an uneventful night, he'd move along and out of Namrena, away from Bill's town.

Bill shook his head, lowering his gaze from the mirror for a moment. He had come so close to pulling out the .357 Colt Python he kept holstered on his hip when he first laid eyes on the drifter. Bill was damn near ready to unload a few rounds into the man, but he continued to walk past the bench seat on the side of the road. If this stranger had stopped at the dead drop for any reason, Bill would have been looking at a very different situation.

The old road on the edge of town barely saw any traffic, let alone hitchhikers. Did this "George" know there was over fifty thousand dollars in cash stored in a box underneath the seat? Surely not. But Bill could tell this man wasn't on his way through. He was coming to town for somebody or something. No one walked Arizona's desert roads for the hell of it. Whoever this man was, Bill got the impression he was the kind of man who didn't want to be noticed.

The drifter was at least six feet two and had to be over two hundred pounds of solid muscle, judging from the man's tattoo-covered arms alone. Bill didn't doubt this guy had some form of training. Be it military or something else, he looked capable and ready to take down a few people on his own in a fight. The baseball cap and sunglasses he wore tried to hide the man he really was, but Bill could see some anger in that face waiting to come alive.

Maybe Bill was being overcautious, coming close to killing a total stranger in broad daylight. But then again, he couldn't be too careful. So many desperate thugs had tried to muscle in on the operation at his farm over the last five years that he'd lost count of the number of bodies he'd dumped out in the desert. The bastards never seemed to learn. And there was always another young punk willing to try their luck.

A few more minutes crept by without George emerging from Rosie's. Bill didn't have time to sit around and stake out the diner like some clock-watching fed. He had a dead drop to retrieve and a business to run. Plus, he had an important meeting later that he needed to prepare for.

Bill cranked the pickup into gear and peeled out onto the main road, turning back the way he came to collect the money. His tires squealed a little. It wasn't his favorite vehicle to drive around town in, but every other car he owned wasn't built for the remote locations he used for dead drops in the area.

Bill could have sent one of his men to retrieve the money, but he figured if he was always the one to grab the cash, he would have no problems. It took little for a trusted individual to give in to temptation and steal the payments his network of local dealers made for him. He'd seen it before. There was nothing worse than having to dispose of a good man because they screwed up and got greedy. Bill learned a long time ago it was better to remove such opportunities from the equation and rely on himself as much as possible.

After retrieving the dead drop, Bill drove out to the opposite side of town and arrived home at Wilkins Farms. Two of his men on the outer perimeter met him. Each was armed with whatever pistol they felt like carrying at the small of their backs, tucked underneath their shirts. In the bed of a nearby pickup, parked off to the side of the paved road, sat a pair of Ruger AR-556s loaded with M855 green-tip ammunition should the need arise. Operating his business from an open-carry state sure had its benefits.

Bill pulled up to the men and gave one a nod while the other opened a reinforced electric gate without being asked. Given the number of attacks the operation had seen in the last year alone, the two sentries guarding the farm's entrance were necessary. Trouble had come up from Tucson, as it always did. Some newly formed gangs whose leaders wanted to expand their operations thought they could muscle in on the farm. Bill dealt with them the same way he'd always handled the competition. It was a messy but necessary part of the business.

Bill primarily supplied a network of dealers in Tucson with methamphetamine he manufactured on the farm in bulk. His farm alone provided the city with almost a third of its meth in a deal Bill had made with a Mexican cartel connection a long time ago. Bill kicked the connection a generous twenty percent of his profits every month to keep the cartels across the southern border happy. It was a small price to pay for the massive sums of cash he saw flow through the farm. Plus, the last thing he wanted was a group of motivated sicarios coming up from Mexico to wreak havoc on his operation. He also had his locals pushing his product in and around town, but the money they made him was spare change compared to the income generated from supplying drugs to Tucson.

Bill drove down a wide driveway he'd gone to the expense of paving a long time ago. He hated driving his beautiful, clean SLK along a dirt road before heading to Tucson or Phoenix, so it was worth the price.

Bill continued past the dozens of illegal laborers he employed to run the actual farm. Their somewhat lawful work was the perfect cover. They tended to various crops that grew throughout the year, including cotton, hay, and wheat. Of course, the farm's legitimate output paled in comparison to the meth that was produced.

Almost twenty years ago, Bill had abandoned the old ways and decided he no longer wanted to bust his back working the land for a dollar. His father and his father before him had done so their whole lives and left a worthless legacy behind. Bill had been the one to break the cycle and not work harder than he got paid. The Wilkinses would never have to struggle to get by. Instead, they would be feared and respected in the region. It had taken a lot of spilled blood, but the Wilkins name came out on top.

Bill pulled up outside the main building and climbed out of his pickup. As the engine began to cool and tick away in the scorching sun, he stretched out his stiff frame and shook out some fatigue.

After dumping the dead drop inside his office into an oversized safe, Bill came back outside and moved to a building across the way that housed the farm's underground meth lab. He walked in via a large opening where expensive crop equipment was repaired and stored as part of the front used to launder his cash. He approached a small, reinforced door that read Staff Only. It came across as a normal enough sight to the untrained eye.

"Hello, sir," said one of his lieutenants, guarding the door. Carl was at least twenty years younger than Bill and wore a white tank top with an open plaid shirt and a pair of jeans. Sweat covered his brow.

"Where is he?" Bill asked, knowing Carl would understand the question.

Carl closed his eyes and shook his head. "Down below, sir."

"Watching the lab?"

Carl gave him a doubtful look.

"Of course not," Bill said, letting a huff of anger flow from his nostrils. "Anything else to report?"

"No, sir. Last I heard, the current batch is running ahead of schedule. They're already making preparations for the next one."

"Great to hear, son." Bill slapped him on the shoulder with a smile. It wasn't Carl's job to report on such things, but Bill encouraged the initiative.

The pair turned around and made their way through the heavy door and down some steps to a small back room. At first glance, the room came across as nothing more than a storage closet. But if someone looked closer, they might find the hidden door behind a movable locker. Inside, a secret entrance led to the meth lab below where the wheels of the business turned and allowed the entire farm to be more than just a hundred-year-old joke.

Carl did the honors and opened the electromagnetically locked door that swung out onto a fresh set of stairs. He gestured for Bill to go first, respecting the chain of command.

Bill took the squeaky steps twenty feet down and came out to a sealed window that overlooked the lab. A dozen of his people toiled over the underground equipment. With more and more rival gangs popping up in Tucson, Bill had to work harder than ever before to yield as much of the drug as possible. He couldn't allow his connections to think he wasn't up to the task. Otherwise, his operation would be taken offline, so to speak.

Bill had fought long and hard to keep up with the demanding output, but it was only a matter of time before someone younger and more aggressive than him took over. It was just the way of the world. He accepted the fact and had an exit strategy ready to go when the day came, but for now, the name of the game was to make as much money as possible.

Bill moved along a noisy catwalk to where his son would be sitting with two of his most loyal idiots. He spotted them making a racket in a small room at the end of the line, playing video games on a big-screen television.

Bill's son, William Wilkins, called Liam by his friends, had taken it upon himself to set up and install the TV along with the comfortable seating and a loudspeaker system. Gangster rap droned from an oversized subwoofer, sending more anger down Bill's spine. The three "men" were supposed to manage the lab and keep watch over the underground operation. They were meant to be ready for action in case the authorities ever raided the farm. Instead, they were always screwing around and avoiding doing their jobs.

"Junior," Bill shouted.

William snapped his head toward Bill with his mouth half open. He wasn't wearing what any of the other men on the farm wore to blend in. Instead, William had taken to dressing like he had come straight from the inner streets of the city in a basketball jersey, baggy dark jeans, and white sneakers. Gold chains swung from his chest, slapping his thirty-year-old frame whenever he moved.

"Hey, Pops. Why you back so soon?" William asked from

the sofa. He had one leg slung over the arm of the seat like he had no problems in the world.

Bill's arms flew out wide as he walked toward his son. "Are you fucking kidding me? You and your two morons are down here jerking each other off when you should be overseeing production in the lab. And you have the balls to ask me why I'm back so soon?"

"There's nothing to do. The lab runs itself. Anyway, what are you worried about? You've got half the local PD looking the other way. There's no raid coming."

Bill chuckled under his breath as he shifted his focus to the floor for a moment. "Junior, I weep for your generation. I really do."

"It's all good, Pops. Maybe you should just chill the fuck out, huh?"

Bill's forced smile turned to a toothy sneer as he stepped closer to his boy. He snapped both of his hands to the front of his son's basketball jersey and lifted him over the sofa to his feet. William grabbed at his father's thick claws.

Bill yelled, "Do you think we can afford to fuck around for even one goddamn minute? This whole operation, this good life you live so carefree, can all fall to pieces in a second. There are people out there who will kill every last person on this farm to take even a slice of what we have. Do you understand?" Bill shoved his son backward, letting him trip over the sofa to the solid floor.

William crashed hard and winced. Once he caught his breath, he glared at his father. "What the hell? You can't treat me like—"

Bill rushed forward and backhanded his son across the face, silencing his protest. "You don't talk to me like that. You do as I fucking say. Got it?"

William's brows dug into the bridge of his nose, flaring his nostrils with scorn. He nodded without making eye contact. His two sidekicks stared on in silence, mouths agape.

Bill eyeballed the pathetic sight before him and cursed again under his breath. He needed to get through to his son the importance of running the business like a man and not some amateur gangster. If the concept didn't sink in soon, Bill would have to consider sending William as far away from the farm as possible. It would be the only way the boy would survive.

Then an idea came to Bill. One that was simple enough. "The drifter," he muttered. He would send his son to keep an eye on the man and make sure he got on his way out of town. The task was just the kind his son needed to prove his worth.

"Drifter?" William said, as blood spilled from his lips. "What are you on about?"

"Get on your feet, Junior. I've got a job for you. Tell your morons here to come along, too."

CHAPTER 5

RANGER

The burger and beer Rosie brought Ranger went down smoothly. He was impressed by how delicious the meal had been. Rosie had even thrown in a handful of fries to help fill his growling stomach. For the most part, it allowed him to put his concerns about the supposed farmer, Bill Wilkins, out of his mind. Maybe he would be able to leave the diner, check in at the motel as suggested, then sneak out to walk to Donny's place without anyone caring. Unfortunately, Ranger's positive thoughts were soon dampened when a BMW X5 pulled into the parking lot of Rosie's diner.

Loud rap music droned from a subwoofer as the X5 parked close to the front door, cutting off a man who was driving a minivan filled with kids. From where he sat, Ranger had a good view as the older driver of the minivan shouted at the X5 driver and made a fuss. He did so until a younger guy wearing a basketball jersey and loose jeans stepped out of the BMW. The minivan driver's hands rose in an apologetic gesture from the steering wheel as the guy in the jersey stared. A moment of unease passed by before the minivan driver was waved off. He reversed his vehicle in a hurry and sped out of the area.

Ranger continued to observe while keeping to his booth as the jersey man muttered something with a sneer and made fists. Two similarly dressed men who appeared to be even younger than the first guy climbed out of the X5 and joined their associate. The three walked toward the diner's entrance with the jersey man leading the way like he owned the place. All had something dangerous tucked into the back of their jeans. Ranger spotted the telltale shape of a firearm on each of the men.

Ranger couldn't explain it, but he got the feeling that the men had been sent by Bill Wilkins to check up on him. Given the way they were dressed, all three men appeared out of place. Rosie's diner didn't match the energy they were giving off. Not in the slightest. If he had to guess, they were involved in something illegal.

Before the three men entered the diner, Ranger tucked his hat low over his eyes. He picked up a folded newspaper he had collected from the next booth over and pretended to read it while keeping his eyes on the new customers. With any luck, Ranger would come across as just another patron of the diner. Experience had shown him that luck was rarely on his side.

The bell above the entrance rang as the three men strolled in. "Hi, Liam," Rosie said from behind the counter as she wiped it. She lowered her gaze and asked, "What brings you here? I'm all paid up for the month, right?"

"I don't give a shit about the rent money," Liam hissed, not seeming to care who could hear him.

Rosie took a step back. "Oh, I'm sorry. I didn't mean any—"

Liam held up a palm and shook his head. "Save it."

"What can I do you for? Are you hungry?"

"I could eat," Liam said as he leaned on the counter. "First, we've got business to attend to. We're looking for a drifter. Bill said he left a man here with some money for a meal and a bed for the night across the street."

Ranger glanced down at the mention of a drifter but kept listening as best he could.

"Oh, him," Rosie said. Ranger could only see the newspaper in front of him, but it was obvious whom Rosie was referring to.

"What's his deal?" Liam asked.

"He hasn't said much. Ate his food real fast and drank his beer."

"He cause any trouble? Does he seem like he's here for anything other than to grab a bite to eat?"

"I don't think so."

"So why am I here?"

Ranger resisted shaking his head. This Liam person had been sent by Bill Wilkins, but he was about as professional as a toddler. There was a sense of entitlement about him that made Ranger question why Bill would have sent this kid of all people to check up on him. He mustn't have been too concerned about Ranger if he'd given the job to a punk like Liam. With any luck, Liam would think Ranger was a nobody. Just some guy who had caught Bill's paranoid attention.

"Screw it," Liam said. "Three burgers and three beers, Rosie. The usual."

Ranger lifted his head enough to see Rosie nod and rush behind the counter to write out the order. She didn't mention anything about the cost and shoved the order ahead of the others despite the restaurant only having three customers.

Liam and his two pals sat down at a booth that had a good view of Ranger and made no attempts to be subtle. Liam, especially, faced his whole body toward Ranger and watched him in his peripheral vision as if Ranger had come into town to ruin his day.

"Yo, boss, what are we doing?" asked one of the two associates after only a few minutes spent sitting in the booth. Ranger figured the two men who were following Liam around were his underlings.

"Just keep your mouth shut unless I say otherwise," Liam said, still speaking louder than he needed to. He faced Ranger for another minute, then swiveled into his booth.

Less than ten minutes later, Rosie rushed over to their table with three burgers and three beers. Each meal had a side of fries, just like Ranger's had.

"About time," Liam said as he dug into the food. He stuffed a fistful of fries into his mouth.

The bell at the front door chimed as a figure came into the building. Ranger flicked his eyes up to see a young woman enter the diner with a little boy. Liam twisted around in his seat with a mouth full of fries. "Well, hello," he mumbled.

The woman kept her eyes downcast and walked straight toward Rosie as if she was hopeful Liam hadn't seen her. Not one to disappoint, Liam jumped out of his booth and cut off the woman's path a second later.

"Hey, girl, what's the rush? You got somewhere else to be?"

"No, Liam. I, uh, just need to pick up my paycheck and get James something to eat."

"Is that right?"

She nodded with a sunken frown, avoiding eye contact. Her body found its way in front of who Ranger assumed was her son.

"Now, now, don't be like that, Laura. I'm only saying hello."

"Please, Liam. I know what this is about."

"Is that right?" he asked, his voice rising. "Then why don't you tell me what this is about, huh?"

The woman named Laura didn't say a word.

"Got nothing to say now, do ya? Well, let me fill you in. You owe me—big time. So if I don't see some goddamn money in the next few minutes, then things are going to get ugly."

"Please, Liam. I'll pay. I swear it. I'll cash this check right now and—"

"Bullshit. The second you get that money, it'll be gone. Besides, I don't want your money. You know what I want." He leered over her and puffed up his chest. Ranger watched the interaction and could see the shape of a handgun at the small of Liam's back poking out.

James inched farther behind his mother as Laura seemed to put on a brave face in front of the people in the diner. Liam's voice was booming off the walls.

Ranger focused his attention on the jackass and watched as he seemed to be contemplating something. Ranger had no idea what the man was thinking, but he knew it couldn't be good. Especially for Laura.

"What's it gonna be?" Liam asked her.

"Please, Liam."

"So be it," he muttered. He grabbed Laura by her hair with his right hand and raised the left like he was going to slap her with an open palm. She flinched and shut her eyes as he held his hand at the ready.

Ranger gripped the newspaper tight in both hands. Was this asshole really going to hurt the girl? And in front of everyone? Ranger rose to his feet in silence. Liam's two buddies didn't notice and seemed to do little else but hang back in their seats and wait for orders. They were busy reveling in the sight of their boss harassing the woman and her child.

Ranger had the perfect opportunity to slip away. In a heartbeat, he could take advantage of the goons' misplaced attention and charge out the back door of the diner via the kitchen. He'd done it before in the past when he was out of options. And the few times he hadn't had almost led to him landing in police custody. So what was stopping him from running this time around?

The answer was obvious to Ranger, even if he didn't want to acknowledge it. The woman and the kid needed help, and no one else in the diner was going to offer it to them. He couldn't stand by and let some punk beat a mother in front of her son. The boy looked to be only five or six years old. Just like his daughter.

"Last chance," Liam muttered. "Come with me or else."

Laura kept her eyes closed. "I'm sorry."

"Wrong answer." Liam swung his arm farther back, ready to uncoil, but stopped when Ranger's steel grip wrapped around his left wrist. Liam turned to find Ranger behind him, holding his arm back from striking Laura. "Let her go," Ranger said.

Liam's mouth hung open in surprise, but soon faded into a wide grin. He stared at Ranger and said, "You just made the biggest mistake of your life."

CHAPTER 6

With Liam's left arm in his grip, Ranger kept his eyes locked on the man. He stared back with a hard, unyielding gaze. Laura was still being held by the asshole while her child cowered behind her for protection.

The two lackeys finally sprang into action and were on their feet. A second later, they drew the weapons Ranger knew they were hiding. The taller of the two had a Glock 19 aimed at his face while the shorter man was wielding a MAC-10, of all things, tilting it sideways. The situation was about to get messy, as Ranger maintained a grip on their boss.

"You're a dead man," Liam spat, refusing to let go of Laura.

Not waiting for the opportunity to pass him by, Ranger twisted Liam's arm behind his back with his left hand and pulled him into a chokehold with the other. Liam released Laura and tried to clutch at Ranger.

"Tell your buddies to drop their weapons," Ranger said to the back of Liam's head as he pulled tighter and applied pressure.

Liam struggled and failed to fight back. Ranger reaffirmed

his control and placed the boss man in the firing line of the two morons with guns. They would have to shoot Liam to get a single bullet into Ranger.

"Shoot him," Liam choked. "Do it."

"Ain't got a shot, boss," said the idiot with the MAC-10.

"Same here," agreed his counterpart.

Rosie stood frozen behind the counter like she was waiting for blood to splatter against the wall. Ranger glanced at her but had no idea whose side she was on. She could easily pull a shotgun from under the counter and put Ranger down, but he figured she wasn't a huge fan of the three scumbags.

Ranger snapped his gaze to the two thugs in case they decided to use their brains and flank him. He dragged Liam a few paces back and spoke to Laura without looking at her. He couldn't afford to lose sight of the two lackeys again. "Are you okay? Is the boy all right?"

"We're good," Laura said.

"Glad to hear it. Why don't you and your son leave? Right now."

"They ain't going anywhere," said the man with the MAC-10. He shifted his aim toward Laura and her son.

Ranger's eyes went wide. If the idiot in front of him lost his cool and fired at the woman and kid, they'd be dead before Ranger took a step. There was no way to miss with a machine pistol at such close range.

"You let Liam go, or I shoot this bitch," the moron said. His finger curled around the trigger. Ranger hadn't thought the goon had it in him to smarten up and use the girl against him, but he did. He'd underestimated the threat.

"Yeah," said the second shooter as he too aimed his Glock at Laura. "You wanna see her die? Let our boss go or else."

Ranger felt the walls of the diner close in on him as he remembered that fateful day he'd come home to his wife. If only he had called the police when his instincts had told him to, maybe he could have saved her. He'd played the scenario out in his head over and over for the last eighteen months, to the point of obsession. But no matter how well things turned out in his mind, reality always reminded him he had failed. His wife had died because he didn't save her.

"What's it going to be, asshole?" one of them asked.

Ranger held his steely gaze on one lackey before he switched to the other. He made an assessment and knew what he had to do to save the girl and her son. There would be a steep price to pay, but he had no choice. His only alternative was to reason with the gangsters, and they didn't seem like the type of people who went for rational conversations.

"Tell you what," Ranger said, "why don't you both put down your guns and walk away? I don't hear any cops coming, so we can all disappear and pretend this never happened."

The two lackeys glanced at one another as if they were considering Ranger's proposal. But the thought mustn't have lasted long with their boss under threat. They held their stance.

"You don't know who you're messing with," Liam said through choked words. "My dad will kill you, you hear me? You're shit out of luck."

"Not yet," Ranger said, knowing exactly who Liam's dad was. Bill Wilkins wouldn't let any of this slide.

"Do it," Liam called out to both of his men. The man with the Glock squared his aim at Laura and tensed. He was going to shoot her without a care, just like the man in the suit had murdered Kaitlyn.

With Liam's left hand firmly in his grip, Ranger yanked hard on his wrist until he felt the man's shoulder dislocate. Cries of agony spilled out of him. The noise distracted the asshole who was about to shoot. But before he or the clown with the MAC-10 could react, Ranger released Liam, reached down the back of his jeans, and pulled out the lowlife's Glock 21. He racked the slide on the pistol while the man fell to his knees in front of him.

"Oh shit," one moron said as Ranger raised the pistol and squeezed off a single round into his chest. Ranger shifted his aim to the shorter goon and popped him in the same spot. The two men fell backward into the booth. One landed on the soft seat while the other collapsed over the fixed table. Without losing focus, Ranger glanced down at Liam and raised the pistol up high, then slammed the Glock down on the back of his head.

In less than a few seconds, Ranger had disabled all three of them. He charged toward the two he'd shot in the chest and grabbed their dropped weapons. He dismantled the firearms and scattered the pieces throughout the diner. Then he rushed back to the frightened woman and child as he tucked the Glock he'd fired into the waistline of his jeans. "Are you okay?"

She cowered away for a moment, most likely upset by the loud shooting she and her son had witnessed.

"I'm sorry you had to see that," Ranger said as he turned back to the groaning pair. "They left me no option."

"Are they going to die?"

He shook his head. "Unfortunately not. They're both wearing body armor. The shots have only winded them, but we don't have much time." Ranger had seen the vests under their baggy clothing and was glad he'd disabled the two armed men without it resulting in their deaths. He could take a life when he needed to, but avoided it whenever possible.

He checked the groaning pair again. They were still catching their breath. "We have to go."

"What? I can't go with you," Laura said.

"You don't understand. These guys aren't messing

around. If you stay here, they'll kill you and your son." She looked down at her cowering boy as he pressed his head into her body.

Ranger held out a hand for her to take. He didn't have time for this. His window to escape was closing fast. Three or four people in the diner had watched him shoot two men and injure a third. Sure, he hadn't killed anyone, but he might as well have.

"Okay," she said, seeming to understand the gravity of the situation.

Ranger nodded. "Give me a second." He got to his feet, rushed over to the two fallen men, and rummaged through each of their pockets. He ignored their cries of agony and found some cash on each of them. Ranger took the money, knowing he'd need every cent to get the girl and her kid safely out of town.

He finished his search and walked back to Laura. "Grab your boy. We're out of here in one minute."

Just as Ranger helped Laura up from her crouched position, he heard some laughter coming from Liam's spot on the floor. The man was facedown and awake. Ranger turned to him.

"You think you can run from us? We'll find you, and when we do, you'll wish you were dead."

Ranger strolled over to Liam and kicked him in the face with a firm boot. The asshole fell unconscious again. He was about to give him another boot to the head for good measure but knew there wasn't time to mess around.

"Wow," Laura said, almost smiling. "That was amazing."

Ranger gave her a wry smile. "Just one second." He moved toward Rosie, who had seen everything from behind the counter. She stepped back a pace as he approached. "Ma'am, do you have any security cameras in the building?"

Ranger had spotted several on his way in, but there was something odd about them.

"We do," she said, pointing to one in the far corner with a shaky finger, "but they're all fake. Just a camera lens and a blinking light. Nothing gets recorded."

He nodded. "Okay. One other thing: why haven't you called the police?"

The woman said nothing. Instead, she shook her head. It was clear to Ranger that calling the cops was the last thought she'd ever have with Bill Wilkins and his son around.

Ranger sighed and said, "I understand. We'll be on our way now. Sorry for the disturbance." He jogged over to Laura and James and guided them out the front door as Rosie continued to gaze at him with an open mouth.

CHAPTER 7

The first thing Ranger noticed when he, Laura, and James escaped the diner was the lack of police officers rushing toward the scene. He thought that with the number of people in the diner, someone would have called the cops. Surely, not every person who lived in Namrena feared Bill and Liam Wilkins as much as Rosie?

"Where are we going?" Laura asked as they rushed behind the diner.

"Give me your cell phone," Ranger said, ignoring her question.

"My what?" Laura snapped.

"Your phone. Hand it over."

"Okay, okay," she said as she rifled through her bag. "If you need to make a call, keep it short. I'm low on battery."

Ranger took the device and placed it down on a large rock. He then retrieved the Glock 21 from the back of his jeans and smashed the phone with the butt of the grip.

"What are you doing?" Laura yelled.

Ranger made a shushing gesture with his finger and continued to destroy the cell phone. He yanked out the device's battery once he'd accessed it and proceeded to break it apart.

"Why did you do that?"

"So Liam can't track you."

"Track me? I could have turned the thing off."

"That's not enough. While it has a battery, even the smallest charge can allow it to emit a signal. Now there's no way for Liam or Bill to find you."

Laura stared at the sight of her destroyed phone with a solemn gaze while Ranger inspected the Glock. Apart from needing a cleaning and oil, its serial number had been filed down. The gun was a throwaway. Perfect for murder.

"Come on," Ranger said, urging her to continue. "We gotta keep moving."

"All right," she said. Her brow was lined with concern. No doubt she was still in a bit of shock with everything that had happened in the diner. Ranger wished he had time to comfort her some, but that would have to come later. They couldn't stop.

He forged a path behind every building along a pothole-covered service lane, constantly keeping an eye out for the local authorities. James was struggling to keep up, so Laura carried him. The weight of her boy then hindered her pace.

"Let me take him," Ranger said. "We're going too slow."

"You can't," Laura said, turning James away from Ranger. "I'm sorry, but he'll scream if you touch him. He's not very good around strangers."

Ranger checked for anyone tailing them again, and nodded. "Okay. I guess just try to keep up."

"I will," she said laboring to breathe, "but you need to answer my question."

"What question?"

"Where are we going?"

Ranger slowed down for a moment and guided Laura

behind a dumpster that would give them cover from the main street. He ducked her gently down and got her to sit as close to the hot metal of the foul-smelling container as possible. "Take a break here for a minute."

"Thank you," she wheezed as she held James close, "but I still need an answer."

Ranger stared at the kid and watched as he nuzzled himself into her chest like he was several years younger than his size suggested. He couldn't quite tell if there was something wrong with James, but it was obvious he had a few mental issues setting him back.

Laura pressed her question by raising her eyebrows.

Ranger couldn't ignore her any longer. "I'm taking us to a buddy's house in town. He'll be able to hide us from those people back there." Ranger glanced over the lid of the dumpster in both directions. Everything was clear for now, but soon Liam would call for his dear old daddy to come back to the diner. What kind of business were the father and son into?

"Wow," Laura let out.

"What is it?" he asked.

"You don't know who you just smashed over the back of the head, do you?"

"I've got some idea."

"I don't think you do. That guy you pistol-whipped, his dad runs this town. He has criminal connections from here all the way to the border. Your buddy's house ain't safe."

"I know it's not. That's why we're just going there to grab what we need to skip town."

Laura held James tighter. "You want me to leave town?"

"Yeah."

"I can't. My whole life is here."

"I get that. I really do, but you don't have a choice," Ranger said, knowing the pain of his proposal better than most.

Laura's eyes sank to the ground, lowering with her voice. "You didn't give me a choice."

He didn't, but what else could he have done back there? He refused to sit idle for another second and do nothing while that armed son of a bitch attacked her.

"I'm sorry," was all Ranger could think to say.

Laura pressed her cheek to James'. "It's okay. I know you were trying to help me." Her eyes started to water. She looked like she had more to say but couldn't bring herself to say the words.

Ranger exhaled a long breath and allowed himself a second to think. "Whatever happens, you need my buddy's help. We don't know who else we can trust around here apart from him. And these roads are too long and open to be on without a plan and some supplies."

She nodded her understanding but didn't cast a glance Ranger's way. He thought about his wanted status. If the police got involved in the incident at the diner, he had to avoid being identified if he didn't want a team of US Marshals to roll into town ready to hunt him down. All led by his eager brother-in-law.

Laura shook her head. "Wait. We need to go to my place first. I have to pick up James' meds and some clothing for him. It's not far from here. I live in the mobile home park."

"I'm sorry, but your home is off-limits."

"Are you serious?"

Ranger scanned the area. "Think about it. Where's the first place Liam will take his men?"

Laura closed her eyes and let out a sigh. "My place."

Ranger nodded with raised brows. "I'm guessing he also knows about your boy's need for this medication. Liam might seem like a moron, but I know his type."

"And what type is that?"

"The kind that enjoys tracking someone down so they can murder them."

"Oh, God," Laura said as her worry line returned. As she stared into the distance, lost in thought, Ranger scanned their surroundings again for threats. There was no one giving chase and no sirens blaring. Despite the relative calm, he decided it was time to go.

Ranger helped Laura to her feet as she held James and pointed them along. "This way."

The trio continued along behind a series of buildings that ran parallel to the main road through town. The service lane was empty apart from a row of disgusting, overfilled dumpsters that littered the way. Ranger led them to a dusty sedan at the end of the lane and asked Laura and James to duck down beside the vehicle. If they were going to drive to Donny's home without hassle, they'd need a set of wheels.

Ranger had stolen a few cars over the last year, targeting older vehicles that were easier to break into. He always felt bad for the owners whenever the need arose, but it wasn't like he could walk into a rental company and hire a vehicle.

With no time to be tactful, Ranger sent his elbow through the driver's door window in one solid motion. The safety glass crumbled into the car without too much noise. No alarm sounded, and no owner came running out in a violent rage.

Ranger unlocked the back passenger door and pulled it open so Laura could hide inside the car with James. They climbed in while he yanked the driver's door open and brushed the crumbs of broken glass to the floor. His callused palms deflected any of the sharp edges that were still present.

"Are you sure we can't stop at my place?" Laura asked as Ranger climbed in.

"Not right now. Maybe we can swing by later, though, before we leave town. Provided they've given up on the idea of you going home."

"How long do you think that will be?"

Ranger pulled out a small knife from his leather belt. The sharp blade of the tool had been concealed in the belt, and its handle looked and acted as a belt buckle. He got started on hot-wiring the old Toyota. "About a week to be safe."

"A week? Please tell me you're joking."

"I wish I were, but Bill and Liam will probably have one of their guys sit outside your home for two or three days at least. Maybe longer."

"How can you know that?" she asked. "You don't know a thing about them."

"I do," he said, not explaining further. Ranger had seen just how far criminals would go to get what they wanted, especially when their egos were at stake. And judging by the way Liam and most likely his two pals were waltzing around with concealed and unregistered firearms in the middle of the afternoon, it meant they were well connected.

"Well, that's great," Laura said, frustration cracking her voice. It was understandable given the circumstances.

"I promise you we'll go to your place as soon as possible."

She shook her head. "A week is too long. I've only got a day or two of his meds with me. Then he'll need his next dose."

"Shit," Ranger muttered. "What's he on? My contact could pick something up."

"Not without the prescription that's sitting in my home. James has severe anxiety and a sensory dysfunction. He can't take anything over the counter."

Ranger nodded in the rearview mirror. "Okay. I'll see what I can do. Let's just go to my buddy's house, and we'll figure everything out from there."

"I hope so. Because if James goes without his medication…" She drifted off mid-sentence.

Ranger felt that familiar pang of guilt. It wasn't the first time he was responsible for making someone's life worse. He couldn't keep his wife safe from harm's way. Kaitlyn's death and Cindy's broken life were his fault, no matter which way he sliced it.

Most days, Ranger wished the man who had murdered Kaitlyn had done a better job of shooting him. Leaving him alive to live with the aftermath of that day had broken his soul. He wondered if he'd ever find out who had destroyed his life and why.

The ignition ticked over. Ranger gave the engine a few solid revs to be safe and pressed in the clutch for first gear. It had been a while since he'd driven stick, so he eased the car through the lane and headed for the nearest exit before anyone realized he was stealing their ride.

"Where does your friend live?" Laura asked.

"Far side of town. Toward Tucson. He's got a few acres of private property that's away from everyone."

"That's good, I suppose. Is he a shut-in or something?"

Ranger turned onto the main road and hit the gas, pushing the noisy sedan up to speed. "Nothing like that. Just a man who values his privacy is all."

"As long as he can keep us hidden from Liam. That's all that matters."

Ranger saw a shudder run down her spine in the mirror. He wanted to ask her the awkward question that had been sitting on the edge of his tongue for some time now but wasn't sure how best to approach the subject. He decided to just come out and ask it.

"All that back there with Liam. Why do you owe him money?"

Laura glanced away from the mirror and focused on the road. "Are you seriously going to make me say it?"

"I don't want to," Ranger said. "What you do in your spare time is none of my business."

"That's right."

"But I need to know how badly you owe him."

Laura sighed and closed her eyes for a beat.

"I know this is awkward, but the more you tell me, the better. It will give me a good idea just how far a man like Liam will go to find you."

"He's not a man," she muttered. Laura continued to avoid Ranger's eyes in the rearview mirror. Finally, she answered the question. "I owe him about two or three grand."

"For drugs?"

Laura huffed. "Yes. Oxy mostly. Sometimes a bit of weed. I hurt myself a while back in a car accident. The doctor gave me a prescription for Oxy for the pain. I guess I liked the way it made me feel and got hooked on the stuff."

"Hey, no judgment here," Ranger said.

"I couldn't afford to buy it off the street. Not on the money I make at Rosie's. But I knew Liam could get me some. I kept seeing him at the diner and knew who he was. His family has a meth lab outside of town. That meant he could get me what I wanted. I just had to give him what he wanted…"

Ranger ran a hand through his beard and tried to change the topic. "Must be a big operation."

"Yeah. I've heard they're connected with a cartel."

Ranger's eyes went wide. "And you owe them money."

"No, I owe Liam. We had an arrangement. One that didn't involve cash."

"But?"

Laura stayed silent for a moment. It was clear she didn't want to talk about any of it in front of James. After a minute of quiet, something made her speak. "He's been getting violent lately. Laying hands on me during our time together. He wasn't always like this. Hell, he used to be kind to me. But in the last few months, something dark has been growing inside him."

Ranger grunted. He'd known Liam's type. All sweet one minute, then psychotic the next. A man like that would eventually snap. And if Liam and Bill were in the business of supplying the underworld with drugs, they wouldn't have a problem murdering the mother of a young boy.

Ranger pursed his lips, pitying the mother. Sure, no one was forcing her to buy drugs from the town's biggest scumbag, but he knew better than anyone how screwed up life could become.

"Sit tight, Laura," Ranger said. "We'll reach my buddy's place soon enough and sort this all out. I promise."

"Thank you," she said.

Ranger focused on the road, knowing he had to stop making promises. Especially ones that were hard to keep.

"Say, what's your name, by the way?" Laura asked. "You know mine."

Ranger stared back in the mirror, contemplating which name to give her. He settled on the name he thought she was worthy of knowing. "Frank. Frank Ranger."

"Frank, huh? You don't look like a Frank."

"What do I look like?"

"I don't know. Maybe a John or a Dave. Just not a Frank."

"Well, I hate to disappoint, but I'm Frank."

Laura chuckled, then fell silent. She faced James and leaned down, whispering something soft into his ear.

Ranger gave them as much privacy as he could and kept his eyes on the road.

CHAPTER 8
BILL

Carl scratched the back of his head as he stepped out of Rosie's diner and approached his boss. The look on his face said it all. Bill was waiting in the parking lot inside his Ram pickup with the windows down.

"What's the damage?" Bill asked.

"Liam's out cold but breathing. His two boys have each been shot in the chest. Luckily for them, their vests caught the rounds."

"I don't give a fuck about those two halfwits. What about George—the drifter? The one who attacked them? Any sign of him?"

Carl shook his head. "In the wind. No trace. Rosie saw him leave with Laura and her kid, along with Liam's piece."

Bill slammed his fist against the dash of his truck. "Useless idiots, every one of them."

Carl nodded in agreement. "From what Rosie said, this guy has some skills. Seems like he knows how to handle himself."

Bill sighed. He'd seen it in the drifter's eyes when he sat in the passenger seat of his truck. This George person had clearly been through some hard times and wasn't averse to violence. Bill had underestimated him and should never have sent Junior to the diner to handle the problem. It was a test he was bound to fail.

Bill glanced at his watch and grunted. He didn't have time to deal with the mess his son had created, not with the meeting he still needed to attend. The thought loomed over his head like a sharpened pendulum.

"What do you want to do, boss?" Carl asked.

Bill flexed his shoulders and pulled himself together. "Let's head in and have another chat with Rosie. See if she forgot to mention anything."

"Got it."

Bill got out of the truck and led the way. He stepped up to the restaurant door, gripping the belt on his jeans as he went. Once he pushed through the entrance, he could see the mess George had left behind. The stranger in town had gotten away from three armed men without killing a single one of them. It was impressive, considering how outnumbered he'd been.

Once Bill spotted his son's unconscious body, a wave of shame washed over him. Junior had failed to do his job. All Bill had asked of him was to watch over the drifter, not engage him. If he couldn't handle something so simple, how would he ever be man enough to take over the farm? "Jesus Christ, son," he muttered.

Bill left William where he was and stepped up to the counter of the diner. Rosie was still at her post, but the customers had all been sent away and had been given money to keep their mouths shut. Only Rosie and her cook remained behind.

Rosie couldn't take her eyes off the two groaning men in the corner, who were busy feeling sorry for themselves. Bill had half a mind to drag them out to the desert and put a bullet in each of their thick skulls, but he knew Junior would never forgive him if he ever went through with it.

"Rosie?" Bill asked. "You okay?"

Her eyes snapped to Bill's. "Uh, yeah."

"What happened here?" Rosie had been the one to contact Bill's people. He'd given her a number to call in case the diner ever saw any trouble, as part of her rent and protection plan.

"I don't know. It all went down so fast."

"Hey, hey," Bill said, taking a step closer to the counter. "Calm yourself down. Everything's okay. Now I need you to take a deep breath and tell me exactly what you witnessed. Every detail."

"All right," Rosie said. She took in a lungful of air as suggested and focused on Bill. "After you left, Liam and his two friends came in. They were here asking about that man whose lunch you paid for earlier today. Uh, George, I think."

Bill held her stare.

"Things seemed fine at first. The guys ordered the usual and were happy enough keeping tabs on the man. Then Laura came into the diner with her son."

Bill knew Laura. And so did everyone else at the farm. His son wasn't discreet with the woman he supplied pills to in exchange for sex. "And?"

"Well, Liam and Laura were talking. Things got a bit out of hand, and he—" Rosie cut herself off.

"The truth now," Bill said. "I'm only after information. This stays between you and me."

"Okay, okay. Well, Liam grabbed Laura suddenly and was about to hit her. I think she owes him money."

Bill sighed again. The sex-for-Oxy arrangement William had with Laura was no secret. He'd given her thousands of dollars of the pills over the past few months alone. She must have grown tired of the payment method. No doubt, Junior hadn't taken it well. "What happened next?" Bill asked.

"The man, he sprang into action. He was over to Liam in a heartbeat without him ever knowing it. Hell, I didn't even hear him move across the room. He was so fast."

"What did he do?"

Rosie stared out at the scene again as if it were replaying in her mind. Bill stepped in front of her line of sight to regain her attention.

"Sorry," she said. "The man. He twisted Liam's arm around his body and held him in a headlock to stop Laura from getting hurt. Liam's boys reacted and pulled out their guns."

Rosie stared into the distance again.

"Then?" Bill said, lightly tapping the counter with his open palm. His wedding ring clattered on the surface.

"Uh, then it all went to hell. This guy did something to Liam's arm. I don't know if he broke it, but it sounded bad. Then he pulled a gun from nowhere and shot Liam's friends in the chest. A second later, he cracked Liam over the head with the pistol. Before I could call you, he kicked Liam hard in the face and took off with Laura and James. I've never seen anything like it."

Bill nodded and ran a hand through his gray beard. He turned around and gazed at the booth where William's two boys sat. The useless idiots avoided his eyes at all costs. Bill spat on the ground and stepped away from Rosie before he lost his temper.

When Bill had spotted the drifter out by the dead drop, he'd given him the benefit of the doubt. He had offered this George character a hot meal and a warm bed, all so he'd pass through town without a fuss. But this man was tougher than a two-dollar steak. And to make matters worse, he'd chosen to make his son look weaker than a sack of kittens. Bill couldn't tolerate the Wilkins name being thrown into the mud in such a way. George, or whoever this drifter really was, would be swiftly dealt with, along with Laura. She'd sided with the enemy and could no longer be trusted. The kid Bill would spare. It wasn't his fault his mother was a useless pill-popping traitor.

Turning back to Rosie with a smile, Bill fished out his wallet and retrieved a thousand dollars in cash. He tossed the money on the counter and shoved his wallet back into his jeans. "Thank you, Rosie. I'll have my men clean this up."

"Not a problem, Bill. Thank you for coming by so fast."

Bill waved her off and moved toward his son, both fists clenched.

"Oh, Bill," Rosie said. "There's something else you should know."

"What is it?" Bill asked with a plastered-on grin.

"The man. Before he left, he took some money off the two boys and then asked me if there were any cameras in here. He had a gun, so I told him they were all fake. Then he asked me why I didn't call the cops. I said nothing, of course, but he seemed to be more concerned about the police arriving than anything else."

Bill stroked his gray beard again and weighed up the evidence he had. "Sounds like our man might be on the run from the law. Thank you again, Rosie. That's most helpful." Bill turned and walked over to his unconscious son. He stared down at his boy and shook his head. A half-empty glass of water sat on a nearby table. Bill grabbed it and poured the contents out over his son's face. "Rise and shine, Junior."

William stirred and tried to avoid the water as it splashed into his eyes. "Goddamn it. What the hell?"

"Get up," Bill said with a kick to William's legs.

"What gives, Pops?" William asked as he held one arm with the other while wincing.

Bill dropped to a squat and pulled his son up by the ridiculous jersey he was wearing. William cried out as he grabbed his shoulder with his good arm. "Listen to me, boy. You fucked up today. And a lot more than normal. If you don't make things right, so help me God, I will…" Bill forced his rage down for a moment to stifle his words.

"I'm on it, Dad. I promise. This guy just crept up on us, is all. We'll find him, and we'll waste him. You'll see."

"You'd better, because people in this town need to respect us. How do you think that's going to happen when you keep screwing things up?"

"Christ, okay, Dad. I'm sorry."

"Sorry's not gonna cut it. Not until George is dead, you hear me? Laura, too. You can spare the kid."

William's eyes twitched.

"Is that a problem?"

"Uh, no. I'll handle it."

"Good," Bill said. He released the steel grip he had on his son and let him drop to the floor. William yelled in pain as Bill stood tall. He glanced at Carl by the door and gave him a nod.

Carl pulled out a morphine syringe from his pocket and dropped to William's side.

While rolling about, William realized something was happening. "What's he doing?"

"Fixing you, boy. Now shut the fuck up and let Carl do what he needs to do."

"All right," William said, showing some trust in his old man for a change.

Carl told William to stay still and asked him to release the grip he had on his dislocated shoulder. He pressed him down flat on the ground and grabbed the wrist of his injured arm. "Don't move," he repeated.

"What the hell are you—"

Carl yanked William's arm and released it. William let out an almighty yell as his shoulder snapped back into place. Carl popped the cap on the morphine and stabbed the syringe close to his shoulder, injecting William with the pain-relieving concoction.

"You son of a bitch," William whispered. "You broke my arm."

"Up, boy," Bill said. "That arm ain't broken. It's fixed. Now get off your ass and bring your two chumps along."

William rotated his shoulder and grinned when he could swing his arm again. "Oh, shit. It's all better. He fixed it, Dad."

Bill ushered his son along as he got to his feet. "Of course he did. Now stop messing around. It's time you and your idiot friends do some work. Go sort out this problem before I send every available man in Namrena to flush these people out."

"Okay. Where should I start?" The question felt genuine for a change. Maybe there was hope for his son yet.

"Head over to Laura's place and go through her things. Do whatever it takes to find her."

William nodded. "Okay. I can do this."

Bill grabbed his son by the back of the neck and pulled him in close. He whispered, "You'd better make this right, boy. If you fuck up one more time, I'm going to have Carl put a bullet in those two mouth breathers you call friends. And this time they won't be wearing vests."

Bill released William and left the diner before his son said another word.

CHAPTER 9

RANGER

Ranger pulled up in the stolen sedan just beyond the fence line of Sergeant Donny Brown's property. He and Donny had served together in Afghanistan in the same platoon. That meant they'd been through hell and had seen the best and worst humanity had to offer.

When Ranger went on the run, he'd wanted nothing more than to contact Donny and tell him he was innocent and that he had nothing to do with his wife's murder. But he didn't want to get Donny involved, not with the scores of police hunting him down. When Ranger was originally heading to Namrena, he felt like enough time had passed, and that it was safe for him to visit an old friend. He didn't know if Donny would be home or if he still lived in the town. He didn't have a contact number to call first. Just an address the soldier had given him back in Afghanistan. Ranger had unintentionally memorized it. It was a habit he'd developed during his deployment as a redundancy policy in case of tech failures. He only wished he had done the same with Donny's cell phone number.

With any hope, Donny would be home when Ranger came

by. He needed his help. Especially with the incident at the diner.

"What are we doing?" Laura asked from the back seat of the sedan. James had his arms firmly wrapped around her body. All the windows in the car were down, but it only made a small difference to the sweltering temperature. "I thought we were going to your friend's place?"

"We are. I just don't know if he's home or not," Ranger said to the rearview mirror.

"What do you mean?" she asked. Her brows narrowed tight. "Wait a second. He doesn't know you're coming, does he?"

"Not exactly, but he'll remember who I am the moment he sees me. We go way back. We served together in Afghanistan."

"You're a Marine?"

"I was a Marine. A sergeant."

"Was?"

Ranger turned away from the mirror. "Yeah. It's a long story." He opened the creaking driver's door and climbed out.

"Hey, where are you going?"

Ranger scratched his head. "To see if my buddy's home."

Laura scoffed. "Wait, you're not seriously going to show up on his doorstep uninvited?"

"Yeah."

"What happens if he's not here?"

Ranger stopped in the dirt road and glimpsed up at the clear blue sky. He let the question hang in the air for a moment before he turned around and walked over to the open window of the back door of the car. He leaned down and stared at Laura. She stared right back at him without budging an inch. She seemed to be finding her feet now.

"Laura," Ranger started, "I know none of this is ideal, I

do, but I need you to trust me and let me do what needs doing."

"Trust you? I don't know you."

Ranger stared at the dusty ground. "That's true. But you know what? I stepped in back at the diner when no one else would. If I weren't on the level, then I would have just up and left."

Laura closed her eyes for a moment and exhaled. "Frank, I appreciate what you did for me, I really do, but here's the thing: this isn't the first time that piece of crap has hit me in front of other people."

Ranger's jaw dropped. He knew he had overreacted to the three morons in the diner. He understood all too well that he'd gotten Laura and James involved in a mess they could never clean up. But he couldn't help what went down. After losing his wife, after failing to keep her safe, seeing another woman in trouble set him off.

"I'm sorry," Ranger said, apologizing again for what he could not undo.

She placed a hand on the one he had planted on the open window. "You didn't know."

"I'm gonna make it right. I swear."

She gave him a forced smile. It was clear to him she didn't think he would be able to save her from these people. Ranger pushed away from the car and ran a hand through his hair. "Stay here. I'll see if Donny is home."

"Okay. But please hurry. This place looks creepy."

She wasn't wrong. The front of Donny's property held a sturdy metal ranch gate. It appeared to have been weathered by the Arizona sun and had faded red letters on an old sign that read KEEP OUT. Desert brush had also gathered around the posts. The gate wasn't just to keep people out. Knowing Donny the way he did, it was meant to make them think twice about entering.

Ranger let out his breath. His first hassle was to figure out a way to move up to Donny's door without being shot. Donny treated home security as a priority. Strolling on up to the man's front door was a risk in itself. Ranger had never been to the place before, but he'd heard all about the setup Donny had when they served.

Ranger left Laura behind with her son in the car, promising he'd be back in a minute. He hoped that was the case as he ran a hand around the rotting gatepost that guarded the driveway up to Donny's private property. Along with the aging KEEP OUT sign, the gate was covered with multiple warnings that made all kinds of threats to trespassers. Ranger felt a pang of doubt run through his core and was unsure if he was making a mistake.

"Too late now," he muttered to himself.

Ranger climbed over the creaky gate. The second his feet hit the ground on the other side, a sting of nerves hit his gut. The feeling continued as he moved along a dirt road that was shouldered with overgrown shrubs. Ahead, he found an old timber house that was surrounded by unkempt bushes. The modest house looked to be abandoned from a distance, with boarded-up windows and doors.

"Shit," Ranger muttered. Had Donny moved on from this address? The only reason he had initially come to see him was to finally catch up with someone from his old life who might listen to him about his innocence. Donny was the only person he trusted to talk to about it. Ranger wasn't sure what the plan was going to be after he'd spoken to his old friend, but now he needed Donny. If the man didn't live in town any longer, then Ranger didn't know where he'd take Laura next.

He continued along the road, ever aware that Sergeant Donny "Hatchet" Brown had been a sniper in Afghanistan who had saved his ass on more than one occasion against the Taliban. If Donny was somewhere close by or in the abandoned home, Ranger only hoped his friend would realize who was walking slowly up his driveway. It was the only reason he left his hat and shades back in the sedan. Leaving the Glock behind under the floor mat in the sedan when Laura wasn't looking was also a wise decision. Donny would spot the hidden gun in the back of his jeans in an instant.

The closer Ranger got to the house, the worse it looked, leaving him to doubt if anyone had lived within its decaying walls for several years. Sure, Ranger and Donny had both lived in crappy conditions over in Afghanistan, especially on long missions away from base, but this house seemed beyond repair.

Ranger reached the front door and discovered there would be no way for him to open it without a claw hammer. Aging boards of timber offcuts had been nailed across to keep the world out. With a soft groan, Ranger realized he was wasting his time and had nowhere in town to go. There was no one else to turn to, and Bill's people would soon find him and end his little rebellion. Laura and James would pay the price for his failings.

"That's far enough," said an unfamiliar and deep voice from behind. The barrel of a pistol dug into the small of Ranger's back. A second later, Ranger felt the cool blade of a knife press up against his throat. He froze on the spot, aware beyond a doubt that someone had gotten the drop on him.

"You've got about three seconds to tell me who the hell you are." The knife pressed into his skin.

"Take it easy," Ranger said. "I'm looking for a friend of mine. Thought he lived here, was all. Didn't mean to cause any trouble. I'll just be on my way." He made a slight move to turn around but stopped the second more pressure was applied from the blade.

"Did I say you could move? Now stay right there."

Ranger gave a small nod as the gun and knife fell away

from his body. The man behind took several strides back, no doubt keeping his pistol trained on Ranger's center mass. One wrong step and he'd be dead.

"Okay. Put your hands on your head and turn around. Do it slow. Nice and easy."

Doing as instructed, Ranger slapped both hands to his head and swiveled on the spot. The man was wearing a baseball cap low over his sunglass-covered eyes and a bandanna over his mouth and nose. He had a Beretta 92FS trained on Ranger's face and seemed quite serious about the intrusion. The combat knife had been returned to its sheath.

Ranger stood firm, waiting for his next lot of instructions. But none came as the pistol lowered.

"No way," the man said. The deep voice had climbed an octave into a familiar tone. "Frank? Is that you?" The man pulled his bandanna down to reveal a thick mustache that sat above an open, confused mouth.

"Hi, Donny," Ranger said, recognizing the man he'd been through hell with.

CHAPTER 10

Donny had lowered his Beretta 92FS away from Ranger's face but kept the gun level. His brow dug into the bridge of his nose as his confusion held firm.

"It's okay," Ranger said. "I'm unarmed."

"Yeah, I got that. That's not my problem."

"What, then?" Ranger asked, with his hands still on his head.

Donny lowered his pistol farther and placed it into the side holster he had strapped to the leg of his cargo pants. He shook his head as he looked Ranger up and down. "I don't know. Guess I'm not used to seeing ghosts this up close and personal." Donny held his gaze for a moment longer, then walked toward his dilapidated house.

"Who said I was dead?" Ranger asked.

Donny stopped and faced him. His eyes stabbed through the hot afternoon air that had blown in from the desert, but he didn't say a word. Donny continued walking, ignoring Ranger's question. He moved at a steady pace past the front door and traveled around to the side of the home. An old refrigerator had been dragged outside and left to lean up against the wall of the property. Donny shuffled the metal box across to reveal a side entrance the refrigerator was concealing. Several newer-looking deadbolts had been installed on the door.

"Don't tell me you live here?" Ranger asked.

Donny glanced back, pausing during the process of unlocking the door. "I don't live here. Well, sometimes." He continued jiggling a set of keys about until the door clicked open. Ranger moved closer but kept his distance. Something seemed off about Donny. He was not the man he knew only eighteen months ago. Then again, the same could be said about Ranger. They hadn't seen each other since Afghanistan.

"You coming in?" Donny asked.

Ranger glanced back to where Laura and James would be through the shrubbery. "Sure."

"Don't worry," Donny said with a twisted smile. "They'll be okay for a few minutes. You can call them in soon."

"You saw them?"

"Yeah."

"Okay. Did I catch you on your way back in here or something?" Ranger avoided using the word "home." A glance inside the nearly blacked-out rooms of the house gave him the overwhelming urge to flee back to Laura and James and get the hell out of there. Donny must have had hidden security cameras or a sixth sense to know they were there.

"Something like that," Donny replied as he stepped inside what appeared to be a living room. It was hard to tell with the lack of decent furniture or a TV. All Ranger could see was a small couch and a coffee table to one side. To the other was a scuffed dining table covered in oil stains, as if Donny had been using the surface as a workbench. He moved through the open-plan home and went straight past an island bench to the kitchen. Ranger ventured inside and closed the door behind him.

"Lock that," Donny said.

Ranger gave him a nod and twisted the locks into place. He scanned the room, locating the front door to the building, or at least the area that was the front door. Donny had covered it with thick lengths of timber and had nailed it shut on both sides.

Two beers came from an actual working refrigerator and landed on the island bench in front of Donny. One got slid in Ranger's general direction as Donny popped the cap off his using the end of the bench. The man didn't wait for the foam to settle before he took a long swig, devouring a third of the bottle in one go. Ranger wasn't so haphazard with his own bottle and gently popped the cap on his end of the bench. He took a sip of the cool beverage and placed it down. It had been some time since he'd drunk a cold beer, and now he'd had two in the space of a short time.

"So tell me, Ranger, what brings a ghost like yourself to my neck of the woods?"

"Why do you keep calling me a ghost?"

Donny took another large swig of beer and released his breath. "Simple. You're dead."

"Dead?"

"You heard me. Dead. That's the official word from my guy in the brass. Last time I bothered to check, anyway. He said the feds got you in a shoot-out up north."

Ranger shook his head over and over. "No. They almost got me, but I'm very much alive."

"So there was a shoot-out?"

Ranger scratched the back of his head. "Yes and no. I didn't fire a single round at those feds, but I was in the middle of a gunfight between them and a gang of bikers."

"You're shitting me?"

"Afraid not."

"Wow. You think you know a guy. Wait, though. Why did they say you were dead?"

"I wish I could say. Unfortunately, I can't tell you how these people think. It was probably easier for them to say I was dead than to admit I got away."

"Yeah, I guess…"

An awkward silence fell over the room. Donny cleared his throat. "Now, I gotta ask you something, and I hate to do this, but—"

"I didn't kill my wife," Ranger said, cutting Donny off.

Donny studied Ranger for what felt like a long time before he said, "Okay. Do you know who did?"

"No. I just know what the guy looks like."

"How?" Donny asked.

Ranger felt a familiar icy rage flood his veins. "I was there when he pulled the trigger. He killed her less than a few feet from me."

"Jesus," Donny said.

"Yeah."

"I had no idea. I'm sorry you lost Kaitlyn like that. I couldn't imagine how hard it must have been."

Ranger took a hefty swig of his beer this time. He went to answer and instead took another gulp. His wife's murder was a hard subject to discuss on a good day.

"You wanna talk about it?" Donny asked.

"Not really. But then again, I've never told anyone much about that day. Maybe I should say something."

"You don't have to," Donny said. "I shouldn't have said anything."

"No, it's okay. I should do this. Eighteen months ago, I got home from Afghanistan after they released us from duty. I was excited to see Kaitlyn and Cindy and put everything we did over there behind me, you know?"

"I get it. We saw some crazy shit I won't soon forget."

Ranger nodded with an absent stare. "So anyway, I walked in the door, but everything felt wrong. It was too quiet. The kind that makes your stomach drop. Still, I moved through the house and tried to shake the feeling. But then I heard a voice from the kitchen. One I didn't know."

Donny held his focus as Ranger spoke.

"So I walk in, and there they are. Three guys in fancy suits. All of them were concealing a pistol. Kaitlyn was sitting at the table, pale as a ghost. The leader of the three said he was from some private security firm, wanting me for a job. But I don't know, there was something not right about him. His offer sounded like bullshit, like there was another reason for him being there. I played along and tried to stay calm. Then the guy brought up my last mission in Afghanistan."

"What mission?" Donny hadn't been part of Ranger's final mission. Only two-thirds of his squad had.

"A recovery mission. We were ordered to find some crates the Taliban had picked up from a supply truck they'd hit."

"And the brass wanted you to go find it? Sounds straight fucked-up to me."

"I had the same thought. Especially when I was told I'd be a fire team down."

"Only the nine of you? You're kidding?"

"Afraid not. It was not exactly what you'd call ideal. Still, I did as I was told. We trekked out into the shit and got some intel from the locals. They said the crates were probably in a certain cave in the area we'd been assigned to search. It sounded like we were walking into an ambush, but I didn't turn back."

"Jesus," Donny said. "Talk about a clusterfuck. And that close to being pulled off the line as well. Not that we knew it at the time. Still."

"You know the brass. Anyway, we got to the cave easy enough. There were obvious signs of the Taliban throughout, so we approached with caution. What we found inside made no sense."

"What'd you see?" Donny asked, leaning toward Ranger.

"Dead Taliban fighters. At least a dozen of 'em. Couldn't have been there more than a day. All shot with 7.62×39mm, from what we could tell."

"Shit. In-fighting? Factions hitting each other?"

"Maybe. Either way, better them than us, right? And guess what? All the crates are there in perfect condition. Not a thing missing."

Donny whistled. "Okay, this just gets crazier by the minute. What did you do?"

"We hauled them in. I thought we'd done the impossible and completed the mission with a fire team down, without a single casualty. Didn't even fire a single round. We took the crates back to base, and that was that."

Donny pursed his lips. "But it wasn't that easy, right?"

"Nope. According to the uninvited asshole who came into my home, the crates had more than just weapons inside them. He claimed there was heroin hidden in the base of every crate. And as if that wasn't bad enough, he said it had all been stolen."

"Holy shit," Donny let out.

"Exactly. I swore up and down that I didn't know anything about it. But this son of a bitch didn't care. He said he wanted his drugs back, or they'd hurt Kaitlyn. I tried to reason with him. I even offered to help track down whoever took it, but it was too late. One of his goons reached for his gun, so I fought back. I managed to take out two of them. But the leader got the drop on me."

Donny didn't say a word and stared.

Ranger forced himself to continue. "Then the monster pulled out a second gun. It was the Beretta I kept in my bedroom. He held it to Kaitlyn's head and made me kneel."

Ranger paused and closed his eyes for a moment as he felt himself being taken back to that moment. "I couldn't move. I couldn't stop him. He shot her. Right in front of me. Killed her with my own gun."

"Frank," Donny started, "I…"

Ranger shook his head as his fist tightened around the beer. He had more to say. "Then he shot me. In the head. The shot grazed me and knocked me out. I don't know if he meant to kill me or what, but he left me for dead and framed me for the murder of my wife."

Donny cleared his throat. "Wow. That's screwed up, Frank. I don't know what else to say."

"There's nothing to say. My only saving grace was that Cindy wasn't there. She was at her nana's place for the night."

"That's lucky," Donny said. Then a moment of silence ran over the room.

Ranger felt a release as he finally got to tell the truth to someone who might believe him. It was almost like a weight off his chest. He only wished his story had a different ending.

"So, what have you been doing since you escaped?" Donny asked, changing the subject slightly. "Apart from getting into wild shoot-outs with feds and bikers?"

"Just surviving, I guess. Running, for the most part."

"Surviving," Donny muttered, shaking his head. "How is this possible?"

"What is it?" Ranger asked.

Donny seemed to be holding back on saying more. He paced around for a second, then came to a stop. "What happened to them, Frank?"

"What happened to who?"

"Your squad. Not all of them. Just the eight guys who were with you on that mission."

Ranger sighed, understanding. He hadn't spoken to any

of his men since he left Afghanistan, and knew they were scattered across the United States. Finding each man to speak to about the heroin claim would be no simple task. Not when he didn't have their contact details or addresses. "I don't know. What am I missing here?"

Donny's brows rose. "You don't know, do you?"

"Know what?"

Donny exhaled a long breath. "Your guys on that mission. They're all dead, Frank. Every last one of them."

CHAPTER 11

"What?" Ranger spat out, stumbling back from Donny in his dilapidated kitchen. Eight other guys from his squad were dead. Instantly, Ranger thought of the man in the suit and what he had said about the stolen heroin. "How did they die?" Ranger asked.

Donny glanced up like he was lost in thought. "Suicides, car accidents, drug overdoses. You name it. Everyone said that you guys were cursed. It was one death after another."

Ranger shook his head. He couldn't believe what he was hearing. He'd been so focused on his own problems and had disconnected himself from the world. Why hadn't he stopped to check on any of them after Kaitlyn was murdered? Why hadn't he tried to warn them?

He thought about O'Connor, Dena, Johnson, and Evans. About Santos, Reed, Mitchell, and Thompson. Ranger had bled with these men, and now Donny was saying they were all dead. It didn't seem possible.

"Eight guys. Dead," Donny continued. "And you were number nine, rumored to be shot dead by the feds after running from your life sentence. The only ones alive are the guys who weren't on that last mission."

Ranger's jaw slackened. "How is that possible?" Ranger had thought a lot about his squad over the last year. Someone in the twelve had to have been involved in the business with the heroin, but he could never work out who. With every person sent on the weapons recovery mission dead except for Ranger, it was obvious now that the fire team who had been suddenly called away had something to do with it all.

"Those sons of bitches," Ranger whispered.

Donny leaned toward him. "Who?"

"Harris, Carter, Rodriguez, and Murphy. It was them. All along. They must have stolen the heroin or something. Then that bastard came looking for it and killed Kaitlyn."

Donny scoffed. "Holy shit." He pointed a finger at Ranger. "Wait a minute. You came here. Does anyone else know where you are? Apart from those two people out there?"

"No. Of course not."

"How can you be so sure?"

"Because I walked into town. Well, mostly. Besides, if they knew where I was, I'd be dead already."

The rest of Donny's beer vanished down his throat. He opened a second bottle and took a swig. "Jesus, Frank. What the hell?"

"I'm sorry."

"Don't tell me you're sorry. Tell me why you're here."

"I don't know. I guess I was coming to see you."

Donny chuckled. "Of course. Why not? I love it when people bring their problems to my doorstep. Hey, wait a minute. Why did you say 'was'? What the hell does that mean?"

Ranger ran a hand through his beard. "On top of what I told you, I'm in a bit of a bind."

Donny crossed his arms over his chest and leaned his

head forward. "Does this bind involve those two people out in that stolen sedan?"

Ranger nodded. He was tempted to ask Donny how he knew the car was stolen, but there was no point. Donny finished his beer and slammed the empty glass bottle down hard enough for it to have shattered.

"All right," Donny said, exhaling. "Enough screwing around. I want straight answers now. Why are there two people in a stolen car with you?"

Before Ranger could say a word, Donny strode back to the refrigerator and retrieved his third beer. He opened it as roughly as he had the last two and took a hefty swig. "Well?" he asked with an open palm.

Ranger shifted his weight. "Let's just say there was an incident in town. I need to take them as far away from this place as possible. I could use your help with supplies. Maybe some cash if you can spare it."

Donny's brows dug into his nose again. "What did you do?"

"It was nothing. I was walking into town to visit you, but I got offered a ride by some good Samaritan. The guy begged me to hop in. There was something about him that told me I couldn't say no, so I accepted."

"Okay," Donny said, his voice level.

Ranger filled Donny in on his chance encounter with Bill Wilkins and how the man in his sixties had placed him at the diner to keep tabs on him. Donny didn't move a muscle and stared at Ranger with a sniper's eye.

"Later, three rough-looking guys showed up to make sure I did what the supposed farmer had told me to do. I'd already worked out that the guy who gave me the ride had a lot of sway around town. Their presence simply confirmed it. Anyway, they were doing a lousy job of watching me until the leader of the trio started harassing this girl. One thing led to another and—"

"You stepped in, didn't you? Just like with that damn village in Marjah."

"She was about to have hands laid on her in front of her own kid. What was I supposed to do?"

Donny didn't reply as he paced up and down the small kitchen with his arms crossed. His beer was tucked under his elbow. With a yell, he threw it across the room. The bottle smashed against the wall and sprayed its contents in all directions. "I'll say it again: you fucking came here?"

"I was careful," Ranger said. "What's the problem?"

Donny slammed both palms flat on the kitchen bench. "Tell me you didn't kill anyone."

"No. I just disabled this guy named Liam and shot his two goons in their Kevlar. They'll all be fine."

Donny held both hands over his face and concealed a muffled shout. "This is bad. You're telling me you attacked Bill Wilkins' son, and you have his girlfriend out in your car?"

"Wait. You know who these people are? All of them? Including Laura?"

Donny continued his pacing and started muttering to himself. Ranger could see his hands squeezing into fists.

"Donny?" Ranger asked. "Talk to me."

"Talk to you? Come on, Ranger. You need to leave. Right now. I don't need this shit. Do you understand me? You got more crap coming your way than you know, and you've brought it to my doorstep."

"She needs our help, Donny, and so does her son. They need supplies for the road and money to relocate. I can't show my face around town for multiple reasons. But you can." Ranger stepped closer to Donny and cut off his pacing. "I can find my way out of here, but these two need to get away from this town and into the next state. Only you can make that happen."

Donny closed his eyes and let his breath flow out of him. "You don't understand. I can't help them."

"Yes, you can. Besides, you owe me."

Ranger's few words opened Donny's eyes in a flash. "You can't be serious? You're gonna cash in that favor for them? Some people you don't even know?"

"They need help. And we can give it to them. If you do this for me, we'll be even."

Donny chuckled and stared at the ground. "This is beyond fucking stupid."

"It's not. You're saving two people from these maniacs. You obviously know who the Wilkinses are and what they are capable of."

Donny muttered something inaudible. The man looked like he had conversations with himself. Had his time in Afghanistan done some damage, or was it all a case of Ranger laying too much on him at once? "Do we have a deal?" Ranger asked.

"Yes, fine. I'll help them. But let's make one thing crystal clear: the second this is done, what you did for me will be forgotten, got it?"

Ranger thought back to their time in the sandbox. Donny had assisted Ranger countless times as part of an overwatch fire team. But one extra hot day during a patrol, Donny and his fire team got cut off from the rest of his squad and came close to being overrun. Ranger and a few volunteers pushed back through the line and made it to Donny's location. Thanks to their efforts, Donny got out, but not before two of his men got cut down and torn to ribbons by rifle fire.

Ranger sighed. "Just get them to safety, and we're square."

Donny scratched his head again. "All right. But then I

want you gone. Between the cops, heroin deals gone wrong, and the Wilkinses, you're bad company, Frank. No offense."

Ranger offered Donny his hand. "We got a deal."

Donny paused for a moment, then took it. "Don't make me regret this."

"You won't."

A chuckle escaped Donny's lips. "Let's get to work. You can start by getting that car off the street. Take my keys. Red one's for the gate."

"On it," Ranger said, heading to the door. He'd never seen Donny so serious in his whole life. Ranger unbolted the door and opened it. He charged outside and rounded the bend to run down the driveway. Less than thirty seconds later, he reached the gate and hopped over it in one graceful motion.

Ranger found Laura and James where he'd left them. Laura had her door open to let in cooler air than was inside the overheating car. He'd left the two of them there for much longer than he should have.

Laura reacted to Ranger's hop over the gate and climbed out of the car. "What is it? What's happened?"

He didn't answer as he undid the thick padlock on the gate. He yanked the chain through and clear before he swung the gate open. He rushed up to the stolen sedan and started the car, guiding Laura back into the rear passenger seat a second later.

"Frank, tell me what's up."

While revving the engine, Ranger glanced at Laura. "It's my friend. He knows about the Wilkinses and the trouble I've caused. He said we need to head inside and keep out of sight."

"Okay, but why the panic? No one's here. They wouldn't have a clue where we are. Just take a breath, okay?"

He nodded and did as he was told, taking a deep breath in

and letting it slowly out. "Thank you. I guess I was just freaked out a little by the look on Donny's face."

"Donny?"

"My buddy. He knows who the Wilkinses are."

Laura held James close and spoke softly. "Everyone knows who they are. And not in a good way."

"I'm sorry. I knew they were bad news before I got involved. But I guess I underestimated them."

"What makes you say that?"

"Simple. Things must be screwed up if the Wilkinses have Donny rattled."

Laura didn't respond as Ranger drove the car past the gate. He cast a glance at the rearview mirror again and saw a thick worry line running across her brow. She'd seemed calm until he came running up to the sedan with concerning news. For her sake and his own, he needed to do a better job at staying in control.

Once Ranger cleared the gate, he tapped the brake and climbed out of the dusty vehicle to swing the gate closed again and lock it.

Within a minute, he had shifted the sedan up and out of view of the road as much as he could. In case he needed to make a quick exit, he kept the car in an accessible location.

"Let's go," Ranger said over his shoulder to Laura and James once they were out of the car. He waited for the pair to move. Then, from under the seat, he pulled out the Glock 21 he'd beaten Liam Wilkins over the head with and tucked it into the back of his jeans. Chances were he was going to need it again soon.

Ranger guided Laura and a concerned James up to the side door he'd left unlocked, only to find it was locked again. Donny had rebolted the door in his paranoia. Ranger had the keys, though, but he wanted to make sure Donny was okay. "Open up, Donny. It's Ranger. We're here."

A few seconds later, the door unlocked and swung open to allow the three inside. Ranger walked Laura and James through the house and sat them down on the sofa. Donny closed the side entrance and checked every bolt twice as he locked up again.

"Thank you," Ranger said, catching his breath. He placed Donny's keys down on the messy coffee table. "What do we do now?"

Donny didn't answer and pulled out his Beretta 92FS again. "We pray no one knows any of you are here."

CHAPTER 12

BILL

Not having the time to deal with Liam's latest mistake—one of many in a long chain of never-ending failures—Bill traveled back to the farm in a hurry. Carl drove while Bill let multiple thoughts run through his head at the same time.

His Tucson contact had called minutes after they'd left the diner, demanding a meetup in the next hour. The meeting he'd been thinking about all day had been pushed forward. Something was up.

It was unlike the people in Tucson to call and change the schedule in such a way, and the thought left a bad feeling in Bill's gut. He wondered what the driving force was behind the meeting: his contact in Tucson or the cartel across the border? Either way, the problem had to be dealt with head-on.

Bill hated anything that interrupted his day. First, there was the delay of collecting one of the dead drops. Then his son and the menace in town were giving him stomach ulcers. Now, the change in schedule was center stage, making him want to pull out his hair. He also had other minor problems to attend to back on the farm, but business with Tucson always came first. If he kept them happy, they kept the cartel element happy.

Bill's Colt Python stirred in his holster. Something told him between the meeting and the problem with his son, he'd be needing the weapon. For what, he didn't know, but he hoped it would only be used to put a few bullets into the man who called himself "George" and nothing more. Bill wasn't looking to go to war with anyone.

When he arrived back at the farm, he rushed inside the main house to change into something that didn't scream hick farmer. He'd spent most of his life trying to convince the people in town he was a farmer. But with his business contacts in Tucson, he wanted them to think the opposite. He dressed in a suit and tie as a sign of respect and to be taken seriously. They never returned the favor, though, but that didn't stop Bill from playing his part.

Inside the primary bedroom of his house on the farm, Bill placed the .357 on his dresser and caught sight of his reflection. He sighed at the figure staring back, only seeing what they all saw: an old man who was close to the end of a long game. But this old man still had plenty of fight left in him, and he would not let anyone think otherwise.

He got changed into a dark-blue suit with a dress shirt and a red tie. Then cleaned the dirt and grit from his hands and strolled out of his bedroom with a straight back.

A knock came at the door. "Come in," Bill called, knowing who it was. Carl opened the door and walked in a few paces.

"What do you suppose this is all about, sir?" Carl asked. Bill turned to Carl as he returned the .357 to his hip holster and concealed the weapon with his jacket. "I got no idea, son, and that makes me nervous." Bill straightened himself up and dusted off his jacket for the third time. He was forever slapping dirt out of his clothing at the farm.

"I've got your back, sir."

"I know you do, Carl." Bill slapped the man on the biceps. "We'd best be getting a move on. Can't keep these people waiting. Let's take the Chrysler." Bill was talking about his Chrysler 300C. It wasn't the most luxurious car a man in his position could afford, but it was one of the few vehicles in his fleet that had been armored. Just like the X5 he had given to his son, he'd spent a small fortune having the windows and panels armored. He'd also gone to the extra precaution of having the gas tank, tires, engine, and even the flooring made to withstand a beating from most rifle rounds. The bottom of the car could even handle an explosion from a grenade and keep on driving. The vehicle damn near rivaled the president of the United States' Cadillac in terms of sturdiness.

Carl escorted his boss to the fleet of pickups, sedans, and trucks the farm had at its disposal. He collected the 300C and backed it out to Bill's side. Bill climbed in and felt safer once the thick, reinforced door was closed. The thought of the meeting had him on edge. His main Tucson contact, a Latino man named Dallas, never deviated from the schedule. Not without giving a solid reason beforehand. The guy had a temper, sure, but he was methodical when it came to their meetings. Bill felt unprepared. He was used to going into a situation with enough ways out to feel comfortable. He prayed the higher-ups in the game hadn't decided it was time for an early retirement for him. Carl swiveled around in the driver's seat and looked his boss in the eyes. "All set?"

Bill nodded. "Get us over there as fast as you can."

"What about some backup? We always take at least ten guys."

"Not this time. Tucson requested it be just me and a driver."

"Shit," Carl said with a heavy sigh. "This is serious."

"Uh-huh. Anyway, we don't have a choice. Get a move on so we can get this crap over with."

"Yes, sir." Carl revved the modified engine on the 300C. It had to bear the extra weight the armor added. He drove up the main driveway and through the open gate, leaving behind a full crew of men who could have been useful if things got out of hand in Tucson.

Bill cursed under his breath. He was confident he was walking into a trap. That, or he was letting his paranoia get the best of him again. Maybe this was the universe's way of telling him it was time to push up his own retirement plans and exit the game before it was too late.

"Screw this," Bill muttered. Before the car got too far down the road, he pulled out his cell phone. He had a decision to make.

CHAPTER 13
RANGER

Donny rattled his Beretta 92FS against his leg as he stared at Laura and James. Laura kept her eyes on him, clearly not loving the fact that the man Ranger claimed would help them was living in a boarded-up house, wielding a gun.

"You can put that away," Ranger said, pointing to Donny's pistol.

"Yeah, sure," Donny replied, keeping his focus on Laura and James. He tucked the weapon into its holster as his brows remained narrowed in on his guests like they were going to steal something. There was nothing in the run-down place worth taking.

Ranger continued to watch Donny. He seemed to be more on edge than when they'd been in Afghanistan on patrol.

Donny stepped around in front of Laura, placing his back to Ranger. "You got a cell phone?"

Ranger answered for her. "No. I destroyed it. They're both off the grid."

"Good," Donny said. "And you're sure no one followed you here?"

"Positive. I took the long way around and drove past the place twice before parking out front. Besides, you live in the part of town no one wants to be in. We weren't followed."

"We'll see, Frank," Donny said as he glanced away toward the back of his house. He moved about the place like there was a team of Navy SEALS outside who were about to smash through the barred-up windows. Why was Donny so agitated? He and Ranger had fought the Taliban, for God's sake. Donny knew something about the Wilkinses that no one else did, and Ranger needed to find out what that was. But first, he had other problems to focus on.

"We need to discuss our next move," Ranger said.

Laura stood, cutting off the conversation that existed between the two men as if she were not there. "What's there to discuss? I say we fill up the gas tank in that car and get out of town."

Donny chuckled. "That easy, huh? Do you think Ranger would have come here if it were as simple as that?"

"It is. The longer we spend in Namrena, the easier it will be for Liam to find me."

"I know," Ranger said. "And that's why we can't just drive out of town. That piece-of-crap car won't take us far before it breaks down. Then we'll be stuck on the road. Bill and Liam will find us in no time. Or one of their people will. I'm guessing the Wilkinses have plenty of contacts in the region. That's why we need to do this right."

Laura avoided Ranger's eyes. She was right to be upset. He hadn't given her an option when he got involved. He had made Liam look incompetent in front of his own people and the public. By siding with Ranger, Laura had destroyed any possibility of being forgiven.

Donny continued with his edgy behavior and paced the room while he stared at Laura. Ranger shook his head and kept the conversation with Laura alive. "I've been thinking, to do this smart, we need supplies and to change our looks. We'll also need some fake IDs. Maybe a passport for you and James if there's time. From what I can tell, the Wilkinses must have connections far and wide in this state. No one in the diner bothered to call the police."

Laura shifted her focus to Ranger and said, "From what Liam's told me, Bill's got half the cops on his payroll. And a few in the next town over."

"Okay. So you understand why we can't take off without being prepared. If any of those officers find us, we're done."

"I know," she said as if admitting it to herself.

"The things we need," Ranger continued, "I can't collect without Liam or Bill noticing. But Donny, you can drive into town without raising any suspicions."

Donny chuckled as he walked away. Ranger observed the soldier to better comprehend where he was at with the idea and the situation. He followed Donny as Laura dropped back down to the sofa, holding herself tight. James stayed close by and made Ranger think about Cindy and the way she used to snuggle in close to Kaitlyn. He'd never see that again.

Donny made some noise in the next room, drawing Ranger's attention. He stepped after his friend and made sure not to stand too close to him.

"She's keen to leave, huh?" Donny said as he moved back into the kitchen.

"Seems that way." Ranger had no idea, if he was being honest. In the short time he'd known Laura, she'd come across as timid. Especially around Liam. She was starting to come out of her shell around Ranger. Underneath her fear, he could see a strength that could only come from taking care of a kid who had challenging difficulties.

"As long as she keeps her head down," Donny said, "we'll all—"

A loud buzz rattled from the benchtop. Ranger glanced at

the source of the noise and saw a cheap cell phone light up with a text. Donny snatched up the device and read the text in a flash.

"Crap," he said.

"Anything wrong?"

"Uh, no. I need to go see someone."

"Right now?"

"Can't be avoided. I'll be back as soon as I can, okay? Maybe work on that list of supplies you wanted while I'm gone." He lowered the phone and shoved it into his pocket.

Ranger didn't know what to make of the text Donny had just received. Whatever it had said, the words got him moving. He watched Donny disappear into the back of his home and reappear less than a minute later with a rucksack over his shoulder.

Donny kept his eyes forward and distant. It was a look Ranger recognized all too well from their time in the sandbox. If he didn't know any better, he would swear Donny was about to head out on a mission of some description.

Ranger walked along behind him, trying to determine if anything about the rucksack would tell him what he needed to know.

"I'll be back soon, Frank. Keep the light to a minimum and don't make any noise. And keep them both in the house at all times. If anyone drives past and spots them, it's over."

"Wilco," Ranger replied. He witnessed Donny leave through the side door and locked it the second he was clear.

"Where is he going?" Laura asked with a furrowed brow.

"Not sure," Ranger said. He inched closer to one of the sealed windows and stared out a small gap in the wooden offcuts that had been hammered to the frame. With one eye open, Ranger followed Donny as he paced out of earshot of the house.

"What the hell are you doing, Hatchet?" Ranger whispered to himself. Whatever reason Donny had to leave left a sinking feeling in the pit of his gut. He walked over to Laura and placed a hand on her shoulder. She glanced up at him and looked ready for more bad news. She was probably getting used to it by now.

"What's wrong?" she asked.

"Something is up with Donny."

"That's an understatement," she said, keeping her voice level.

Ranger removed his hand from her shoulder and placed it on his hip. He had a decision to make, and realized whichever way he went, things could end badly. "I'm going to follow him."

"You what?"

"I need to work out where he's going."

"Why?"

"I'm just worried. He's an old friend."

Laura's mouth fell open. "You can't be serious. You drag us out to this weird house, claiming your friend can help us, and now you're going after him when he ups and leaves? Maybe he's just got somewhere he needs to be. You didn't even know if he would be home."

Ranger didn't respond as he crept back to the same boarded-up window. He peeked through the tiny gap again to see Donny open a tucked-away shed where a late-model Ram 1500 Express was sitting. Donny opened the driver's door and climbed in with his rucksack. A second later, he fired up the V8 engine and drove the large vehicle down to the locked gate. He sat idle in the pickup for a moment instead of jumping out to open the gate. Ranger saw his opportunity. "I'll be back soon."

"Please don't go," she begged. "You can't leave us here."

Ranger let out his breath. He didn't know what to say. It was becoming more and more clear that he'd made a huge mistake in bringing them to Donny's place. He faced Laura with as much reassurance as he could find and said, "I promise I'll be back as soon as I can."

CHAPTER 14

DONNY

Donny kept his eyes glued to his cell phone as he waited for another text from his contact. This was the worst part of the job. Well, not strictly the worst, but it was one key aspect he detested. He was a man who liked to plan things down to a T and know what lay ahead. Not knowing where his skills were needed until the last moment pushed his patience to the edge.

The throwaway cell phone in Donny's hand lit up again with an address. It was near Tucson. These jobs he was given took him between Namrena and Tucson whenever they came up. Occasionally, he'd receive a job in Phoenix, but not this day.

Donny had been on call, so to speak. He knew there was a chance he'd be sent a job today. It was the only reason he had been at the crapshack he used as a staging ground for jobs. Ranger had gotten lucky when he showed up and set off Donny's silent security system. Any other day of the week and the place would have been empty.

A sinking feeling cramped Donny's gut as he thought about what this sudden request could all mean. Usually, the text came with more time to prepare. Not as much as he'd like, but enough to get things done. Donny didn't like to think of himself as a gun for hire, but there was no other way to rationalize what he'd become.

He jumped out of his Ram 1500 Express and gave a sweeping glance back toward the house. It was one of many run-down homes he owned in the area. Each had been cheap to acquire. They were all listed under a dummy corporation and not in his name. No one knew where he lived, and that was the way he liked it. This crapshack had once been the only place he'd called home until he got out of the Marines.

He'd given Ranger the address a long time ago, before things had changed. He never expected the dead man to show up the way he had, especially with Liam Wilkins' girlfriend and her kid, of all people. Ranger had tripped a proximity alarm when he approached the gate in the stolen sedan, prompting Donny to find out who was at his place.

He let his gaze run over the exterior of the house. It was clear. Ranger wasn't trying to follow him. The ghost had other things to worry about and couldn't risk leaving Laura and the kid on their own. Donny was happy the man had enough sense not to tail him. He didn't want to go through the pain of having to bury an old war buddy out in the middle of the desert. Not that you could really bury a person in Arizona without heavy equipment.

He opened the gate and got back in the truck. The truck rolled forward past the fence line.

As Donny exited his vehicle again to close the gate, he thought about the war and what it had done to him. He'd once had a life out here. A fiancée and a decent home and plans to have kids. But what he'd brought back with him from that part of the world only served to destroy the life he once knew.

He hated being a cliché, but he'd hit the bottle hard the second he got home. He never dealt with any of the nightmares the war left buried in his soul. Eventually, it all came to the surface, and he lost everything. His wife-to-be, Diane, fled eight months ago when matters got out of hand. She didn't want to deal with the reality of it all. Things could have been different if she hadn't left. At least that was what he liked to tell himself.

Another buzz from his cell phone snapped Donny from his thoughts. He blinked a few times to clear the memories and checked the text. It told him the amount of money he was going to get for his efforts today. He had to look twice, as the figure was double the normal rate. "Holy shit."

Donny pocketed his cell phone and climbed back into the pickup. Knowing where he had to be, he sped up faster than he needed to, kicking up dust and rocks as he started his journey out to the location he'd been provided. He was only given a time and a place and nothing more. The final piece of the puzzle always came to him at the last possible moment: the target.

———

THE DRIVE OUT to Tucson was a peaceful one at this time of day. The sun was easing down but still had a few hours of light left in it. Traffic was all outbound as commuters made their trips back home from work in the city. He wondered how many of them realized how good they had it, that they could hold down an actual job and go back home each night to their families without needing to drink themselves into a stupor. Donny might have had an offshore bank account with enough money in it to retire ten times over, but he'd trade it all for the ability to forget the past. Doing what he was about to do was the only thing keeping him going.

He reached the outskirts of Tucson and realized he was less than a few minutes away from where he needed to be. He still didn't know who he was taking out—if that was even the goal. The boss was cutting it closer than normal.

Donny drove his pickup along a single-lane road around the perimeter of an active quarry. He glanced out the window and noticed that the workers were mostly gone or packing up for the day. It was the perfect place to use the bolt-action .308 Surgeon 591 Short Action CSR he had folded away in his rucksack. The concealable sniper rifle was his only option, with Ranger poking his head around. His former brother-in-arms would have identified a rifle bag from a mile away had he taken one of his regular rifles.

Rolling to a stop, Donny lined up his truck for a quick exit. He parked a few minutes' walk away from where he would be working. Most of these jobs required subtlety and discretion. There was no sense in allowing his vehicle to be identified should things go south.

No one had ever spotted him, at least not on home soil. There had been a few incidents in Afghanistan where an enemy sniper had pinned him down. One time, he had to stay prone behind a small wall for six hours while under heavy fire, waiting for a delayed airstrike to take out a lone shooter. He came close to dying that day, but it wasn't his worst moment in the war.

When Donny got behind his rifle, he felt like a god hovering above the target, waiting to take a shot. Seeing the faces of the people whose lives he held in the palm of his hand through a long-range scope gave Donny a sense of power unlike anything else. With a single squeeze, he could silence a man's existence. The fifty-plus confirmed kills he had in Afghanistan were etched into his mind forever. Each shot seemed justified, like he was a shepherd protecting his flock from harm. Now, though, when he pulled the trigger, he understood he was just ending the life of a person who had wronged his employer and nothing more. Those faces, he wanted to forget.

Moving with purpose while keeping low, Donny edged up to the top of the quarry. He lowered himself down to his belly and placed the rucksack in front of him. He pulled out the concealable sniper rifle and set it up, complete with a suppressor. After laying out his DOPE book and loading up three magazines with five rounds of custom .308 Winchester, Donny took a breath. He pulled out his spotting scope and stared down at the location of the meeting over one thousand yards away.

Donny exhaled when he found his employer, Bill Wilkins, and his main lieutenant, Carl, where they were supposed to be. Opposite stood two men. All four were armed and appeared to be on edge. From such a distance, none of the men would be able to see or hear Donny. Unless he screamed at the top of his lungs, no one would notice him there.

Shaking his head, Donny thought about Ranger. He still couldn't believe what he had done to Liam, not to mention the business with some unknown private security firm that was involved in the heroin trade. The ghost had dragged a world of shit to his doorstep, and Donny had every right to send Ranger packing. Still, he couldn't bring himself to do that to an old friend. One who had been through the same pain as him.

Ranger would have no way of knowing about the professional relationship Donny had with Bill. Otherwise, he wouldn't have come within ten miles of Donny's address. Ranger had been all noble back in the war. And apparently, those traits had lasted, even after someone had framed him for the murder of his wife.

Donny had no idea what he was going to do with Ranger. He owed the man his life. Maybe once the current contract was completed, he'd help Ranger and Laura, then get out of town himself. He had enough money to find somewhere remote to hide and drink himself slowly to death. It wouldn't be a bad way to go, all things considered. Maybe the sudden arrival of a phantom from his old life was a blessing in disguise.

Donny received a text. His heart rate increased as he read the words on the crappy burner phone. He'd been given a target, but the message also said not to take the shot until Bill sent through a final text to confirm. Donny must have been there as part of a backup plan. Whether or not he pulled the trigger, he still got paid.

"Okay," Donny whispered as he placed the spotting scope down. He jotted down some notes in his book and made some adjustments to his rifle for the light breeze that was blowing over the quarry. Everything was ready for him to take the shot. He kept his weapons zeroed and clean and practiced, using them all at the range he had made at the back of the crapshack. He had to keep his skills sharpened.

Donny settled into position and was on standby to kill. He knew who his target was and had a clear shot lined up. All he needed to know was when he had the green light to fire.

CHAPTER 15
BILL

Bill stared at his Tucson contact as the text to Donny went out into the ether. His man could start raining down bullets the second Bill gave him the go-ahead. All Bill had to do was tap out one last text with a single word: yes. Once that was sent, Dallas Jaramillo Chapa would be no more.

Bill and Dallas had been meeting to discuss the operation for longer than Bill cared to admit. Things had never been that friendly between the two businessmen, but an understanding that what was good for one was good for the other had always existed.

"Dallas," Bill said to the small Latino man with a thick handlebar mustache. He was wearing a dark-gray collared shirt and black sunglasses. His short sleeves revealed a series of tattoos that ran from his wrists to his neck. Bill could only assume the rest of his body was also covered in the faded ink.

Dallas was in his early fifties and had lived a hard life of crime in Tucson. Bill had heard stories about his violent temperament and his inclination to make an example of those who crossed him. Bill understood the purpose of hauling people over the coals when they had wronged you, but Dallas had a knack for taking the task to the next hideous level. He wasn't above carving a man up with a machete and parading his body parts around town for all to see. Again, it was another area where Bill preferred discretion over the dramatic.

Despite his flaws, Dallas was Bill's connection in Tucson and the man who kept the cartel element at bay. If things broke down with Dallas, Wilkins Farms would cease to exist shortly after. It was a fragile business model, but in a lot of ways, Dallas needed Bill as much as he needed Dallas. Bill produced a hell of a lot of meth, and Dallas distributed the product to the hordes of eager customers.

Dallas had an equally tattooed man at his side—a young Latino in a white tank top who looked like he'd committed dozens of murders in his career. Bill didn't know his name, but the man did his best to stare down Carl. Carl held his ground all the same and ignored the gawks with a level head.

Dallas and his bodyguard were standing beside a shiny Cadillac Escalade with twenty-four-inch chrome rims. A heavy bass rhythm pounded from inside the car. The meeting was meant to be limited to the four men in total. Bill wondered how many other armed individuals were hiding behind the tinted windows of the SUV. Having Donny up on the hill made him feel better about the game in play.

"Wild Bill," Dallas said. "What brings us here today?"

"I don't know, Dallas. You called this meeting. We weren't supposed to meet each other until tonight at the usual spot."

Dallas gave Bill a sneer and chuckled to himself like there was a joke on the tip of his tongue. The thought sent a chill down Bill's hand as it sat in his pocket. There, his cell waited, ready for him to issue the order to Donny. One press of a button would be all he'd need to send a bullet through cold Chapa's brain. But there would be hell to pay after.

"And why do you think I called this meeting, gringo?" Dallas continued.

Bill shrugged. He hated being called "gringo," but he tolerated the term for the sake of business. "To shoot the breeze? Just get to the point."

"Hey, fuck you, old man. You don't give me orders."

Bill raised a hand to apologize. He had to find a balance with Dallas. He couldn't come across as weak, but he also had to let Dallas think he was in charge. "Please enlighten me."

Dallas spat on the ground and muttered something in his native tongue. Bill ignored the obvious insult. "Your last shipment is why we are here."

"The last shipment? What about it?" Bill asked.

"It was light, gringo. Way off the mark."

"What are you talking about? I inspected that shipment myself. It was all there when we delivered it to your people, down to the last gram."

"Bullshit," Dallas yelled. "It was out by ten keys. Someone is taking a slice off the top on that gringo farm of yours."

"Not possible," Bill said as he took a step closer to Dallas. Dallas' sidekick reached down for the custom Sig Sauer 1911 he had visibly tucked into the front of his baggy jeans.

Dallas stopped his man with a single gesture and stabbed a finger toward Bill. "Choose your next words wisely, old man. Tell me what the hell's been going on or so help me God."

"Not a thing. I swear to you the weights were correct. We have the best people working in the lab. Every last one of them is loyal. None of them would steal from me. Ever." Bill found himself seething at the accusation that was flying his way. He knew he had to dial it back before things got out of hand.

Dallas stretched his arms out wide. "Someone's got sticky

hands in the operation, Bill. What are you going to do about it? Probably nothing. You know why?"

Without meaning to, Bill's teeth bared. "Why?"

"You're too old for this game, gringo."

"Damn straight," added Dallas' counterpart.

Carl stepped forward, this time with his chest puffed out. Bill steadied his man. "Back down, son. I guarantee you there are more hombres in that Escalade. This is what he wants."

Carl gave Bill a near imperceptible nod and eased back.

"Dallas," Bill said, "I'm not too old to know when I'm being pushed into a fight. Let me assure you, we don't want to start a war. This arrangement has always benefited us all. Let's keep it that way."

Dallas sneered at Bill with an icy stare. It was clear Bill's words were not the ones the gangster wanted to hear.

"Tell you what, Dallas. As a sign of good faith, I'll throw in an extra twenty keys on the next shipment. No charge. That covers the ten you say we were short on, to make up for the shortfall, and gives you a bonus ten. What do you say?"

It was a decent offer. One that Dallas couldn't refuse without leaving money on the table. Plus, Bill knew he didn't have another supplier lined up to take over. Not one that could handle the production levels of Wilkins Farms. This was a test from Dallas. Maybe even a reminder of who was in charge.

Dallas spat and muttered something in Spanish.

"We got a deal or what?" Bill asked.

"Fine, gringo. Twenty keys. Not a gram less, you hear me?"

"Twenty. All for you, friend." Bill eased his hand off the cell phone in his pocket. He didn't need to send the text to Donny. That would come another day, though. It was only a matter of time.

"Let's get out of here," Dallas said to his sidekick.

Bill kept his eyes forward, waiting for the pair to climb into their Escalade and go. He wasn't one hundred percent certain Dallas wouldn't change his mind and put a bullet into the back of his skull for the sake of it.

A sigh escaped Bill's nostrils as he watched the Escalade open. He saw other men inside, each of them armed for a fight. Dallas had come prepared, but so had Bill. He would have given anything to see Dallas' corpse lying still on the ground before him, his brains spilled over the quarry.

"Let's move," Bill said to Carl. "I've got other shit to deal with."

"Understood, sir," Carl replied. He rushed over to the 300C and opened the rear passenger door.

Bill took a step toward his ride. He didn't hear the shot until after the bullet landed. A sonic boom echoed and cracked across the quarry. Carl fell toward the 300C with wide eyes. It took him a moment to realize he'd been shot in the stomach. He slid down the side of the car to the dirt as blood seeped through his shirt.

Dallas and four other men all spilled out of the Escalade, weapons drawn.

Bill's eyes drifted to the top of the quarry to where he knew Donny would be prone on the ground.

"We're under attack," Dallas called. "Get down, old man."

CHAPTER 16
RANGER - A FEW MINUTES EARLIER

Ranger crept up to Donny and found his former brother-in-arms lining up a shot on a group of people down in the quarry. He had to squint to determine how far away they were, but it was a shot Donny could make. The only question running through Ranger's mind was, why? What the hell had Donny gotten himself into?

Twenty minutes earlier, Ranger had climbed into the back of Donny's pickup and hid himself under a camouflage tarp that had been stuffed into the truck's bed. Ranger had pulled off the risky move while Donny had been distracted closing his gate.

After a bumpy ride, the pickup had come to a rough stop inside a quarry of all places that looked to be located on the outskirts of Tucson. Ranger waited a few minutes before exiting the bed of the vehicle and following Donny along the edge of the quarry. He didn't know what Donny was up to, but when Ranger saw a compact sniper rifle emerge from Donny's rucksack, it confirmed his worst fears.

The discovery made Ranger think about Harris, Carter, Rodriguez, and Murphy. Had there been any signs of what they had planned before it happened? He didn't even know if what he suspected was true or not.

With no other choice, Ranger drew his stolen Glock 21 and approached his friend. He waited until Donny's focus was drilling down the scope of the sniper rifle before he declared himself. "Whatever it is you're about to do, don't do it, Donny. I've got you dead to rights."

Donny flinched as he spun his head to Ranger. "What the fuck?"

"I should ask you the same thing," Ranger said, steadying his aim.

Donny groaned. "Goddamn it, Frank. Why do you always have to get involved in shit that doesn't concern you?"

"Don't put this on me. You're the one out here about to murder someone. Who are those people down there?" Ranger flicked his eyes in the group's direction for a moment. From what he could tell, there were four people and two cars. The group had to be at least one thousand yards away, maybe more. It would be a tough shot with good conditions, but Ranger had seen Donny make harder kills while under a barrage of mortar fire.

"Walk away, Frank. Just leave it. Take the girl and the kid and get the fuck out of town."

"I can't do that. Not while you're doing this."

"This has got nothing to do with you. It's just business."

"Business? So you're a mercenary now? Is that what you chose to do with your life after we came home?"

Donny glared at Ranger with bared teeth. "It's better than what you did."

Ranger shook his head. "I told you I had nothing to do with my wife's murder."

Donny chuckled. "So you say."

"I wasn't lying. She was butchered in front of me, and I couldn't do a thing to stop it."

"I don't care. Whatever happened to your wife isn't my problem. And besides, even if you weren't the one to kill her, it sounds like it was your fault."

"What did you say?" Ranger said through clenched teeth, thrusting the Glock at Donny.

"You heard me. Now, if you don't mind, I have a job to do."

Ranger's grip on the pistol tightened. "Don't do it. I swear I'll put you down."

"Do what you gotta do, Frank. I came here for a reason. And as soon as I get a text from Bill Wilkins down there giving me the green light, I'm pulling this trigger."

"Bill Wilkins? You work for him?"

Donny smirked. "Don't act so surprised."

Ranger shook his head as a lump in his throat formed. "I don't understand. You're better than this."

"Am I, Frank? How is this any different from what we did in Afghanistan? They paid us to kill. They told us who to shoot and when to do it."

"That was different, and you know it. We were fighting an enemy hell-bent on killing innocent people. Are you really trying to justify what you're doing right now?"

Donny ignored Ranger and gazed down the scope again as if he had his target lined up.

"I'll shoot," Ranger said. "Don't think I won't."

Donny scoffed. "I'll believe it when I see it." With his trigger finger resting on the guard, Donny adjusted his aim with slight movements. He was close to firing. Ranger was certain. But he had no idea when he was going to do it. Then Ranger spotted Donny's cell phone sitting in the dirt. He'd said something about waiting for a text from Bill Wilkins. There was still time to save Donny from himself, but he'd have to move fast.

Ranger kicked a sharp spray of dirt at Donny's face. The

sudden attack forced the sniper's eyes to close, but he didn't budge from his position. Ranger dropped to one knee and reached for the rifle, but Donny let go of the weapon and pounced at him. He grabbed Ranger's wrist and attempted to take the Glock 21 out of his hand. Ranger spun sideways as they both wrestled for control of the pistol.

"Give me the gun, Frank," Donny said, keeping his voice down. He clearly didn't want Bill to hear them.

"No. You need to stop. I won't let you do this." Ranger elbowed Donny in the gut and gained the upper hand. He twisted the pistol toward Donny's face and lined up a kill shot at point-blank range. It was one he could never take, but he needed Donny to think otherwise. "It's over. You're coming with me, away from this bullshit."

"You're not going to kill me, jackass. You forget, I know you, Frank. You think you're some kind of Boy Scout sent to save the world. But you couldn't save Kaitlyn, could you? You said it yourself; you failed her."

Ranger clenched his jaw and resisted the urge to wrap a finger around the trigger of the Glock. He wasn't going to kill his friend, but one more comment about his dead wife might change the equation.

Donny drove a left hook into Ranger's temple, sending a bright flash into his eyes. He fell to his knees and saw the glimpse of a follow-up kick to his ribs. The breath flew out of Ranger's lungs and sent him to the rough ground.

"Screw you," Donny muttered as he scooped up the Glock. "This is my life. You don't get to tell me how to live it."

Ranger rolled around in the dirt as Donny muttered to himself some more. He tossed the Glock out of Ranger's reach beside his gear. He then settled back behind the compact sniper rifle and lined up his target for a second time.

"Got a clean shot, Frank. Just need the okay from the

boss," Donny said as he leaned sideways and collected his scuffed cell phone from the dust. He checked the screen and didn't react. Ranger prayed a message hadn't come through from Bill Wilkins telling Donny to take the shot.

"Nothing yet, Sergeant," Donny said, using Ranger's former rank.

"Then walk away," Ranger wheezed, short of breath.

Donny laughed. "You don't get it, do you? You don't walk away from Bill Wilkins. Especially when you humiliate his piece-of-shit son. I don't have a choice."

Ranger shook his head. "There's always a choice. We can help each other. Just like old times."

Donny stared at Ranger with a hard line across his brow, then returned his focus to the scope. He settled his hands into position on the rifle, ready to fire. "That world is gone. We didn't know it, Frank, but those were the best days of our pathetic lives. For guys like you and me, it's over."

"Not yet," Ranger said. He shot to his feet and bolted around behind Donny, taking advantage of his distracted thoughts before it was too late. He went for Donny's right arm and tried to yank his hand away from the rifle.

"What the fuck?" Donny let out as he kept hold of the weapon. Ranger didn't see it happen, but Donny's finger must have gotten caught on the trigger of the rifle. The weapon discharged.

The booming sound forced Ranger to let go of Donny. He fell away from Donny into the dirt. For a moment, both soldiers stared at one another, their mouths open.

Ranger shot to his feet first and rushed at Donny. Before Donny managed to get up, Ranger threw a right cross at his skull and followed through with as much power as he could muster. Donny fell sideways into the dirt and didn't move.

While Ranger's breath flew in and out of his lungs, he retrieved the Glock, then squinted toward the group of people in the distance again. One of the two vehicles had sped away. The other did the same a moment later in the opposite direction. The gunfire must have scared them.

Ranger hastened to Donny's side and noticed his Beretta 92FS in its holster. Donny could have drawn it at any time and shot him. Ranger claimed the pistol and stepped back. He tried to understand how things had gotten so out of hand for his friend. Had he really been killing people for a scumbag criminal like Bill Wilkins?

With Laura and James to worry about, he didn't have time to understand. The second Donny was functioning, he'd want blood. Ranger had just screwed up the job for him and had no doubt destroyed the working relationship Donny had with Bill Wilkins. He needed to go.

Donny groaned again with what sounded like words. Ranger kicked Donny square in the head and knocked him out again. He checked his pulse and made sure he was breathing fine on his own; then he fished through Donny's pockets until he found some car keys.

Ranger retrieved Donny's rifle, as well as his scuffed cell phone. With speed and efficiency, he ripped out the device's battery and smashed it against some rocks. Then he found his way back to the pickup and got the engine started.

Speeding back to Namrena, Ranger realized there would be no time to gather supplies or buy fake IDs for Laura and James. He only had one move left: get the mother and son the hell out of town.

CHAPTER 17

BILL

With his foot to the floor, Bill drove his 300C out of the quarry as fast as he could. When he glanced into the side mirror, he spotted Dallas fleeing in his Escalade in the opposite direction. Dallas seemed to believe the meeting had been under attack by a rival gang. Bill didn't tell him otherwise, not while he was outgunned and down a man.

The 300C bounced onto the solid road as it came out of the quarry. Bill prayed no police cruisers would spot the blood and damage on the side of the car where Carl had been hit. The round had passed straight through Carl and slammed against the armored 300C, leaving a visible dent in the metallic paint. Until Bill was certain Dallas wasn't following him home, he had no choice but to keep going.

"How you doing back there, Carl?" Bill called out to the rearview mirror. Carl sat in the back seat, clenching his gut. Blood was all over the seats.

"I'm fine, boss. Just get us out of—" Carl cut himself off to groan, seeming to be incapable of finishing his own sentence. Bill could see in the man's eyes he wasn't going to last another ten minutes. And there was no point in taking him to a hospital. It would result in a police investigation beyond the jurisdiction of Namrena. Bill didn't have control over the police in Tucson.

He slammed the steering wheel. Nothing had gone to plan. Donny wasn't supposed to shoot unless he gave him the all clear. Bill had paid the soldier a ridiculous amount of money for the overwatch protection. So why had Donny fired? And why at Carl? Had someone offered him more money to shoot his top lieutenant to send Bill a message? Too many possibilities ran through his mind.

The disastrous meeting was another problem Bill would need to sort out—provided Dallas didn't wise up to what really happened. Dallas and his men had reacted the instant they heard the sound of the shot catch up to the bullet that hit Carl. Even though Donny used a suppressor, it wasn't enough to hide the immense decibels that spewed from the powerful weapon. The main purpose was to conceal Donny's location.

When Carl went down, Dallas and his enforcers must have assumed the shot had been meant for Bill and Bill alone. Dallas had even come to his aid for a moment. The second Dallas had figured they were under attack from an invisible sniper, he'd ordered his men to all flee back into the Escalade.

At the same time, Bill had rushed Carl into the 300C and crawled into the driver's seat. He didn't know if Donny was out to kill him or if someone else was up on top of the quarry pulling the trigger.

"Boss," Carl groaned, his voice low.

Bill looked into the mirror again. Carl was leaning sideways.

"I need the hospital. I don't think I'm going to make it. Please, I…"

"Keep pressure on it, son."

"Bill, please, you gotta take me now. I'll be dead by the

time we get to—" Carl coughed. Blood sprayed the air and ran down his chin.

The writing was on the wall for his man. "Okay, we're on our way. Just close your eyes, son. We'll be at the hospital soon. I promise."

"Okay," Carl whispered as he closed his eyes.

Bill continued driving toward home. A minute later, Carl slumped all the way to his left and fell silent, leaving a messy streak of blood on the seat.

The man's death was a damned waste. He was one of the few people Bill trusted. He would be a great loss to the business. But Carl's end didn't matter in the grand scheme of things. Every person he hired understood the risks when they entered the business. Each day, they rolled invisible dice and played the odds. Carl's time was simply up.

The only thing that mattered to Bill was why Donny had failed him. Never in their arrangement had Donny let Bill down. Every target given to the former Marine sniper had been taken out with a sense of professionalism that was refreshing to witness. Something had caused Donny to screw up the job and had cost Bill a loyal man. Not to mention the headache he'd have trying to explain things to Dallas the second he worked out what had happened and decided to call. And Dallas would call.

Bill's list of problems continued to grow. He pulled his cell phone out of his pocket with bloodstained fingers. He kept one eye on the road as he found Donny's latest burner on his contacts list and hit the call button. The call failed, and there was no way to leave a voicemail, not that Bill ever would. Donny had most likely destroyed it.

Bill tossed his phone onto the front passenger seat and let out a yell. He gripped the steering wheel so tight his bloody knuckles turned white.

Once Carl was dead, Bill drove the car off the main road

and found somewhere remote to pull the 300C over. With the sun going down, he had a bit of luck on his side. He dragged Carl out of the back seat and moved the dead weight to the edge of a dried-up drainage system. The kind that was used to stanch the flow of a flash flood on those rare occasions when rain graced the land.

Bill stared down at the sight before him and shook his head. He'd thought Carl was going to be one of the few who made it. The man had brains and knew how to handle himself. But it wasn't Bill's fault he was dead, and he didn't have the time or the energy to accept any blame.

Bill removed every item from Carl's pockets that could tie him to Wilkins Farms. With a fatigued leg, Bill rolled Carl's body over and watched it tumble down into the drain. It wouldn't take long for someone to find him, but by then Bill would be back in Namrena.

He climbed into the 300C with a groan and got underway, taking the back roads wherever possible on the journey home to the farm. The side of the car would need to be cleaned, repaired, and resprayed, and the interior would require detailing with strong chemicals. Bill had a mechanic who would handle the job—no questions asked.

Bill's cell phone buzzed on the seat. He reached out and swept the device into his hand and found a blocked number on the screen. Bill rarely answered such a call, but he thought it might have been Donny calling to explain.

"Hello?"

"What the hell was that, gringo?" Dallas yelled down the line. Gangster rap played in the background.

"I don't—"

"Someone's out to get you, old man."

Bill thought about the situation from Dallas' perspective and realized there weren't many other explanations. "It looks that way."

"Is it going to be a problem?" Dallas asked, revealing whom he was concerned about.

Bill thought about Donny and couldn't understand what had gone wrong. Dallas seemed genuine in his belief that Bill was under attack from an unknown entity.

"Because if we've got a problem on our hands—"

"I'll take care of it," Bill said, cutting Dallas off.

"See that you do, gringo. And by the way, about your offer. Make it forty extra keys on the next delivery. Twenty won't cut it."

Bill closed his eyes and suppressed an urge to yell. "Understood."

The call disconnected, leaving Bill to wrap his mind around what needed to happen next.

CHAPTER 18
RANGER

Revving the engine as much as Donny's truck would allow, Ranger rushed out of the quarry. He sped back onto solid roads, cutting off a sedan. He ignored the blaring horn behind him and accelerated well past the speed limit.

Ranger had to find his way back to Laura and James before someone else did. He didn't want to believe that Donny would harm them, but everything he thought he knew about his friend had been wrong. A man he had once considered a brother had become a contract killer for the sleaziest man in town. Ranger and Donny might have killed people in Afghanistan, but they were all military-aged men from the Taliban armed with AK-47s, PKMs, and RPG-7s. The two situations didn't compare.

Donny was lost. Ranger had heard the anger in his voice. He'd practically dared Ranger to shoot him as if he wanted his life to end. Once a man started down such a path, there was no turning back.

Ranger wondered how Donny could work for Bill Wilkins. And for how long? How many people had Donny killed for the supposed farmer? His reaction to Ranger upsetting Liam and Bill earlier now made perfect sense.

Not only did Ranger have to contend with a murderous crime family to save Laura and James, but possibly an old friend who had the skills to shoot them all dead from up to two thousand yards away. Ranger could only hope interrupting Donny would make the man fall out of favor with Bill Wilkins. Maybe Donny would have to skip town and cut his losses.

Ranger brought his fist down hard onto the dash of the truck. How had things gotten out of hand so fast? He'd done it again and had made things worse. The police, a US Marshal, and some shadowy private security company already wanted him locked up or dead, but it wasn't enough of a headache to deal with. He'd pissed off every person there was to anger in Namrena.

The impromptu trip into town had gone sideways. He was supposed to stop off to visit an old friend from the past before pushing on through. Now, Ranger was up to his eyeballs in hot water, with no idea what to do next. All he could do was pick up Laura and James, then keep them safe as they fled the state.

Ranger only had a few thousand dollars in cash that he'd stolen from Liam's men. It wasn't enough for the mother and son to start a new life somewhere else, let alone change their identities. Long term, they'd need more to survive. He owed it to Laura to make things right.

"Just get them out of town first," Ranger told himself. The rest would have to wait.

Exhaling, he accepted the thought and focused on the road ahead, the road he could see. There was no point trying to figure out what problems might jump out at him around the next bend. He'd fight through each hell as it came.

Ranger didn't know Namrena all too well. Not beyond the

main roads Bill had shown him. When he had been hiding in the truck on the way to the quarry, he couldn't risk too many peeks at his surroundings. Not with Donny behind the wheel. Once he saw a familiar sight in town, Ranger got his bearings and drove to Donny's run-down house. The state of the home made sense. Donny didn't live there. It was a hideout.

How many places did Donny have access to now that he was a gun for hire? He'd mentioned the run-down property was just one of the locations he stayed in. How much blood money had Donny earned killing civilians on US soil? Ranger shuddered at the thought. Donny was one of the best he'd ever seen and had been well respected by his fellow soldiers. What had happened to the fiancée he was supposed to marry after coming home? Had Donny thrown that life away for this?

Ranger arrived at the gate to Donny's house before any answers formed in his mind. Instead of unlocking the barrier, Ranger left the truck running and hopped the fence. He charged up the driveway and tried to think of what he would say to convince Laura to grab James and come with him. So far, he'd turned her life upside down and had only made things worse. How could she trust him to do the right thing?

Ranger had thought he was saving Laura at the diner. He'd thought he was protecting an innocent woman from a public beating. Yet he hadn't known a thing about Laura before he intervened, other than that she owed money to a violent prick. One he knew was armed. The situation might have turned deadly without him meaning it to. As hard as it would have been to do nothing, Ranger knew he'd made a mistake the second he'd laid a hand on Liam Wilkins.

Ranger reached the side entrance to the house and went to unlock the hidden door using Donny's keys. But the door was partially open. "What the hell?" he let out. When Ranger went inside, what he found was the last thing he'd hoped to see.

Laura and James were gone. They had vanished from Donny's place without a trace. Ranger darted from one messy room to the next, shouting Laura's name louder and louder as he went, but no one answered.

Ranger cursed out loud and charged back outside. When he took a good look around, he realized the stolen car was missing. He'd left Laura with the spare set of keys to the house and main gate Donny had given him. She must have worked out how to open the gate and had known how to hot-wire the stolen car. She'd even gone to the trouble of locking the gate after herself. Again, Ranger had underestimated the woman.

Laura and James were long gone. Ranger had no way to find them. It wasn't like he could call Laura. He'd destroyed her phone. It left him wondering if she even wanted to be found. He doubted she took off with James to find him. "You stupid son of a bitch," Ranger whispered to himself. There was no one else to blame for the chaos he'd created.

He sat on the floor in Donny's house, wishing he had someone to talk to. Someone who could give him all the answers and tell him what to do to fix his life. Maybe it was time to call the police and finally let them haul him in. Kaitlyn's brother would gladly take that call. Deputy US Marshal Dane Briggs had been chasing Ranger since his escape from justice in Montana. He was based in Billings but had come close to catching him in Wyoming during the incident with the feds and the bikers. Fortunately, Ranger had slipped away at the last minute.

The thought of Dane being hot on his heels had never sat well with Ranger. He and Dane had been close before Kaitlyn was murdered. They didn't see each other often, but when they did, they got on like a house on fire. Dane was now just another person who longed to see him rotting away in prison for the rest of his life.

Since his escape, Ranger had gone from one disaster to the next. He'd broken the law more times than he could keep track of and had even been forced to kill in self-defense. All the while, his wife's murder remained unsolved. His focus should have been centered on finding the man in the suit, but it seemed easier to take on the burdens of strangers than to face his own hell. That needed to stop if things were ever going to change. Or better yet, maybe it was time to run from it all.

He could leave Namrena and never look back. Ranger could forget about Donny and Laura and especially the Wilkinses and continue along his path to nowhere. That way, he could blend into the background of society and pretend his life wasn't a total mess.

When Ranger climbed into Donny's truck, he put the pickup into reverse. He was ready to go. Ready to get back to what he did best and split. He could go farther south and cross the border. No one would search for him in Mexico. It wasn't like he could bring Kaitlyn back from the dead. And Cindy was better off without him. If he ever went back to Montana, he'd be risking her life. It was time to run.

But something tugged at him. A nagging question he wanted answered.

How would Laura and James survive? They had Liam and Bill Wilkins on their tail, wanting them dead. Maybe Donny too. Laura was a survivor, sure. That was clear, given the way she'd stolen the sedan and fled with no one's help or approval. But how would she disappear with her son without being caught in the Wilkinses' network of thugs, killers, and lowlifes? And was Ranger prepared to leave them on their own and abandon them the way he had abandoned his daughter?

He couldn't leave. Not without making sure they were okay. He shut off the engine as a better thought hit him. He knew where Laura had taken James, and the only way he could help was to go there right away.

Ranger fired up the truck and got back on the road. Now, he just needed to find Laura's house at the mobile home park she'd mentioned living in. Ranger was positive that was where she would be heading. James needed his meds to get by. Ranger only hoped he wasn't too late.

CHAPTER 19

DONNY

By the time Donny came to, the sun had almost set over Tucson. "Goddamn it," he groaned through a mouthful of dirt as he sat up. A pain in the side and front of his skull throbbed, making itself known. With every passing second of agony, fresh memories of what had transpired came through the fog in his mind.

"Oh, shit."

Donny stumbled to his feet and tried to dust off his clothing. There was no getting the filth of the quarry out of the material, though. He looked like hell. Some of the grime on his hands had combined with the blood he'd wiped off his head to form a caked muddy layer.

Donny took in his surroundings and noticed everyone was gone. Bill, Carl, and the people Bill had met were all in the wind. Ranger was nowhere to be found, either. That was when Donny realized his keys and Beretta had also been taken.

"Ranger," Donny coughed. The idealistic madman must have stolen his gear so he could run back to Laura and the kid. What crap was Ranger trying to pull? He was a wanted man. Getting in between Laura and Liam was about the dumbest idea possible. Now Ranger had extended his heroics into Donny's world and had caused a headache the size of Arizona for him. Was all the involvement in strangers' lives to do with the death of his wife? It had to be. Nothing else made sense.

Donny took a minute to close his eyes and recover. He wiped the dirt from his face and mustache. Ranger's punch and follow-up kick had sapped him of energy. He didn't bounce back as swiftly as he used to when he was younger.

"Wait a minute," Donny said. The sound of his suppressed CSR echoed in his mind. Another memory came flooding back, one he'd hoped was a dream.

Ranger had wrestled with Donny when he was staring down the scope of his Surgeon with a finger on the trigger guard. Then they'd fought over the weapon. In the blur of that fight, Donny's attempt to keep the rifle out of Ranger's control had caused an accidental discharge.

"Shit, shit, shit," Donny said, both hands clutching the back of his head. He had no idea how close the single round came to striking anyone at the meeting, but the sound of the shot alone would have been enough to screw everything up beyond repair. Bill had not given Donny the all clear to fire. He had to call the old man and make things right.

Donny slapped his body for his cell phone and remembered it was on the ground. No doubt Ranger had taken that, too. He was always one for the minor details. "Fuck, Ranger. What have you done to me?" Donny asked the world. No one answered him in the empty quarry.

Donny had no way to contact Bill and tell him that what had happened wasn't intentional, that it wasn't his fault. After giving himself a minute to think, he realized it didn't matter. What was done was done. Bill wouldn't see reason and would only assume the worst. Even if Donny delivered

Ranger's head on a silver platter, Bill might not be able to forgive him for the screw-up at the meeting. How many chances did you get with a man like Bill?

Donny hobbled his way along the quarry. All of his gear was gone, along with his truck. Ranger had left him with nothing but the knife he kept on his side. "Big mistake, Frank."

Spinning in circles, Donny swept the quarry, looking for a vehicle or anything useful to steal. He needed to head back to Namrena. He didn't know if the gunshot had been reported to the police yet. With any luck, none of the remaining workers on the far side of the quarry had noticed it. It might have sounded like a bit of heavy machinery banging about or some rocks falling.

In the distance, Donny spotted a pickup with some company logo written on the side. A lone worker with surveying equipment was staring out in the opposite direction. He was going to regret his little overtime assignment. Donny used the opportunity to sneak up to the man and hit him over the head with a rock. The worker fell in silence and looked worse for wear. He'd have one hell of a headache, but he'd live.

A minute later, Donny was on the road and had put the quarry behind him. There was no point looking backward. He knew the smart play was to collect a go-bag and run. He had plenty of them around town ready for such contingencies. Each had clothing, food, a pistol, money, and fake IDs. He also had enough funds in offshore accounts to retire to a tropical island and never be heard from again. He could live out the rest of his days getting hammered on a beach somewhere in the Southern Hemisphere, away from the world he knew. But something about the idea didn't sit right.

"Screw that," he said out loud. He refused to let Ranger off that easily. The son of a bitch had single-handedly ruined

Donny's reputation in one fell swoop. He couldn't let that kind of disrespect slide.

Laura, Liam, and Bill. None of them were his concern. But if they got in the way, he wouldn't hesitate. There was only one person on his list to kill, and the prick had just sped away in his truck.

All Donny needed was some supplies, and he could finish the fight between them that Ranger had started.

CHAPTER 20
RANGER

Ranger reached the only mobile home park in town as night fell over Namrena. Using Donny's pickup was risky. Any one of Bill's people might recognize it in town, but time wasn't on his side. He drove Donny's pickup up to the entry of the unkempt network of roads that ran in and out of the park, and killed the engine. A local was sitting out front of their property on a torn sofa, staring him down the entire time.

Taking in a breath to focus, Ranger stepped out of the truck. With sure reluctance, he went into the area on foot. The place had seen better days. Its inconsistent layout was filled with neglect and decay. Some of the mobile homes had broken windows and exposed insulation. Rusted swamp boxes sat on roofs next to deteriorated satellite dishes. Half-standing chain-link fences surrounded most of the mobile homes.

Ranger had both the Glock and the Beretta tucked away in his dirty jeans but hoped he wouldn't need to use either handgun. He'd heard enough gunshots for one day.

As Ranger strolled, doing his best to blend in, he couldn't help but feel exposed on all sides from an ambush by Bill's people—if they were even watching and waiting for him. At least one person from Wilkins Farms had to be in the area, monitoring Laura's home, so Ranger knew he needed to tread lightly and stick to the shadows.

The plan to find Laura at her home was based on nothing but a gut feeling and some honest desperation. He didn't know where she lived or if she had even come home. Still, he had to try.

Some homes in the park had their external lights on. He avoided them as best he could and stuck close to the ones that only had a few lights on, inside or out.

After wandering the streets, Ranger noticed some teens hanging around on a corner at one of the small intersections in the park. They were listening to loud music while drinking and swearing at one another.

Ranger was about to bypass the group when he realized one of them kept checking over his shoulder at a particular mobile home. It might have been where the kid lived, but he checked the front door every thirty seconds. Ranger got the impression that someone had asked him to keep an eye on the place. No doubt a person connected to the Wilkinses.

It wasn't much to go on, but Ranger had no other leads. He backtracked and walked over to a narrow lane that sat behind the property being watched. If he was quick and quiet enough, he could reach the back door of what he hoped was Laura's home without being detected.

Keeping his head low, Ranger stepped as lightly as the dirt road allowed and made his way to the back of the house. No one noticed his approach, and none of the young kids were watching the lane. He felt like he was back in Afghanistan on a night raid. Except he wasn't armed with an M4 carbine and didn't have his squad backing his play. The squad who was mostly gone.

He thought about the four men from his squad who

hadn't been on the fateful mission. At the time, they had supposedly been pulled aside to assist some higher-up with a logistics operation. It was highly unusual. Ranger knew all too well that a squad could only have operational effectiveness when they were working together. So why had four of his people been strangely removed from his command right before a dangerous mission? Four men who had avoided death.

Their names ran through his head again. Harris, Carter, Rodriguez, and Murphy. He didn't know how, but if he managed to find Laura and James and help them to safely leave Namrena, he would hunt every last man in that fire team down and ask them questions they probably didn't want to hear.

The snake who'd entered his home and destroyed everything he held dear did so because of a drug shipment Ranger had no clue about. What efforts had the man taken to punish Ranger and the Marines who had been on that mission? Faking suicides and car crashes couldn't have been easy or cheap.

A teenager yelled, pulling Ranger from his thoughts. The kid was shouting at one of his friends about something unimportant. Ranger resisted the urge to mutter his contempt for the unruly teens and continued to Laura's place.

Even in the dark, most of the homes appeared to be rundown. A few were in good condition. Their owners had put in the effort to maintain every aspect of the house and land they called home. Others, though, let their properties be ravaged by time and neglect.

Ranger had thought about moving into a mobile home park. One that was somewhere remote where he could keep a low profile and never be found. But it seemed too much like settling down in one place. He preferred to keep moving and not slow down. It was the only way to survive. For now, though, he needed to locate Laura and James and get them as far out of town as possible.

Ranger found the back door to what he hoped was Laura's place and stepped up to it. There were no lights on inside. If it was indeed Laura's home and she was in, she was at least being smart by keeping things dark.

Ranger tried the door, but it was locked. The cheap lock wouldn't take much effort to smash open, but the task would require noise. Plus, he couldn't be sure what would meet him on the other side of the door. It might be a frightened Laura or a loaded gun.

Ranger contemplated the best way to break in without making a lot of sound. As he thought, his eye caught sight of an open window down the side of the narrow home. It was only open the slightest amount—a few inches at most—but it would be enough for him to work with.

With only moonlight guiding him, Ranger crept over to the window and slid it sideways as far as it would go. It made a horrible squeal as it went, but no one came running to investigate. The loud music might be enough of a cover. Using the palm of his hand, Ranger struck the window's mesh screen into the house. A drawn curtain dampened the sound as it flapped about on the floor inside. The gang of teens still failed to notice the racket over the babel they were making in the street. Whoever had given them the task of watching the house had chosen the wrong people for the job.

Ranger climbed into the mobile home and slid the window back across. He drew the curtain closed and moved along the creaking floor as softly as his boots would permit.

It was dark inside. Laura, or whoever the building was occupied by, had every window covered with curtains or bedsheets, most likely to reduce the amount of heat the home received during the day. Ranger took full advantage of the setup as he moved about, but it left him to do so in a near pitch-black environment.

There didn't seem to be anyone at home. It was only early in the night, so most people would still be awake. God help those who needed to sleep, though. The teens outside sounded like they were planning on partying long into the night.

After rummaging around in what looked like the kitchen, Ranger came across a flashlight. It didn't work at first, but after a few solid bangs, it jolted into action. The battery was weak, but he didn't plan on needing the tool for long. The home could be searched top to bottom in a matter of minutes.

Ranger took a second to think and clear his head. He'd rushed around town in such a flash, he'd almost forgotten his reason for coming to the mobile home park. Laura wasn't there, so he needed to make use of the break-in and find something to point him in the right direction.

There was only one reason Laura would risk coming back to her place, and it was her son. Specifically, to collect his medication. Ranger used the waning flashlight to search for the medicine Laura was desperate to secure for her son. If he couldn't find anything, it meant Laura could have come and gone from the house while he'd been busy wrestling Donny at the quarry. If that was the case, he didn't know what he'd do next.

Ranger started in the bathroom and searched for James' medication. He could only guess what the tablets looked like or if they'd be in a pill jar or a sleeve. A medicine cabinet behind the mirror proved fruitless. All Ranger found inside were expired aspirin jars and a few antacids.

He moved on into one of the bedrooms. The flashlight went out a few times as he searched through what had to be Laura's room. He found a photo of her and another person on the floor. The glass in the frame had been smashed. He figured Laura had either dropped it or didn't care about the picture. He didn't mean to judge, but experience told him that someone in her position might have put a low priority on anything they couldn't sell or swap for drugs. Laura had already admitted to swapping sex for pills and God knows what else with Liam.

"Stop it," he said to himself. He was frustrated and letting his own pain make him think less of Laura. He couldn't judge her. She was just trying to survive in this world like everyone else. He took a breath and refocused.

As Ranger was about to move on from the room, he realized something. He had thought the house was messy and unkempt, but he'd been looking at the place through a biased lens. What he had failed to notice were the telltale signs others had been in the house who didn't live there.

"Liam," he muttered.

Had the spoiled brat been through Laura's home already? It was possible given the presence of the teens out front, who were on the lookout for any visitors. How many eyes did the Wilkinses have in town?

Ranger picked up the pace. The flashlight flickered more and more with each passing minute. Soon, its batteries would be dead.

He finished searching Laura's room and found James' past the bathroom. Just as he got inside the cramped space, he tripped over a mattress that had been pulled from its frame. When he landed on the floor, the flashlight fell from his grip and smashed against something solid, extinguishing the light.

"Shit," he muttered in the dark. He used the wall to stand and felt a wave of fatigue hit him. It would be so easy to drop back down to the soft mattress and fall asleep. The day had taken its toll. Before he gave in to temptation, the rattle of a key entering the back door lock sounded.

Ranger pulled out Donny's Beretta without thought and

held it level in two hands. He disengaged the safety with his thumb and kept his trigger finger pointed along the guard. Ranger moved away from James' room, back to the main area. He leaned around the corner to get a good look at whoever was using the back door to come inside.

Was it Laura? Had she come home to get James' pills and spotted the rowdy group of teens out front?

The door swung open. It closed a moment later once the lone person had entered. They didn't turn on any of the lights and activated the flashlight on their cell phone to guide their way. They seemed to be avoiding detection as much as Ranger was.

With a squint, Ranger spotted the outline of a woman. It had to be Laura. Who else would be sneaking into the house with a key? He kept his gun level, ready to fire, in case the stealthy individual wasn't Laura.

The woman tripped on a toy on the floor and almost fell over. She cursed as she got a grip on the phone in her hand. The beam of light ran up her face. It was the woman from the diner, Rosie. She was standing in the middle of Laura's kitchen.

"Don't be scared," Ranger said as he stepped out into the room.

CHAPTER 21

Ranger engaged the safety on the Beretta and stared at Rosie. The owner of the diner by the same name held up her hands in submission. The phone she was using as a flashlight stayed firm in one hand, its light still shining.

"Please don't shoot," she begged, stumbling backward into the closed door behind her.

"I'm not going to hurt you," Ranger said, hearing the rapid increase in her breathing. He placed the Beretta back into his jeans.

Rosie squinted at Ranger in the dark. A look of recognition soon registered on her brow. "Wait, you're him, aren't you? You're Frank."

"How do you know my—?" Ranger cut himself off. Laura had told Rosie his real name. That meant she was alive and had gone to Rosie for help.

"Where is she?" Ranger asked.

"Laura? She's at my place."

"James too?"

"Of course."

Ranger let a sigh escape him. They were okay. Liam and

Bill hadn't found Laura and James. At least not yet. And neither had Donny. Although Ranger figured Donny would only be after him and no one else.

Grateful nothing awful had happened to Laura and James, Ranger realized he could still help them. He could still save the pair from the town's surplus of psychopaths.

"What are you doing here?" Rosie asked as she lowered her guard.

"Looking for Laura and James. We were holed up somewhere else earlier but—"

"You left them," she said, cutting in.

"I didn't leave them. I had to go. My friend—"

"You don't have to explain it to me, Frank. Tell it to Laura."

Ranger sighed. It sounded like Laura was upset with him. She had every right to be. He'd left her and her son on their own in Donny's "creepy" home that wasn't a home. It was no surprise she ran.

"Thank you for taking them in," Ranger said.

Rosie shrugged. "She didn't give me a lot of options. She showed up at the diner in a car that I know doesn't belong to her. I gave her my house keys and told her I'd be home as soon as possible. I had to close up early and send my regulars on their way. Half of 'em don't even know how to cook a meal on their own. They'd probably starve if I went out of business."

Ranger smiled at the comment about Rosie's customers. "I'm sure Laura was grateful for your help."

"I suppose. Again, she didn't give me a choice. I know what them Wilkins boys are like, so I did what I had to."

"Thank you," he said, exhaling. "And why are you here?"

"James needs his medication. Laura said she keeps it in his room."

Ranger shook his head. He'd been close to finding it before Rosie showed up. "His room's over here."

"I know where it is. This ain't my first visit to Laura's place." Rosie brushed by Ranger, using her phone's light as a guide.

"What the hell happened here?" she asked when she reached James' room. "What did you do?"

"Wasn't me. Liam, I'd say."

"He was here?"

"Him or one of his people. I'm not sure what they were looking for, but they tore the place apart trying to find it."

"My Lord," Rosie muttered. She stepped over the mattress on the floor to reach the opposite side of the room and stopped at a dresser. The top drawer had been ripped free and was on the ground. Rosie knelt down and retrieved a small box that had James' name written on it.

"Is that it?" Ranger asked.

"I think so," she said, giving the box a gentle rattle. Some tablet sleeves within made a swishing sound.

"Okay. Time to leave. How did you get here, by the way?"

"In my car. And don't worry. I parked it a few streets over and walked. I spotted those dumb-ass thugs watching the front door, so I came through the back."

Ranger chuckled. He was impressed. It seemed that Laura and Rosie both knew enough to get by in Namrena. The thought only reminded him it was his fault they were in this mess to begin with. Fortunately, there was still time to make things right.

"Let's get moving," Ranger said, motioning for the back door.

"About that. I don't think Laura will be too happy to see you."

"I know. I messed things up and shouldn't have taken off before, but she still needs me."

Rosie sighed and broke eye contact. With her gaze set on the floor, she spoke. "I think it would be best if you moved on, Frank."

"You mean leave town?"

"Yeah. I can help Laura and James until things blow over."

"Blow over? Things won't blow over. You know what the Wilkinses are like. They clearly have some kind of control over your diner. Do you think they'll just forget what happened today?"

"Probably not, but Bill Wilkins is a reasonable man. I think with enough time, an understanding could be arranged."

"An understanding? What do you mean?"

Rosie shook her head and huffed. "I'm saying that when all this shit calms down, Laura could offer her services to the Wilkinses and pay off her debts. There's no need for any blood to be spilled."

"You want her to hand herself in and let that psycho Liam decide if she lives or dies? You've got to be out of your mind."

Rosie stared at Ranger with a telling look in her eye. It took him a minute to work it out, but he realized what needed to be said. "You're speaking from experience, aren't you?"

"Yes," Rosie said in a shaky voice. Tears formed in her eyes and threatened to flow. "Not that long ago, I owed Bill money for the same reason Laura was in debt to Liam. I understand what she's going through. But Bill gave me a chance to make things right. He let me live."

"In exchange for what?" Ranger asked, taking a solid step forward.

Rosie shook her head and sniffed. In her eyes, Ranger could see memories coming to the surface. He knew what the answer was and said nothing more.

Ranger cleared his throat. "I came looking for Laura and James so I could help them run away. Isn't that better than what's happened to you?"

"No."

"It has to be."

"No, you gotta face your problems head-on. You may have to go through hell first, but you'll come out the other side a stronger person."

Ranger took a step back as he thought about Kaitlyn. He didn't want to, but Rosie had forced the memory to the forefront of his mind. He'd been running for a year, but in his mind, the clock had started the moment she died. How long did he plan on keeping his head in the sand about her death? How much distance did he have to put between himself and home before the pain would disappear?

And there was more than his wife's unsolved murder, than heroin deals and private security firms weighing him down. He had to live each day knowing that his daughter thought he was a killer who had come home from war and snapped.

With a weakness in his knees, Ranger soon found a wall. He pressed into it and slid down to the creaking floor of the mobile home.

Was Rosie right? Would Laura's best chance to survive the mess he'd created for her be in the supposedly merciful hands of the Wilkinses? No. He couldn't accept such a reckless plan. Running was the smart move. Despite how well Rosie knew Bill, her idea had one giant problem. One variable that her own experience was missing: Liam.

Ranger recognized it in the kid's eyes. He wasn't like his old man. There was a darkness within that would never allow Laura the same chance Rosie was given.

"I need to go," Rosie said. She stepped by Ranger and didn't look back.

"This is a mistake. Liam's not like Bill. He won't forgive her for what happened."

Rosie stopped and faced Ranger. "It doesn't matter. Bill is the only one she needs to convince. He'll rein his son in, you'll see."

"And what if you're wrong? What if Bill can't control him?"

Rosie didn't answer and continued out the door.

Ranger didn't move. He was tired. Or maybe self-doubt was pinning him in place. He didn't know anymore. Maybe Rosie's plan was the best decision.

He closed his eyes and saw his wife's face. She'd died because he had failed to save her in the moment. He should never have charged into his home without thinking. He should have called the police when he still had the chance. Running away was always the answer. And any time he ignored his own advice, bad things happened.

Rosie shut the door behind her, leaving Ranger in the dark.

CHAPTER 22

BILL

When Bill reached the farm, he said nothing to the guards on duty, and they knew best not to ask. He parked his 300C as close to his house as possible and stumbled inside. He trudged upstairs and removed his necktie as he went. A minute later, he sat on the end of his bed with his gaze on the floor. His cell phone hung loose in his hand.

The image of the bullet striking Carl in the gut played on a loop in his head. Sure, Bill had seen death countless times. He'd killed men and ordered the deaths of more people than he cared to remember. Carl's end wasn't the thing bothering him. It was the reason behind it. What game had Donny been playing? Bill had paid the man good money to do what he did. Surely, he hadn't received a better offer?

Bill thought back to the first time he'd met Donny eight months ago in a sports bar in Tucson. It was during a business trip at a bar he liked to frequent when he was in the area. Bill loved their buffalo wings, the eager waitresses, and the chance to escape the pressures of the farm.

He'd been watching the Diamondbacks on the big screen while enjoying a cold beer and some hot wings when he noticed a lone man. He stood out from the rest of the patrons, as he was the only one in the bar not watching the game—or any of the others. The man just sat there with the noise of the place and drank—one beer after the next. Being the curious person that he was, Bill sat down on an empty stool beside the man and got to talking.

After an hour of conversation with Donny, Bill learned about the man's military service and the work he'd done in Afghanistan. He also heard about the fiancée the man had lost and how messy their breakup had been. Donny had given his ex most of his savings despite not needing to. And when he went to order another beer, he'd run out of cash.

"It's on me, friend," Bill said, paying for Donny's drink. It was the perfect opportunity for Bill to offer the man a job, one that would pay him more than the military ever could.

"What would I have to do?" Donny asked. It was a delicate question. One that required some finesse to form an answer. When Bill gave Donny the details of the job, Donny told Bill to go screw himself and stormed out of the bar. But Bill wasn't worried. He'd seen something in Donny's eyes that night and knew he'd change his mind.

It only took twenty minutes for Donny to come back inside and ask Bill when and where he'd be needed.

The first job Donny accepted didn't go to plan. He'd hesitated when the order came through to shoot. Bill thought he'd made a huge mistake in hiring the man, that he wasn't cut out for the kind of work he needed him for, but then he saw Donny's worth. The target was about to get away and was on the run, realizing what was happening. Bill bore witness as a single shot from over one thousand yards away dropped the prick into the dirt.

From then on, there were clear skies ahead. Donny set the standard Bill would come to expect for every job he took thereafter. The work was always the same. Bill would send

Donny to a remote location out in the desert and tell him to wait for more information. Hours later, Bill and the target would arrive for a meeting roughly one thousand yards away from where Donny was set up. Donny would receive another text telling him who the potential target was. One of two things would happen next. A text would be sent that said "yes" or "no." Most of the time they said "yes," instructing Donny to take out the target.

The former sergeant would do what he did best and cut down Bill's enemies from afar. They never saw it coming. Not once. Bill could have killed the people he needed dead in a less elaborate way, but he loved the power he held in his hands when he was deciding which text to send.

Whatever reason Donny had for betraying him was irrelevant. Bill had to remove the expert marksman from the chessboard before Donny followed up his betrayal with an attack on the farm. Bill had once seen Donny shoot a man between the eyes from over two thousand yards away. His entire operation would be at risk if he let such a threat go unchecked.

Until the problem could be dealt with, it was best to call all his people back to the farm and go on the defensive. He started with his son. Bill dialed William's cell phone and waited for him to answer. He picked up after five rings.

"What's up?" William said, out of breath.

"Where are you?"

"Doing what you asked. What do you want?"

Bill had to pull his phone away from his face for a moment to contain his building rage. The disrespect his son regularly sent his way was enough to shoot his blood pressure through the roof.

"I need you back at the farm, now."

"Why? I'm out here taking care of business like you asked."

"Forget about the drifter and the girl. We've got bigger problems."

There was a pause on the other end of the line.

"Forget them? You sent me on the road to make things right again."

"Doesn't matter. Just get your ass back to the farm."

William muttered something.

"What did you say?" Bill shouted.

"I said screw you, old man. I'm done taking your orders. One minute, you're telling me to go kill these people; the next you're calling me back in like you don't trust me to do the job."

"I don't trust you, Junior. If it weren't for me, someone would have put a bullet through your thick skull a long time ago. Your mother is lucky she died. She never had to see what a disappointment you became."

Bill ran out of breath and realized what words had come out of his mouth. He wasn't sure how much of what had been boiling up in his head for years had made it into the conversation, but he knew he'd done some damage.

"We're done, old man," William said, as calm as Bill had ever heard him speak. A reaction of any other kind would have been preferable.

"Son, I—"

"Don't you 'son' me. Just shut the fuck up and listen for once in your goddamn life. I'll come back to the farm when I'm good and ready. Got it?"

"Junior, please—"

"Stop calling me Junior. My name is Liam. I'm not some carbon copy built for your legacy or whatever sick fantasy it is you've dreamed up for my life. I'm my own person. So unless the world is about to end, I don't want to hear from you." William ended the call.

"Liam, listen to me," Bill yelled, but it was too late. His

son was already gone. Bill called William's cell phone again, but it went straight to voicemail.

"Leave it," the message said. The recording William had made was unprofessional, but to the point.

"Fuck," Bill roared. He threw his cell at the mirror opposite him and felt shards of broken glass spray into the air. One sliver caught his cheek and sliced through it. The sting of pain was hardly noticeable over the bile forming in his throat. "That dumb piece of shit."

Bill paced back and forth in his room over the shattered glass. As furious as he was, he needed his son to come back home to the farm for his own safety. And despite how much of a disaster William had grown to be, Bill couldn't bear the thought of losing him. It was a reality that entered his thoughts each and every day he ran the business.

With his cell phone destroyed, Bill pulled out a backup, placed the SIM card from his broken phone into the new one, and plugged the device into a wall socket to charge. As soon as the phone powered up, he unlocked the screen and made a call to another one of his lieutenants, retrieving his number from an old-school address book Bill kept in his jacket pocket.

Xaver Braun wasn't currently at the farm. He was out doing what he usually did for Bill, making sure the Namrena Police Department stayed away from Wilkins Farms. It was Xaver's job to oversee the monthly bribes certain officers were paid and to make sure these people stayed under Bill's influence.

"What can I do for you, boss?" Xaver asked when he answered.

"Where are you?"

"On my way back into town. What do you need?"

"I gotta job for you."

"Okay," Xaver said, drawing out the word. "Shoot."

"I need you to do a pickup for me."

"Easy done. What am I pickin' up?"

"Not a what. A who. And he won't come easy. You'll need some help. Could get messy, if you know what I mean."

"Well, all right," Xaver said. Bill could almost hear the man's smile over the phone. Xaver wasn't only good at distributing bribes, he was adept at taking out anyone who thought they were above taking cash for their cooperation.

"I'll text you the details now," Bill said. "Make this a top priority." He sent Xaver everything he needed to haul Liam to the farm. His two pals could go fuck themselves for all he cared. If they were dumb enough to get in the way, Xaver would know what to do. Bill needed his son where he could see him.

CHAPTER 23
RANGER

Ranger pushed himself to his feet and rushed out the back door of Laura's home. He spun left and right until he spotted Rosie walking away in the dark. As silently as possible, he followed her from a distance. He didn't know where the business owner lived, so trailing her would be his best chance of finding Laura and James.

Ranger wasn't going to run, but he also wouldn't force Laura and James to leave town, either. What he had in mind was far more irrational.

Rosie's words got into Ranger's head and wouldn't leave. She thought the best thing for Laura to do was face the Wilkins family head-on and beg for their forgiveness. It was the opposite of anything Ranger wanted to do. He wanted to get the hell out of town. But running was the reason he came through Namrena in the first place. And he hadn't run when he had the chance to back in the diner, so why was he so hell-bent on forcing Laura and James to abandon their lives for a pointless existence on the road? He wouldn't wish his life on anybody, let alone them.

There was no point in running, but having Laura and

James lay themselves at the mercy of the Wilkinses wasn't an option either. Ranger had other plans.

Rosie got into a white Ford Focus sedan. The engine ticked over while Ranger hid in the shadows of the mobile home park and waited for her to drive.

She did a U-turn, casting her headlights over Ranger's position for a second. She didn't seem to notice him hiding behind one of the locals' vehicles. As soon as she was far enough away, Ranger bolted for Donny's truck.

Fumbling with the keys, he got the pickup running and sped out over the dusty road that was covered in rocks and gravel. He careened around a bend and spotted Rosie's car in the distance.

The traffic was light. Most people in the area would be settled at home in front of their TVs with a cold beer after finishing dinner. The thought made Ranger's stomach growl. He had eaten not too long ago, but prior to this, he'd been living off some MREs in his rucksack.

Everything Ranger owned was in the rucksack, and he'd left it at Donny's. In his haste to find Laura, all he had on him were the clothes on his back, the two guns, a foldout map with his wife and daughter's photo on it, and access to Donny's truck. The Ram had a few decent items in it, including the sniper rifle Donny had taken to the quarry, but Ranger was no long-range marksman. He was more comfortable with an M4 carbine than anything else.

In Afghanistan, most missions saw Ranger getting in close to the action, close enough to feel the air rush against his face when a bullet whizzed by within inches of his helmet. He'd lost count of the number of enemy combatants he'd killed during his five tours. After a while, it all became a blur from one day to the next. He'd witnessed horrors and atrocities he wished he could forget and had killed fighters as young as fourteen. The Taliban leaders were experts at recruiting kids to die for a pointless cause.

Each time Ranger had returned home on leave, he wondered if anything he'd done in the sandbox would ever make a difference. Would the death and destruction he'd been a part of amount to any change?

Death haunted Ranger whenever he slept. Some days, it was memories of the war. But most of the time, he dreamed about Kaitlyn. She was always staring at him from the shadows, her eyes fixed with an utter look of betrayal. Then the nameless man in the suit would approach her from behind and shoot her in the head. Even after the shot, her eyes remained open and would stare at Ranger as if he had pulled the trigger himself. Once the dream had reached critical mass, he would snap awake in a pool of sweat, unsure what day it was.

Rosie drove across town and led Ranger to a small block of homes a short drive away from the diner. The roads were cracked and half-buried in gravel. Almost a third of the streetlights were broken or failing, and chain-link fences surrounded each home.

The houses were all about the same size. They were most likely built from the same floor plan. Only the facades and structural materials gave off any distinction between each property.

Rosie pulled up at the end of a street that came to a sudden stop. It wasn't a cul-de-sac in the traditional sense and seemed to be the end of a road that had once been planned. For whatever reason, this part of town had been abandoned midway through development.

Rosie's house was a step up from Laura's. Not much of one, but at least one rung up the ladder in terms of size and quality.

Ranger pulled over, killing the engine and lights on the pickup a moment later. When Rosie stepped out of her sedan, she glanced back down the street but didn't seem to spot Ranger following her. She was probably tired from a long, eventful day.

Rosie soon disappeared inside her home and left her external lights on. Ranger crept along the road with his head tucked in tight to keep a low profile. The last thing he needed was for one of the street's residents to think he was up to no good and call the cops.

He also had the added stress that Donny was still out in the world, alive and relatively well. Ranger had no idea what the man would do when he found his way back to town, and was starting to regret following him to the quarry. He hated the fact that Donny had been working for Bill Wilkins, but it hadn't been enough of a reason to kill his friend.

When Ranger reached Rosie's home, he hopped her fence in one swift motion and moved down a narrow path along the left side of the brick house. He came to the backyard in a short amount of time. The house wasn't very long or wide and sat on a medium-sized block of land that was covered in dirt and gravel. Maintaining a healthy lawn required a lot of water and money most people in the area couldn't afford to waste.

Ranger's footsteps were as quiet as he could make them over the crunching surface of Rosie's backyard. He listened in toward the house and heard mumblings between Rosie and Laura. Mumblings that were turning into an argument.

It seemed that Rosie wasn't wasting any more time and might have told Laura about her idea of going to Bill and asking for his forgiveness. Laura sounded like she was against the insanity given how loud she was responding. Her timid side was fading away without Liam around.

Ranger backed away from the house and dropped behind a tree that had overgrown into the neighbor's yard. He sat on the cooling ground and waited for the discussion to fizzle out. There was no sense in him barging in during a fight.

Getting comfortable, Ranger thought about Laura and James. Why did he care so much about what happened to them? Sure, he'd made things difficult for the mother and son when he got involved in the mess at the diner, but they were safe with Rosie. At least for the time being. In some ways, she was right. He could leave. Maybe things would blow over. Maybe nothing bad would happen. But if they did, there would be two more people Ranger could add to his list of failures.

But there was more than just their safety plaguing his mind. When Ranger looked at James, he saw a child without a father and remembered his daughter. She lived with her nana in Montana and had lost both of her parents in different ways. The loss of her mother was obvious, but if Ranger was being honest, Cindy had been without a father since the day she was born.

He'd been in and out of her life on active deployment every day of her life, only spending two to three weeks with her every seven months. He hadn't been there when she was born and had missed some of the most important moments in her existence. All she knew of her father was that he was a sick monster. One who needed to be caged away until he eventually died. And according to the feds, he was dead.

Laura and James were safe for now, but if Rosie convinced Laura to go through with her plan, Ranger knew he'd have to stop them from leaving. Going straight to Wilkins Farms would be suicide.

Maybe Bill was a reasonable man on his own, but his son would never agree to anything. Putting any trust in Liam would be a death sentence.

There was only one way Ranger could help Laura and James. He didn't see any other option to fix the mess he'd created. He would have to take out Bill and Liam Wilkins.

CHAPTER 24

The argument inside Rosie's home came to an end. Ranger gave the girls a few minutes of quiet before he decided to move. As much as he wanted to sit in the dark and look at the night sky, he had work to do.

Ranger pulled himself to his feet and knocked on the back door to the house. He stepped away from the door with raised hands so Rosie and Laura could see who was there.

The back entry had a window with a curtain over it. Rosie pushed it to the side with the barrel of a shotgun. She pointed the weapon at Ranger.

"Can I come in?" he asked.

"My God, can't you take a hint?" Rosie said through the glass. She withdrew the shotgun and closed the curtain. A short time passed before she unlocked the door and let Ranger in. He wasn't sure if she was going to welcome him in or shoot, but he entered.

"Make yourself at home," Rosie said, sarcasm taking over. She pointed the shotgun toward the ground away from Ranger but didn't put it away. He wondered if the thing was loaded.

The two continued through a small laundry space that housed the back door to a living room. Ranger couldn't find Laura anywhere, but he noticed traces of James in the home in the form of children's toys scattered on the floor. He had no idea if Rosie had kids of her own, but he couldn't see any family pictures on the wall. And given her history with Bill Wilkins, he wouldn't have been surprised if she lived alone.

Rosie spoke first. "What are you doing here? I thought we decided—"

"No, you decided, Rosie."

"Unbelievable. So what? You're here to drag Laura and James to safety?"

"No."

"Then let me ask you again: why the hell are you here?"

"Can I see her?"

"Answer the question first," Rosie said, her grip tightening on the shotgun.

Ranger sighed. He didn't want to explain himself to her. He just wanted to talk to Laura, but Rosie seemed to be her gatekeeper.

"I'm not here to take them away. I promise."

Rosie placed the shotgun down and crossed her arms over her chest. "Okay, so leave. She doesn't want your help. You're the reason she's in this mess. You said so yourself."

Ranger blew out a sigh. "I might have pissed off the Wilkinses, but I wasn't the one who was about to slap a woman in front of her kid, was I?"

Rosie chuckled under her breath. "You think she wanted that to happen? Do you think she enjoys being an addict who owes the biggest asshole in town money?"

"No. Of course not." Ranger ran a hand through his hair and took a seat on the sofa a few feet behind him. It was lumpy in all the wrong places.

"So again, why the fuck are you here? And don't tell me

you 'want to talk to her.'" Rosie held her stance with a raised eyebrow, waiting for an answer.

Ranger stared at the ground for a moment. "I came here to offer Laura a solution."

"A solution? This should be good."

"Just listen. It's not the best idea, but it's the only thing I can think to do besides running."

Rosie's gaze narrowed for a moment. She seemed to have worked out what Ranger was about to say. "Wait a minute. You're not seriously considering—"

"Yes," Ranger said.

"They'll kill you before you reach the outer perimeter of the farm. You know that."

Ranger shook his head. "I was a Marine."

"Yeah, in Afghanistan. Laura told me. So what? I'm sure half of his boys are ex-military."

"Maybe, but they're just there for a paycheck now. It's not the same thing as duty."

Rosie shook her head, blowing the air out of her lungs. "I don't doubt your commitment, Frank. I saw you in action at the diner. But you're one man. Bill has dozens of people. Like I said, some are former soldiers. The rest are hardened criminals. You know, psychopaths for hire. Hell, even the police are on his side. He's got at least half of them on his payroll, ready to look the other way when needed. Do you really think you can take on that many people and win?"

Ranger wanted to ignore the obvious. He understood how insane his proposition was. Even if he hadn't enraged Donny out near Tucson earlier, the task at hand would still be impossible. Regardless, he wasn't going to stand by and wait for a solution to magically appear.

"Why are you doing this for me?" Laura said from the far end of the room.

Ranger turned on the sofa to see her standing on a

threshold that most likely led to the house's bedrooms. He opened his mouth to speak, but Laura cut him off.

"Why are you so desperate to help me?" she asked. Her voice was stronger than he'd ever heard it.

"I'm sorry for leaving you at—"

She held up a hand. "Please, Frank. I don't want to hear excuses. I just want to know one thing: why do you give a damn about what happens to me?"

Another sigh came from Ranger. One loaded with eighteen months' worth of exhaustion. He didn't have it in him to tell Laura or Rosie about his motivations. They didn't know about his dead wife, and he intended to keep it that way.

"Tell us now, or we'll call the police," Rosie said.

Ranger's eyes shot to Rosie. She must have already worked out that he had trouble with the law. And now she had played the card to perfection.

Ranger stood from the sofa and stepped closer to Rosie. "Don't do this."

"What? You think I won't make the call? I don't know what you did, but I can tell when someone's on the run from the cops."

Ranger stared down at Rosie. He took in her features as he absorbed her threat. The years hadn't been kind to the restaurant owner. Ranger could sense a familiar pain hovering behind her eyes. She'd lost someone close to her. He was sure of it.

Ranger turned away from Rosie and sat back down on the sofa. He took a deep breath in and let it slowly out. Finally, he stared up at Rosie with tired eyes, then Laura, and said, "What do you want to know?"

CHAPTER 25

DONNY

Donny returned to the run-down house Ranger had found him in, using the pickup he'd stolen from the quarry. He sat back from the place at a distance for ten minutes in case someone was waiting there for him.

Donny knew Ranger wasn't going to kill him. He could have done so at the quarry at least twice. Maybe more. Donny was more concerned Bill would now send one of his men out to do the job. He'd never disclosed to Bill where any of his houses were, but it would only be a matter of time before the old man found them. He had the resources on his side to find anyone in the entire state.

When Donny crept inside the house, it looked like Ranger had come and gone, taking Laura and the kid with him. He'd left his rucksack behind, but there wasn't much inside the bag apart from some rations and a few spare changes of clothing.

No matter how far Ranger ran, it wouldn't take Donny long to find him, especially once he'd retrieved what he was looking for in the back room of the house.

Ranger had stolen Donny's pickup truck at the quarry. It was one of five vehicles Donny had at his disposal in the area.

He didn't care about the truck, but it had one item inside it that was now more valuable to Donny than anything else.

Donny wondered if Ranger would have thought to check the truck over for a tracking device. He doubted it. Not in his panic. He'd have been too hung up on saving the girl and the kid to take a second to think straight.

"You asshole, Ranger," Donny muttered. He didn't want to kill his friend, but what choice did he have? The man had ruined everything. Donny couldn't just forgive and forget. Could he?

The time he'd spent in Afghanistan had shown him the type of person Ranger was. He always put his brothers first, but he also cared too much about the civilians. One time, Donny had witnessed Ranger risking his life just to save a couple of goat herders from getting too close to an airstrike that was set to take out a half dozen Taliban fighters. He crossed an open field with no cover to get the message across, all as a pair of F-16s came rolling in to drop JDAMs on the enemy. He got the word out and found cover before the bombs reached their target, but five more seconds would have seen him sent home in a coffin with an American flag draped over it.

Civilians died. That was part of war. How Ranger had never caught a bullet during his time in Afghanistan was nothing short of a miracle.

Inside the house, Donny climbed into the attic and walked over to a large gun safe he kept hidden behind some junk. After entering the code and pulling open the heavy door, he stared inside the box at a small arsenal of pistols and rifles. He had a near-identical safe in each property. All of them were complete with an electronic device he'd need to locate any of the vehicles he had around town.

The tech was old school. He could have run a tracking system through an app on his phone, but Donny liked to use equipment that could never be traced back to him. Unless, of course, the authorities raided one of his houses. Even then, there was no proof he owned the trackers or the guns he had in any of the safes.

Donny grabbed a long rifle bag and loaded the tracker inside along with some heavy-duty batteries to power it. He then collected a Sig Sauer P320 and screwed on a titanium and stainless-steel suppressor. He stored the pistol and five preloaded magazines of 9mm Luger ammunition in the bag. It had been one he'd purchased through a man in Bill's circle, Rico Casias. Donny had acquired most of the guns he used for Bill's jobs through Rico. That was over now.

Donny took the pistol out of the bag for a moment to inspect an oil streak he noticed on the barrel. He gave it a wipe and checked the slide. The handgun would come in handy if he had to get up close and personal with Ranger. He placed the Sig Sauer down again and moved on to the next piece in his arsenal.

"Hello, gorgeous," Donny said to his APR Custom .338 Lapua bolt-action rifle. The long-range weapon could hit targets that were over a mile away. Donny had used the rifle many times over to do Bill's dirty work, but now he was going to use the expensive firearm to put Ranger in the dirt where he belonged.

Donny figured he'd be doing Ranger a favor. The man looked miserable and had a list of problems he could never fix. Plus, he deserved to die for the shit he'd pulled at the quarry. Donny knew, when he agreed to be a contract killer for Bill Wilkins, that it would only take one mistake to end the arrangement, and Ranger had ruined it all in a matter of minutes with his damned noble intentions.

By now, Bill would consider Donny to be his enemy. No amount of explanation or pleading would change things. Bill might have come across as a charmer to most people, but

Donny saw the real man underneath the public persona every time he was ordered to take out a target. Bill enjoyed killing. Hell, he thrived on it.

Donny would need to run once he'd dealt with Ranger. There were no two ways about it. Taking on the Wilkinses wasn't worth the time or energy. Sure, he could hit the farm from a distance and kill a few of Bill's people or the old man himself, but then what? Nothing would be achieved. Killing Ranger was the right thing to do. At least in theory.

Was Donny being petty? Was revenge on a man who'd saved his life in the past the smart call? He didn't know. Maybe he was letting his emotions get the best of him, but Ranger had to pay. Somehow. He'd destroyed the only purpose Donny had left in his life and had thrown his moral superiority in his face the way he always did.

"He has to go," Donny said, unsure if he'd convinced himself yet. Time would tell.

He loaded the rifle and some ammunition into the bag along with some MRE rations, some water, a flask of bourbon, a combat knife, some new clothing, a Level IIIA vest, and several scopes. He wasn't sure where Ranger had taken his truck or what kind of environment he'd be facing once he tracked him down, but Donny would be ready.

After clearing out what he needed from the house, Donny strapped on the body armor underneath a fresh set of clothes. He locked the hidden side entrance to the home and climbed back into the stolen car with his rifle bag. He'd need to swap the vehicle for one of his own as soon as possible. If a police officer pulled him over, he'd be in a world of trouble. More so if they were one of Bill's dirty cops.

Donny drove along the main road in town as he activated the tracker. He found where Ranger had taken his truck in a matter of seconds. It was only a short drive away. He pulled out the flask of bourbon and unscrewed the cap. With a quick swig, he tossed back a shot of the whiskey and clenched his teeth.

"I hope you ditched my pickup, Frank," Donny said as he screwed the cap back on the flask and placed it in his hip pocket. If Ranger was still using the vehicle, he would have no clue what was coming for him.

CHAPTER 26

RANGER

Laura moved farther into Rosie's living room and sat down opposite Ranger. Rosie remained standing with her arms folded across her chest and stared him down. He was still sitting on the sofa, ready to tell the women what they wanted to know.

"Ask me anything," Ranger said. "I'll tell you."

Rosie took the lead. "It's obvious you're on the run from the police. Tell us why."

Ranger closed his eyes for a moment. "It's a long story."

Rosie shrugged. "We don't have the time, but what the hell, give us the short version."

"Okay. Here goes. It all started around eighteen months ago. I was returning home from active duty in Afghanistan. The US military had begun scaling back the number of troops they wanted in the country, and I was one of the lucky ones being sent home."

Rosie paced the living room for a moment. "That's right. The withdrawal. It was a big deal."

"It was. For me and a lot of the guys I knew. We'd been fighting for years and had each completed several tours.

Coming home was all we ever wanted. But it wouldn't be easy. War changes you in ways I can't explain. You just have to be there."

"I get it," Rosie said. "My old man served in Vietnam. He didn't last long afterward."

"I'm sorry to hear that."

Rosie waved him off and didn't expand on her experience or what had happened to her father.

Ranger continued, "There I was, coming home from war, ready to settle back into society. The best part, my wife and daughter had no idea. I was going to surprise them in the flesh. For once, I'd be coming home to stay. Needless to say, I was excited. Hell, even a little nervous."

"Nervous?" Laura asked.

Ranger nodded. "Telling them what seemed like an impossible thing was more nerve-racking than anything I'd faced over there. I'd been in and out of their lives for too long. I was worried I'd screw things up or be a nightmare to be around."

Rosie stared off into the distance. Her eyes suggested she understood what Ranger meant.

"As I said, I was coming back from war. I had traveled for a long time, had taken a half dozen flights, and finally reached my home in Montana. But when I got there, something wasn't right. More than something. A bunch of things. The gate was unlocked. I found a fancy car in the driveway I'd never seen before, and the front door was partway open."

"What did you do?" Laura asked.

Ranger told them what had happened to his wife and why, including the detail about the man in the suit and the missing heroin. He revealed every sorry aspect of his hell, the fallout, and the life sentence that was handed down to him. When he finished, their mouths had both fallen open.

"Oh my God," Laura whispered, holding a hand to her chest.

"Who was he?" Rosie asked about the man in the suit.

"I don't know," Ranger said. "But he sure as hell knew me. And he also knew that I was going to arrive. He was using my wife as bait, all so I'd walk into the middle of my home, where he wanted me to be. And I didn't disappoint." Ranger looked away from both sets of eyes, unable to say more.

"It's okay," Rosie said. "You don't have to tell us anything else." She stepped closer to Ranger and stared at him as if he were no longer a threat. Maybe she was seeing the real man underneath.

"Wait a minute," Rosie continued. "I remember this story in the news. It was like you said. The media said you'd snapped after returning home from fighting in Afghanistan and shot your wife. Holy crap."

Ranger exhaled. "Like I said, I was set up. Someone murdered my wife that day, right in front of me. And I don't know his name. Only what he looked like. He didn't care what I had to say, either. The psycho wanted me to suffer."

"That's putting it lightly," Laura said. "So how did you escape the police? I'm guessing you did, seeing as you're here talking to us about it all."

"Another long story. I managed to break free and run when the cops were transporting me from court to prison just after I'd been told I was going away for life."

Rosie whistled. "Wow. You must have really wanted to run. Not many people escape a transport."

"I got lucky," Ranger said, thinking back on that day. It was an ordeal, to say the least.

"What about your daughter?" Laura asked. "You said you were coming home to see her, too."

"I was. Her name is Cindy. Four years old. Well, at the

time. She's five and a half now. I missed her last birthday. Fortunately, she was away at her grandmother's house at the time of the murder."

"Wait. So you haven't seen your daughter in a year and a half?"

"Longer," Ranger said, forcing back a choke in his voice. "I was halfway through a tour when I got pulled off the line. She's growing up without me."

Rosie planted her hands on her hips. "What are you doing all the way down here, then? Why aren't you up there fighting to win her back?"

"It wouldn't be much of a fight. The cops would lock me up before I got close. Not to mention I had a psycho murder my wife. He also went after most of the guys in my squad. Eight of them. All dead now with bogus cover stories of suicides and car accidents."

Laura's shoulders dropped. "No wonder you're on the run."

Ranger shook his head. "I don't want to be, but it's an impossible situation. And as if that weren't bad enough, Kaitlyn's brother is a US Marshal. If I show up in Montana trying to clear my name, I have to assume he'll hear about it."

"What the shit?" Rosie said. "And I thought my life was screwed up."

"Thanks," Ranger said, shooting her a pained grin.

"Sorry. You know what I mean."

Silence crept into the room for a moment as Ranger's words sank in.

"This brother-in-law," Laura said. "He's family. Can't you just tell him you're innocent?"

"I tried to at the start, but he refused to believe me. He's been hunting me since I fled."

Rosie muttered to herself. Ranger narrowed his gaze and chuckled. "What smart-ass thing have you got to say now?"

Her attitude had been hiding back at the diner. She was quite the firecracker when there wasn't someone firing a Glock indoors.

"Oh, nothing. Guess it's just hitting me. You've got a US Marshal hunting you down. We could both be arrested for aiding and abetting you."

"I know. And again, I'm sorry. The last thing I want is to drag you both into my mess."

"It's a little late for that, don't you think?"

Ranger exhaled, doing what he could to let Rosie's comment slide. There was no point in him apologizing again. It wouldn't make a difference.

"Is that what this has all been about?" Laura asked. "Have you been trying to help me to make up for the loss of your family?"

"I guess." Ranger shrugged. He didn't want to say it out loud, but she was right. The death of his wife and losing his daughter were pushing him to take risks for Laura and James. "Hey, forget about my problems. I need to take the fight to the farm and kill Liam and Bill."

Rosie scoffed. "Are you still dreaming about that stupid plan? It's suicide."

"It's the only thing I can offer you both. I'm sure as hell not gonna let you go through with your idea."

Laura glanced at Rosie and back to Ranger.

"What idea?" Laura asked with wide eyes.

Ranger glared at Rosie. "You haven't told her, have you? I thought with all the yelling before, you might have."

"That was something else," Rosie muttered.

"What is it?" Laura asked. "Rosie?"

"Go ahead," Ranger said. "Tell her the grand plan." He couldn't help himself.

Laura stood and placed her hands on her hips while Ranger moved out of the way.

"Well," Rosie started, "I was thinking we should go to Bill and talk to him."

"Talk to him? Are you crazy?"

"Hear me out."

Rosie and Laura discussed Rosie's plan to reason with Bill Wilkins through gritted teeth, seeming to be conscious of Ranger's presence. Laura was not on board. The conversation grew loud enough that James came out from whatever room he'd been sleeping in, rubbing his eyes.

"Mommy, why are you and Rosie mad at each other?"

"Oh, hey, it's okay, honey. Go back to bed. Momma didn't mean to wake you."

James shifted his gaze to Ranger. The kid flashed him a hint of recognition and stared at Ranger until Laura guided him along and out of the room, back to bed.

"He's a sweet kid," Rosie said, breaking the calm James had created.

Ranger nodded. He was as innocent as they came. He liked to imagine that James and Cindy would be friends. His daughter had a caring nature about her. It was all the more reason Ranger needed to do something. He didn't want James to lose his only parent in the world—not that Ranger knew what had happened to James' father. He could only assume he was out of the picture or dead.

"Just tell me one thing," Rosie said.

Ranger faced her and waited for another grilling question.

"If you go ahead with your idiotic proposal to take on Bill and Liam, how the hell will you pull it off?"

Ranger smiled out of the corner of his mouth. It was a fair question. Talking about killing the Wilkins boys and actually achieving the impossible goal were two different things. "I guess I just need to get in close and catch them off guard."

Rosie huffed. "That easy, huh?"

"That easy," he said. It wouldn't be, of course, and they

each knew it. Plus, he still had Donny out there somewhere, pissed off and lively with skills no one in town could match. If Ranger survived, if he pulled off the downright ridiculous, he would deal with Donny later and add it to the never-ending list of crap he had on his plate.

Making things right for Laura and James was his top priority. It was only a matter of time before someone connected the dots between Rosie and Laura. Failing them all was not an option.

Laura came back out to Rosie's living room and fell onto the sofa. She kept her eyes low. "I won't ask Bill for forgiveness."

Rosie started. "Laura, please—"

"No. It won't work. Not after the embarrassment that was handed down to Liam. There's no coming back from that."

Rosie sighed again and crossed her arms over her chest. "Okay, Frank. You win, I guess. Let's hear more of your crazy plan."

CHAPTER 27

Ranger had little in the way of a plan to take down Bill and Liam Wilkins. He was outnumbered, outgunned, and would be attacking the father and son on their home turf. It was an inconceivable goal, but Ranger had a few things working for him: two people who knew the enemy better than anyone else.

Rosie understood Bill inside and out, and Laura recognized Liam's weaknesses. Ranger spoke to them both for an hour straight and gained as much insider knowledge as he could absorb.

They couldn't tell him much about the farm or how many men the Wilkinses had at their disposal. They couldn't tell Ranger what kind of weaponry he'd be up against. Nothing beyond any rumors they had each heard. And the one useful piece of information they gave Ranger only added another layer of difficulty to it all.

Both Bill and Liam traveled in armored vehicles. Their rides didn't look armored from a distance, but each man rode around in cars that would deflect his 9mm and .45 APC rounds like they were raindrops on a windshield. He did

have Donny's .308 CSR, but he wasn't sure if it would penetrate the glass of an armored vehicle. There was a good
chance he'd need to hit the same section of glass multiple
times just to make a hole.

Attacking either man when they were on the move and
driving around would be a risky venture. Ranger only had
one advantage to play, and it was a hazardous idea at best.

"I need to lure them out. One at a time. And the only way
I can think to do that is to use each of you."

Laura and Rosie focused on Ranger in the living room.
They sat on the sofa while he paced the small space with a
knitted brow.

"I can't ask either of you to do this. If you don't want to
have any part in what I'm thinking, I'll find another way."

"We'll do it," Rosie said, answering for herself and Laura.

Laura nodded, confirming her commitment to the forming
plan.

"Okay," Ranger said with a sigh. The reality of what he
was about to attempt sank in. He was going to use the people
he was trying to save as bait. It sounded insane, but nothing
better came to mind.

"Question is, who do we hit first?" Rosie asked.

Ranger could see she was thinking two steps ahead. He
should have been doing the same, but fatigue was messing
with his brain.

"Liam," Laura offered. Ranger and Rosie gave her their
full attention. She continued, "He's less critical to the farm's
operation. Plus, he often goes off on his own, away from Bill.
If we hit Bill first, Liam will be hard to track down."

Ranger nodded. "All right. We've got our first target, then.
So where do we do this? What's the ideal location to catch
Liam off guard?"

The two women cast their eyes away in thought.

"The diner," Rosie said. "I could tell Liam that Laura

called me, wanting to meet him there. He'll rush in without thinking."

"That's good. But what about his two sidekicks?" Ranger asked.

"They'll be with him like always. I've served those losers a hundred times over at the diner. You'll need to take them down somehow, too. They'll be armed, of course."

Ranger noticed Laura glancing away from the conversation as if a bad memory had struck her. He wanted to ask if she was okay. He knew he was the source of her stress, but there wasn't time to worry about the consequences of what they were planning. That would have to come after. If there was an after.

"Noise will be a problem," Ranger said. "I'll need to deal with the three of them as silently as possible." He thought about the combat knife he'd left behind with Donny at the quarry. In his haste to get the hell out of the quarry, he'd taken what he could and ran. The blade would have come in handy for the grisly task he had ahead of him. Ranger did have his own concealed belt-buckle knife, but it was small and not ideal for what he had in mind. It was no pigsticker like the one Donny had swiped at his throat. He would have to find a better way to silently kill the trio.

Ranger shook his head at the thought of committing a triple homicide in such a public place. He wondered if there was a way to spare Liam's two morons. The less killing he had to do, the better.

"Whatever you have in mind," Rosie said, "you'd better make it fast. Those two idiots he has with him know how to make a racket."

Ranger pursed his lips. If by some miracle things went well at the diner, he'd have to move on to Liam's father as soon as possible. "How do we handle Bill?"

"Same location," Rosie said. "We take Liam's phone and text the old man to meet him there."

"Won't that make Bill suspicious? He doesn't seem like the kind of guy who falls for a trap all that easily."

"He's not, but if he also gets a call from me about Liam being at the diner, he'll take the bait. After you've dealt with Liam and his boys, you could wait in the back for Bill to come by. When he arrives, I'll tell him that Liam took off. But I'll also tell him I need to talk to him in my office."

Ranger scratched his beard. "It could work. I guess it'll depend on how many guys he brings with him." The plan—if it could be called that—was coming together. Now all Ranger had to do was execute it flawlessly while keeping Laura and Rosie safe. He also needed to avoid being caught by the police or Donny. Anything might go wrong. Laura and Rosie were still in the dark about Donny and who he really was, but Ranger figured the less complicated he made things, the smoother it might all play out.

"Are those two pistols the only thing you've got on you?" Rosie asked as she stood from the sofa. Ranger had shown Rosie his limited arsenal when they'd started planning.

"Pretty much. I've also got something outside in a truck down the street that might help. I just need to go get it."

Rosie gestured to the opening that led through to the laundry. "No time like the present." Ranger headed for the back door while Rosie followed.

"Stay here. I'll be as quick as possible." Ranger glanced at the shotgun Rosie had placed down on the way out. "Keep that handy."

"Sir, yes, sir," she said with a mock salute.

Ranger chuckled at her poor joke and resisted telling her he hadn't been an officer. He crept outside into the dark. Then he edged up to the corner of the house and took his time checking for signs of anyone from the farm or Donny.

The street was quiet. So quiet Ranger could hear the sound of people's TVs playing in the background. Some were watching sports, others the news. It was a typical thing to hear in a suburban setting during the evening. Peaceful normality. He'd give anything to have it back again.

Ranger didn't know what his future had in store. If he survived the next few hours, he would most likely get back on the road and leave Namrena behind. In what direction he'd travel, he would decide when the time came.

Ranger reached Donny's truck and fished around in the truck bed until he found the CSR. There was also a leather cartridge pouch with ten rounds that he hadn't seen before. It would come in handy. The bolt-action rifle hadn't moved from where he'd thrown it. The casing from the previous cartridge hadn't even been ejected after the round discharged.

Not wanting anyone to see the weapon, Ranger wrapped it up in a spare tarp he found in the bed and pulled the package out. It would be safer to inspect and fieldstrip the rifle inside Rosie's house and clear out any dirt the weapon had collected from the quarry.

Taking a few long glances around, Ranger made sure no one was watching him from their homes. Before he went back to the house, he took a minute to take in a few breaths of fresh air, hoping to clear his head and squash the voice inside that was casting doubt on his every decision. If he was going to take on the Wilkins boys, he needed as much clarity as he could find. The exercise made a slight difference and got him moving again.

When he reached the front of Rosie's property, he spotted her coming out. He was greeted somewhat warmly by the woman who had aimed a shotgun at his face only a short time ago. She had opened her front door to let him in.

"Hurry up, will ya," Rosie said as she impatiently walked farther out the door. "We ain't got all night."

"I told you to stay inside."

"Yeah, you say a lot of things, Frank."

Ranger let a chuckle free and realized he'd left the cartridge pouch behind in the truck. If he was going to mount any kind of assault on the Wilkinses, be it up close and personal with a pistol at the diner or elsewhere with the CSR, the spare rounds could come in handy.

"I'll be back in a second," Ranger said.

"All right," Rosie said, barely masking the impatience in her voice.

Ranger held on to the CSR and rushed back to the pickup. He retrieved the cartridge pouch and held it to the tarp, hopeful he could get his head in the game. The smaller details could make or break his chances at taking out Liam and Bill.

When Ranger got back to the front of the house, Rosie had a hand on her hip and was shaking her head at him. "You look suspicious as hell, you know that."

"I know."

"Come on. We've got a couple of assholes to—"

Rosie's head snapped back before she could finish her sentence. A dull boom sounded as her knees buckled, collapsing her body.

"No," Ranger yelled as he dropped the bundle in his arms and grabbed her before she hit the ground. He dragged Rosie into her house and kicked the front door closed. On autopilot, he continued to pull her away from the front windows as if there were still a chance of saving her.

"Fuck," Ranger spat out as he punched the floor with a fist. The shot he'd heard told him the bullet had come from a heavily suppressed rifle. It was close, but he knew who had taken the shot, and Ranger had led the man straight to the people he was trying to protect.

CHAPTER 28

Rosie was dead. She'd been shot between the eyes by a large-caliber rifle round from a distance close enough that Ranger could only guess the general direction it had come from. He'd been right in front of Rosie when she got hit. Close enough that a mist of her blood had sprayed on him.

As Ranger held Rosie's corpse, he noticed that the round had passed clean through her skull and proceeded into her home, tumbling sideways as it punched through the wall behind where she'd been standing. Her life had been taken in milliseconds.

Laura screamed and shoved Ranger hard in the side. He couldn't hear what she was saying as he stared at the chaos he'd created. He'd led Donny straight to Rosie's home, sealing her fate. The bullet should have been for him, but Donny had shot and killed Rosie. Ranger knew it wasn't a mistake. Donny was too skilled to miss in such a devastating way. And at close range.

"What did you do?" Laura yelled through a wall of tears. James was standing in the hall at a distance, covering his ears with his hands.

"What did you do? What did you fucking do?" Laura hit Ranger over and over until he responded.

"It was Donny. He's out there."

"What?"

"Donny. He did this."

"Your friend?"

"Yes."

"He killed Rosie? Why?"

Ranger took a moment to think of an answer, but he could only say one thing instead. "He should have hit me."

Laura broke down. "Oh, God. This isn't happening. It's not real." She lowered herself to the floor with shaking knees and fell silent. A paleness washed over her features as she rocked back and forth. James did the same, matching his mother's reaction. The more she broke down, the worse he got. After a moment, she seemed to regain some control and took her son into her arms. She held him tight and whispered into his ear.

Ranger snapped out of his daze when he realized how exposed they were. He grabbed Laura by the arm.

"Take James into the bathroom and hide wherever you can."

She shook her head. Not in defiance, but out of a sense of fear. He could see it in her eyes.

"Please," he begged.

After a few seconds, she seemed to comprehend what was being asked of her and nodded.

Staying low, Ranger dragged Laura and James out of the room. He turned back to the front door and drew the Beretta 92FS from his jeans. He scooted up close to the wall by the entrance, keeping it between him and certain death. Not that it would make much of a difference. If Donny got a fix on his location, the caliber of the round he was using might penetrate the cheap wall with ease.

Ranger didn't have time to mess around. He reached out to a switch and killed the lights outside along with the ones by the entrance. It wasn't much, but the cover of darkness might help keep him a fraction safer. Then again, Donny probably had a night-vision scope he could swap to.

Donny could have followed up on his attack and killed him. Ranger might have reacted fast, but he knew Donny had the skills to drop multiple targets before they had time to think.

The shot wouldn't have roused too much attention given the rifle was suppressed. It still made a decent enough boom in the night, but it wouldn't have been the kind of noise that would pull people away from their televisions.

Ranger gripped the pistol tight in his hands. With closed eyes, he focused on getting his breathing under control. There was no way to win the fight otherwise.

Donny had him pinned down. He could run out the back of the house with Laura and James, but then what? The street ran alongside empty farmland. Nothing but an open expanse awaited them. Donny would have no trouble killing all three of them if they went that way.

The CSR entered Ranger's mind. It was just outside Rosie's front door. If he could retrieve it, he might be able to use the rifle to return fire on Donny.

"No," he said aloud. It would be suicide. Donny had him cornered. The instant the door opened, a second round would come sailing through.

"Dammit," he muttered as sweat poured down his forehead. Ranger stared at Rosie's body and saw the glassy look in her eyes. The only thought running through his head was why Donny had shot her and not him. Like a ghost in the night, a sharpshooter like Donny Brown could have killed Ranger and been on his way by now. He was an elite sniper who rarely missed his target. He had intended to kill Rosie when he fired. And during the time Ranger had fumbled to get her body inside, Donny could have taken another shot and put Ranger down.

What made him kill Rosie?

CHAPTER 29

DONNY - AN HOUR AND A HALF AGO

Donny had found Ranger in less time than he'd anticipated. The optimistic soldier was still in town, blissfully unaware Donny could track the location of the pickup he had stolen from him. It was almost too easy. When Donny had activated the tracker, he realized Ranger was on the move. Donny rushed across Namrena and stayed back from the coordinates as far as he could. After a short drive, he tracked the pickup as it came to a stop in a street in a part of town that was filled with run-down properties.

And sure enough, Ranger was inside the vehicle. Donny killed the lights on his truck and came to a stop as well, watching Ranger through a pair of binoculars as he got out. It wouldn't be hard for Donny to find a location nearby with a clean line of sight to take the bastard out.

Donny continued to observe Ranger as he snuck up to a small home at the end of an incomplete street. He moved down the side of the house and sat beneath a tree. "What the hell are you doing, Frank?"

More time passed before Ranger pulled himself to his feet

and slipped to the back of the house. Donny waited ten more minutes and was satisfied that Ranger had gone inside.

Donny could have taken out his APR Custom .338 Lapua bolt-action rifle and put Ranger down before he vanished, but he wanted to do things clean and from a distance, where no one could see him. He would wait all night to kill Ranger if he had to. Besides, the lengthy weapon wasn't a piece of hardware you could whip out in a hurry. Time needed to be spent setting the rifle up before Donny could dispense justice.

Needing somewhere to fire from with no locals to interrupt, Donny pulled his Ford Maverick away from the home to put some distance between himself and Ranger. Donny had swapped out the stolen car from the quarry in a hurry for one of his pickups as soon as he'd collected everything he needed to take Ranger out. The last thing he wanted was to be pulled over by some overzealous traffic cop looking to fill their quota for the day. The pickup he'd left a few streets away from his Maverick would have been reported as stolen by the quarry worker he beat over the head with a rock by now, but the cops wouldn't discover the vehicle until morning at the earliest.

Donny found an abandoned home a few lanes over. There were plenty of them in this part of town. But strangely enough, if Donny traveled a little farther, he'd cross an almost visible line in Namrena that would take him from the rows of unorganized and dilapidated boxes to neat streets filled with large modern housing. That was Namrena. A clash of the old and new. The well-off and the poor.

Donny made sure there were no drug addicts squatting in the abandoned one-bedroom home, then grabbed his gear from the bed of the Maverick and scaled the roof of the worn-out building. He did a walk around to find the right spot and went prone, utilizing the limited height of the structure to give himself a clean line of sight of the house Ranger had disappeared into.

Donny pulled out a spotter's scope and ran his eye over the area. The pickup Ranger had stolen from Donny was parked up the street, meaning Ranger hadn't run off in the short time it had taken to find a suitable location to fire from. Wherever Ranger was, Donny was willing to bet Laura and her kid were inside. Why Ranger hadn't grabbed them both and bolted for the state line was a genuine mystery. He was a man being hunted by the authorities, a US Marshal, a psychotic private security firm, the Wilkinses, and now Donny himself. Did Ranger have a death wish?

Donny didn't have enough energy in him to make sense of Frank Ranger. The soldier he'd once known and loved as a brother was dead to him. Ranger had destroyed Donny's life in Namrena and, most likely, Arizona. After Donny ended Ranger's meaningless existence, he would need to activate one of his bug-out plans and put a lot of road between himself and town. The thought closed Donny's eyes. He was tired, and the waiting game to put Ranger down was only just beginning. There was no telling how long his target would remain indoors before Donny would get an opportunity to take him down. But whatever it took, Donny would get the job done and do things his way.

Whenever Donny had been waiting on one of Bill's targets, his mind wandered back to Afghanistan. How many times had he found himself flat on his stomach at the top of some mud-brick shithole, waiting on a supposedly important Taliban leader who never showed? How many stressful hours of his life had he spent as part of an overwatch unit covering his fellow soldiers under insufferable conditions? All while his comrades were on patrol in a part of a remote village the brass knew was filled with hidden Taliban fighters and IEDs?

Did he really care if he no longer got to sit at the end of a long rifle and play God with people's lives? Maybe he did. Maybe it was all he had left, and the money Bill Wilkins had offered him wasn't the driving force that made Donny pull the trigger time after time.

Donny sighed and took out a flask. He'd had a few more swigs on the way over. He didn't like to think of himself as someone with a drinking problem, but he depended on the liquid. Donny unscrewed the cap while monitoring the house and sucked down another shot. All he could do now was wait.

———

DONNY RUBBED his hands together and blew some of his breath into his palms to keep his fingers agile. The desert was cooling down the way it always did at night. He should have been wearing the fingerless gloves he had with his gear, but he didn't want to take his eyes off the house for more than a second at a time.

After only an hour or so, Ranger emerged from the house. "Got you now," Donny muttered. He tracked Ranger as he attempted to creep along in the night back to the stolen pickup. The sheer arrogance Ranger displayed would be his end. Did he think he could attack someone like Donny and steal from him without consequence? It was laughable. It made lining up the shot on Ranger all the easier. But then a thought hit Donny.

While keeping Ranger in sight, Donny pulled out his new burner and called the only contact he'd saved to the device from a backup notepad. Bill Wilkins answered after a few short rings. "Who is this?"

"It's Donny."

A brief silence filled the line. "Listen, Donny, whatever it is you have to tell me about what happened back there, I'm not interested. What's done is done."

As Donny tried to think of a response, he watched Ranger remove his CSR from the bed of the pickup and begin to wrap it up in a tarp.

"I can make things right again," Donny said.

"Oh, you can bring my head of security back from the dead?"

"What?"

Bill huffed. "Don't play dumb with me. You shot Carl. He's dead."

"Carl's dead? I…" Donny trailed off. He was about to give up on talking to Bill and end the call. There was nothing more to say to undo such a screw-up. Then an idea came to him. One that was as pathetic as it was simple. "Ranger did it."

"Who? What are you talking about?"

"Frank Ranger. The man's been causing you problems since he arrived in town, right?"

Bill groaned. "So the asshole's name is Frank Ranger. He told me it was George."

"Of course he did. He always uses a fake."

"You know him?"

"I do. We go back a ways. At least we did until today. Anyway, my point is, I wasn't the one who killed your man. Ranger did. He attacked me when I was lining up the shot on your target in Tucson. My rifle discharged during a scuffle. It was a bad bit of luck, but that shot must have hit Carl."

Bill growled down the line. "I don't give a shit whose fault it was. I blame you, Donny. I paid you top dollar to deliver. Not fuck around with some asshole you used to know. So if you don't mind, I'd prefer you never contact me again. Otherwise, I'll have to send someone to find you. Understand?"

"I can make things right."

Bill chuckled. "No, you can't. Like I said, what's done is done."

"I have Ranger in my sights."

"You what?"

"I have a shot lined up on him. Right now. I can kill Frank Ranger for you."

Bill didn't say a word. Donny waited for a response. Only a few seconds passed by, but it felt like time had stopped. Finally, Bill spoke. "Where are you?"

"In Namrena. I can tell you where, but first I want some assurances that we can do business again." Ranger remained still beside Donny's pickup, still in his sights.

"What is he doing?" Bill asked. "Is he with a woman and some kid?"

"No, he's alone by a pickup near a house. I'm guessing this woman and kid you're speaking about are inside." Donny made sure to play dumb about Laura and James.

"Ranger's at a house? Tell me the address, Donny."

"I will, but like I said, I want some assurances that—"

"Screw your assurances. Tell me where Ranger is, and I'll forget Carl ever existed."

"I could kill him for you and send through a photo."

"No. Tell me where this house is, dammit."

Donny sighed. He removed his scope from Ranger and shifted it to the half-broken number tacked onto the facade of the home Ranger had come out of. He gave Bill the address, but deep inside it felt like a mistake.

"Son of a bitch," Bill said.

"What is it?"

"That lying whore."

"Who?"

"Rosie," Bill muttered.

Donny took a second to make the connection. "Wait,

Rosie? From the diner?" He'd eaten at her diner enough times to know who she was.

"Yes. That's her house you're watching over. She's helping one of her waitresses, Laura. And her damned kid."

"Helping them do what?" Donny asked, playing along.

Bill muttered something inaudible. "Doesn't matter. But tell you what, if you want to make things right between us, Donny, you need to do as I say. Got it?"

Donny shifted his aim back to Ranger as he moved away from the pickup. "I'm listening."

"Keep an eye on Ranger, but don't kill him unless I tell you."

"Easy enough. He's heading back to the house."

"Good. Keep talking. Tell me what you see."

"He's got my rifle. The one I took to the quarry. It's wrapped in a tarp."

"Okay. Does he know how to use it?"

"Yeah, but he's no sniper."

"Sounds like he's desperate."

Donny came to the same conclusion. As far as he could tell, Ranger had a few handguns on him and the rifle. All with low ammunition.

"What's he doing?" Bill asked.

"He's approaching the house. Someone is opening the front door. Ranger doesn't look happy about it."

"Who is it?" Bill asked, an eagerness to his voice Donny couldn't shake.

"Rosie. She's ushering him inside."

"Good, good. Kill her."

"Wait? What?"

"You heard me," Bill said.

"You can't be serious."

"If you don't do this, then you might as well hang up the phone and start running. You get me?"

Donny's voice filled with panic. "No, I can't. It's Rosie." She wasn't some criminal target he was being asked to take out. It was a woman who had served him food and coffee at the diner.

"Do it, soldier," Bill said. "Do you want to give up this life? Do you want to go back to sitting alone in bars, drinking away your miserable existence?"

Donny's chest tightened as a pang of unease filled him. Dark clouds gathered around his thoughts. He kept his scope trained on Ranger and watched as he moved back to the pickup. Rosie remained by her front door, stationary.

"What about Ranger?" Donny asked.

"Kill him, too. But do Rosie first. I want him to see what happens when you poke your head where it doesn't belong."

Donny didn't reply as sweat coated his brow.

"What's it gonna be, Donny? Do you wanna throw it all away on these losers? They're dead either way. If you don't do this, I'll have one of my other guys kill them. You know I will."

"Okay," Donny whispered as Ranger walked back from the pickup.

"Be a good soldier," Bill pressed. "Take out your targets. Rosie first."

Donny burrowed deep within himself. He pushed all emotion from his body and tightened his aim on Rosie. When he squeezed the trigger, it was as if he weren't the one behind the rifle. Merely an observer on the sidelines witnessing unstoppable destructive power.

Rosie's body fell into Ranger's arms a moment later. The shocked man then pulled Rosie's corpse from the front of the street and into the house. Donny had time to cycle the bolt and fire another round straight into Ranger's body, but all he could do was stare.

"Is it done?" Bill asked.

"Rosie's…dead." Donny shook his head as his hand fell away from the trigger.

"Excellent work," Bill said. "And Ranger?"

Donny released his grip on the rifle entirely. "He ran back into the house. I didn't have a shot."

"Dammit," Bill muttered. "No matter. Keep him there. I'm sending a few of my guys to you now. If Ranger tries to run, you put him down."

Bill disconnected the call before Donny could say another word.

CHAPTER 30

BILL

Bill hadn't expected the call from Donny. And more so, he never envisaged that the man's desperation to get back into his good books would work out so well for him. If anything, Bill had been prepared for an attack on the farm at Donny's hands. Not the opposite. It was a shame Bill would still need to take Donny off the board once Ranger and Laura had been dealt with. In this line of business, you didn't get many second chances.

Bill listened on the phone as Donny took the shot that ended Rosie's life. She didn't deserve such a clean death. After everything he'd done for her, she thought it was right as rain to betray him. If Rosie were still alive and on her knees in front of him, he would ask two simple questions: Was it worth it? Was the life of some whore waitress worth trading for your own? Bill should never have given her the chance he had all those years ago. He wouldn't make that mistake again.

Ranger was still alive, but soon enough, he'd be joining Rosie.

Bill's cell phone rang. It was one of his men calling from the front gate. "What is it?"

"It's your son. His X5 is at the gate, but something weird is going on. I don't think it's him or his boys inside."

Bill understood who was driving the X5 and didn't want to involve the men at the gate any more than he had to. "Let the car through."

"Boss, are you sure?"

"Do as I say, dammit!"

Bill's patience was running low. And no doubt, the same could be said for Xaver, who'd been tasked to bring in his son. The job hadn't gone down the way Bill had expected it to. The matter was growing more complicated by the minute.

Xaver had called Bill earlier when he found William at his home. Considered to be the more affluent area of Namrena, William had bought a large block in the suburban paradise a few years ago and built a two-level, six-bedroom home in the recently developed estate. The boy always complained that it was undersized and too conventional for someone of his standing. He couldn't see reason or understand that they couldn't be seen drawing too much attention to themselves with mansions, supercars, and other extravagances.

Xaver was originally supposed to extract Bill's son and encourage his two pals to take a hike and not get involved in the family affair. But what Xaver had discovered at Junior's home changed everything. Bill had had no choice but to respond.

Bill had been down in the lab when he'd taken Donny's call. Years ago, he'd had one of his people install some expensive tech in the underground area to allow him to make and receive phone calls. The last thing he wanted was to miss an important call while checking on the latest batch—a job his son failed to do time and again.

Bill came up from the lab and strolled out the secured

door on the surface as his son's X5 arrived. Bill signaled for Xaver to head down to where the fleet of vehicles sat. Nearby was a small shipping container.

The X5 moved ahead of Bill and came to a stop. It idled while Xaver waited for Bill to catch up. When Bill reached the start of the fleet, he ordered anyone in sight to move in the opposite direction. He needed the space clear.

The tint on William's X5 was darker than what was legal. To the point where Bill could barely make out Xaver behind the driver's wheel, sitting next to one of his trusted soldiers, Buck Fraley.

The window on the driver's door rolled down. Xaver stared out at Bill with a slight frown but didn't speak.

Bill rested a hand on the front quarter panel of the X5 and shook his head. "You got the job done?"

"Yeah."

"I'll deal with it from here."

"You sure about this, boss?"

"Just back this thing up to the shipping container and unload."

Xaver's mouth opened to speak, but he paused as if reconsidering his words. He gave Bill a nod instead and started to roll the X5 toward the shipping container.

Bill continued walking. He didn't want to hear what Xaver had to say. All he needed the man to do was finish the job and keep his mouth shut about what he'd discovered. At least for the time being. Word would spread soon enough.

In less than five minutes, Bill found himself standing in front of three unconscious, blindfolded, and gagged men. All of them were restrained in place with thick chains that were connected to oversize metal loops that had been welded to solid chairs inside the container. The word "men" was an exaggeration. William and his two idiots were as far from men as three boys could be. And worse still, William was the oldest of the three by almost a decade.

While Bill stared at his son, he thought about the chaos the day had brought his way. When he'd woken up in the morning, he hadn't expected to have to deal with so many problems at once. There were always issues to handle on the farm, but most difficulties could be overcome without much thought.

Donny and his drifter pal were at the core of the calamity. Bill was tempted to send Xaver and Buck to Rosie's home to help finish off Ranger, but Bill had already dispatched two of his men to take out the wanderer and haul Laura in. He was still going to have the woman killed, but before she left her mortal coil, she would serve one more purpose that centered around his son William.

By the time Bill's men returned, Frank Ranger would be dead, Laura would join William in the container, and if Donny was dumb enough to hang around, he would have a round put in the back of his skull for good measure. The two men Bill had sent out had been given orders to kill Donny once Ranger had been dealt with.

For the moment, though, Bill had other problems to handle. His son was stirring, so he removed Junior's blindfold and gag.

"Rise and shine, boy. I think it's time you and I had a little chat."

CHAPTER 31

RANGER

Ranger's leg cramped as he held on tight to the Beretta. He was still squatting close to the front entry of Rosie's home, pinned down by what he knew had to be Donny's sniper fire. It wasn't a novel experience by far. He'd spent countless hours under enemy fire. But never had the threat been at the hands of a friend.

Rosie's motionless body lay where Ranger had been forced to leave her. He still couldn't believe she was dead, or that Donny had been the one to pull the trigger. He knew in his heart that it was Donny. Who else could it have been? One of Bill's men? He doubted it. Donny had tracked him down to Rosie's house, most likely via the damn pickup Ranger had stolen from him.

"Stupid son of a bitch," Ranger muttered to himself, tapping the cool metal of the pistol in his hand against his head. He should have known better. Donny had seemed unhinged from the moment he'd found him at the run-down property. Of course Donny would have a tracking device in his vehicle. Once again, Ranger had made a snap decision that had cost someone else dearly. And this time, it was lethal.

There was no other way to sugarcoat it. Rosie was dead because of Ranger. He slumped down against the wall and kicked his legs out.

James' crying could be heard from where he sat. The kid had gone through hell since Ranger showed up in town. He'd seen nothing but carnage delivered by Ranger's hands. How many years of therapy that Laura could never afford would he need to recover from the damage caused? All assuming Ranger could take James and his mother to safety.

Ranger thought about the single shot Donny had placed between Rosie's eyes. He replayed the sound over and over in his head. Donny had to be a few hundred yards away at best. Had anyone else on the street noticed the shot? And if so, did they think of calling the police? He couldn't hear any sirens in the distance.

Ranger wanted to call the cops. It might scare Donny off. But the hell it would rain on Laura would not be worth the trade-off. She'd have to explain why she was in a house with a fugitive and the dead body of her employer. And if the responding officers were tied to Bill Wilkins, then the crime boss would learn her location in an instant. Then again, maybe Bill already knew. Whoever had killed Rosie had to have been in contact with the man.

Ranger couldn't understand how he was still breathing. Sure, Rosie had gone against Bill and had been helping him and Laura, but she was hardly a threat. If Donny had been the one to kill her, why didn't he shoot Ranger first?

Ranger closed his eyes. He was exhausted and had been for a long time. How much more could he take? How much longer could he run from the pain that filled his life?

The crying in the next room settled down after a few minutes. The lack of noise opened Ranger's eyes. He needed to go check on Laura and James. Keeping low, he crawled across the room, leaving Rosie's body behind. He only stood once he was clear of danger and moved with purpose toward where he thought the bathroom would be. The hushed murmur of Laura singing confirmed he'd found the right room.

Ranger couldn't make out the words, but it sounded like she was singing a lullaby to her son. Thanks to Ranger, the boy had been taken from childhood to the opposite end of innocence in a heartbeat. It was like the incident at the diner all over again, but ten times worse.

Ranger put the pistol in his hand away for the time being. With a gentle tap, he knocked on the thin door of the bathroom. Laura stopped singing. A moment later, she opened the door a few inches and whispered, "What do you want?"

"Is he okay?"

"What do you think?"

Ranger exhaled. "I'm sorry."

"You're sorry, are you? Is that supposed to make it all better? Will that bring my friend back?"

"Laura, I—"

"Just leave me alone."

James started crying with the rise of anger in her voice. Laura glanced back at her son, then returned a glare at Ranger. He closed the door and let her be. For the moment, anyway. There wasn't time to process Rosie's death. Donny or whoever had killed Rosie was still out there, keeping a sniper's eye on the building. And a feeling in Ranger's gut convinced him they had been told to keep him, Laura, and James pinned down until Bill Wilkins arrived.

Ranger let his feet take him out to the kitchen area as his mind tried to formulate a plan. There had to be a way to get Laura and James to safety. One that didn't involve charging out to certain death. With Donny's CSR still sitting outside the front door, Ranger only had Liam's Glock and Donny's Beretta in hand. Neither would be useful when he couldn't even get a fix on the shooter's location beyond a general direction.

The sniper had all the advantages. It was night, the lighting in the streets was poor, and their rifle was powerful and clearly suppressed. Ranger couldn't rely on spotting a muzzle flash. Not that anyone could miss at such close range. Not unless they wanted to.

Ranger paced the kitchen with his arms crossed over his chest. He hated being stuck while a threat loomed close by, unable to fight back. Nothing short of a miracle would change things. He had no lifelines or cavalry rushing in to save him. It was just him, alone, with no way to escape the pressure closing in.

Ranger stopped pacing and took a breath in. As he exhaled, he pooled all the focus he could muster and pushed away his every thought. He needed to find a solution. He stomped back to the bathroom door and knocked, opening it before Laura responded. "I need a small mirror."

"A mirror?"

"Yeah. Does Rosie have one?"

Laura stared at him like he was insane.

"Please," he begged. "I need your help."

"Okay." She sighed. Then she rummaged through some drawers on the vanity and produced a scratched hand mirror. "Here."

Ranger took it with a nod and inspected the rectangle.

"What are you going to do?" she asked.

Ranger stared at the mirror. "Find Donny."

CHAPTER 32

Ranger crept up to the front door, keeping his focus away from Rosie's body. Like his wife, she was gone, and he now had other people to worry about. If he pulled off the impossible, he was going to punish the man responsible for her death.

With the hand mirror firm in his grip, Ranger edged up to one window that had its curtains closed. Turning off the lights near the front section of the home, inside and out, had hopefully given him some level of cover. Still, he knew Donny would be watching with a keen eye and military-grade equipment.

Ranger held up the mirror and slowly raised it to the curtains. He slid it behind the material in front of the glass and angled it to glimpse the world outside. It was a dark night, making it difficult to distinguish what was what, but Ranger soon got his bearings. With a slight adjustment here and a twist there, he found a few potential locations from where Donny might have made his shot. Based on where Rosie got hit, Ranger believed he'd located two likely sites where Donny could be. There were two houses that seemed like viable options. Knowing Donny, he'd be on one of their roofs, staring down at the world.

Rosie's death played on a loop in Ranger's head. As much as he wanted to forget it ever happened, the damning moment was helping him pinpoint where Donny might be, provided he hadn't relocated.

As Ranger saw the life leave Rosie's eyes again and again, the image was soon replaced with another woman's face. One that no amount of time would ever erase from his mind.

The mirror fell from his fleeting grip and struck him in the face, jolting him back to the present. The physical pain was a welcome relief. It reminded Ranger of where he was and what he needed to do.

Shaking the fatigue from his brain, Ranger cleared his throat and placed the mirror in his pocket. He scooted away from the front wall and made his way through the small home toward the back door.

"Tell me you're not going out there," Laura said from the side hallway opening.

He shrugged. "I have to."

"No, you don't. You'll die if you step one foot out that door. Look what your supposed friend did."

"All the more reason to go out there and stop him. He's got us pinned down. I need to find out why."

"What do you mean?" she asked, inching closer.

Ranger let his eyes wander around the room. He didn't want to get into what had happened with Donny at the quarry, but she had a right to know. "There's something I need to tell you."

Laura didn't say a word and stared at him like she couldn't take another piece of bad news. Ranger told her the truth. He told her about the quarry and what he'd discovered his friend doing. He told her whom Donny had been working for and in what capacity.

"Oh my God. You can't be serious."

"I wish it weren't true. I wish this were all a bad dream, but it's not. Donny works for Bill Wilkins as a gun for hire. Specifically killing targets from a long range."

"And you didn't think to mention this to us when you showed up here?"

The question was like a swift blow to his gut. It was another one he couldn't answer. "I'm sor—"

"If you tell me you're sorry again, so help me God."

Ranger stopped himself from saying more. She was right. Apologizing wasn't going to change a thing or bring Rosie back.

Laura faced away from Ranger and muttered something inaudible to herself with fresh tears streaking her skin. He could see it was all catching up to her. Everything he'd caused. He had to set things straight for her.

"I'm going out there. Not just to stop him, but to find out why Donny didn't kill me. It couldn't be as simple as him missing. Not this close."

Laura faced him again. "Maybe he's keeping us here for a reason."

"What do you mean?"

She inhaled and took a few steps toward him. "You humiliated Liam. I ran away with you. Maybe Bill wants us to suffer. Death isn't enough for these people."

"Jesus," Ranger said, letting the word hang in the air. He didn't know if she was right, but she knew Bill and Liam better than him. "If that's the case, time is against us. If I don't do something now, we'll run out of it." He continued to the back door, the one accessed via the tiny laundry. Rosie's shotgun was still leaning on the wall. He picked it up and faced Laura. "Ever use one of these?"

"Yeah, a few times. My daddy used to take me hunting before he left us."

Ranger stopped himself from apologizing for her absent father. Her low prospects, her run-down home, and her pill addiction all made him think of Cindy. What impact would his absence have on her after she'd lost her mother? It was a sorrow he didn't have time to think about.

Ranger walked over to Laura and handed her the shotgun. "Whatever the circumstances, I'm glad your father did that much for you. While I'm gone, I want you and James to sit inside the bathtub and keep this aimed at the door. If it's me, I'll call out a code word to you."

"Okay. How about 'Rosie'?" Laura offered.

He smiled, respecting the suggestion. "That'll work. You hear anything else, you shoot. Got it?"

"Got it."

Ranger let out his breath. He was about to head through the door when an idea came to him. "I need a cell phone. Did Rosie have one on her?"

"I think so," Laura said, closing her eyes. "It'd be in her back pocket."

Ranger nodded, knowing he'd need to search the dead woman's body to retrieve her phone.

"Why do you need it?" Laura asked.

He scanned the room and let the crazy idea that was in his mind marinate. "With any luck, to flush Donny out. Do you know if her phone has a pin code?"

"Uh, yeah. It does, but I don't know it."

"That's okay. I should be able to do what I need without it." Ranger crept back into the front room to Rosie's body. He felt sick taking anything from the dead, but Rosie's cell phone might be just the thing to save Laura and James.

Ranger returned to the main room, then ducked into the back bedroom. Inside, he unlocked a sliding window in case he needed another way back into the home. It wouldn't be hard for Donny to cut off his retreat when the time came.

Ranger emerged from the bedroom and walked by Laura. He paused and glanced at her sideways. "Lock the doors once I go. I'll knock and call out if I need you to let me back in."

"Okay," she said, still gripping the shotgun.

Ranger continued with his plan, feeling his heart rate pick up its pace as he came closer to the laundry room where the back door sat.

"Frank?" Laura asked, slowing him up for a moment.

"Yeah?"

"Kill the son of a bitch. For Rosie."

"Yes, ma'am."

Ranger made his way outside and kept his body to the wall, clinging tight to the cell phone for dear life.

CHAPTER 33

BILL

William groaned awake, opening eyes he swore had been glued together. "Where the hell?" he muttered like he was trying to make sense of his surroundings. It was dark. Only a single source of light was in the room, hanging above his head.

Bill knew the smell of oil and exhaust fumes would have confused him, but it wasn't until William reached up to rub his swollen temples that he realized he'd been restrained and wasn't in his home.

"What the fuck?" William groaned. He was sitting on a hard metal chair with his hands facing forward, bound in thick handcuffs that were connected to a heavy chain that ran between his legs. The chain limited his movement, stopping him from raising his hands higher than his chest. Bill watched as he discovered his legs were also restrained with ankle cuffs that had a central chain running up to his waist.

William attempted to stand. but fell back down. There was no way to achieve the simple task. A final chain ran around his midsection and was connected to the seat itself. It was the kind of setup someone might find in a federal penitentiary, but William hadn't been arrested.

From the shadows of the shipping container, Bill watched and saw the panic fill his son's chest as he tried to make sense of the situation.

"Motherfucker," William spat, seemingly blind to Bill's presence. The boy squinted at the dusty light above. The naked bulb barely lit the rest of the space. As he scanned the room, he found the only other person in the container.

"Whoever the fuck you are," William said, "you're a dead man. You hear me?"

Bill didn't respond and continued to study his son like he was a drugged lion in a zoo.

"I'll kill you," William spat. "I promise you. And if I don't, my old man will bury you alive."

Bill chuckled.

"Wait, no. It can't be."

Bill stepped forward into the light. "Hello, Junior."

William lurched forward but fell back into his seat a moment later once his range of movement had been reached. "What the hell is this?"

Bill scratched at his beard as if he were pondering the question. "How about we call this an intervention."

"Fuck you. Let me out of these fucking chains, or I'll—"

"You'll what? Kill me? Don't be so dramatic, son."

William's breath slammed in and out of his body as he stared at his father with a burning intensity. He was seething with so much rage it made his hands shake.

The boy had to know where he was. He'd been in the room before, but on the other side of the chains, standing where his father now stood. Bill remembered the first time he'd forced Junior to be in the room with him. He'd asked him to extract information from a person who had found themselves in the chair William now sat. It was bolted to the flooring of the shipping container.

There was no point in yelling. William knew firsthand that the container had been made to be almost soundproof. Plus, it was away from any of the workers at the back of the main building. If you found yourself waking up in chains in this shipping container, it could only mean one thing.

"Where's Mack and Roll?" William asked.

Bill crossed his arms over his chest and gestured with his chin for William to glance over his shoulder at his pals. William twisted back as far as possible and found both Mack and Roll in similar setups. Each man was slumped over. The crucial difference was their hands. They'd been cuffed behind their backs.

"Are they dead?" he asked.

Bill strolled by his son and walked up to Mack. The kid had been gagged and blindfolded. Bill grabbed him by the jaw and yanked upward. Mack reacted with a cowardly sob. Bill chuckled and did the same thing to Roll a moment later and got an identical response. "They're alive, Junior."

"Don't fucking call me that," William yelled.

"I'll call you whatever the hell I want."

Both men stared at one another, breathless and unblinking. Time seemed to come to a standstill.

"Why are you doing this?" William asked, speaking first.

Bill laughed. "Are you serious? You can't work it out?"

"Tell me."

"This, my boy, has been a long time coming. How many chances have I given you to respect me? How many opportunities have I allowed for you to prove your worth? If you weren't my son, I'd have killed you a long time ago."

"Screw you. I'm twice the man you'll ever be. This business would be ten times the size if I were running it."

"Is that so?" Bill asked with exaggerated brows. "I guess

you should go right ahead and take over. I'll gladly step aside and watch how a real man gets it done."

"Go fuck yourself."

Bill laughed. "And there it is. The words of a pathetic loser."

"Take these chains off me and I'll show you who is pathetic."

Bill snickered. "What? So you can kill me? Isn't that what you had planned?"

William squinted and glanced over his shoulder.

"It wasn't them, Junior. They didn't sell you out, if that's what you're thinking. I sent a few of my guys out to collect you, seeing as you were refusing to come to the farm. Like I said, you were in danger. I just wanted you back here where I could keep you safe. But imagine my shock when it was reported to me that you had your X5 loaded up like you were about to invade France."

"I was hunting down Laura and the drifter. Like you wanted. I needed weapons."

"Really? You needed an arsenal of long guns, grenades, and heavy body armor to take out two people? I suppose that would explain why you also had blueprints of the farm laid out on the hood of the BMW—you know, the expensive ride I bought you for your damn birthday."

William shook his head and laughed. "You sent someone to spy on me? Couldn't handle the job on your own, could you?"

Bill stomped over and grabbed his son by a fistful of his hair. He craned his head up into the light. "I sent my guys out to bring you in for your own goddamn good. At least that's how it started. Tell me what you were really doing."

William shook his head. "Nothing."

Bill laughed. "Nothing, huh? So you weren't coming here to throw me an early retirement party? You weren't coming to this farm, the one that I built with my own goddamn hands, to put a bullet in your own father's skull?"

William stared Bill down. "What choice did you give me?"

Bill stabbed a finger at his chest. "I gave you everything. I gave you the world, but it was never enough, was it? You always wanted more without doing a goddamn thing to deserve it."

William tried to pounce at his father again, but the sharp jolt of the chains stopped him. "I'll kill you. I swear to God, I'll be the last person you ever see."

Bill sneered at his son. "Not today, Junior." He reached down and pulled out his .357 Colt Python.

"What are you doing?"

"Something I should have done a long time ago." Bill held the gun low as he walked toward his son. With flared nostrils, William didn't flinch and raised his chin. Apparently, he had found his balls in the last five minutes.

Bill went straight past William and aimed the gun at Mack. Mack craned his neck and tried to scream through his gag. The revolver went off with a single, deafening blast. Mack's head snapped backward as chunks of his brain sprayed against the container wall.

Roll also attempted to scream through his gag and met the same fate a few seconds later.

William yelled as his fists balled up. An enveloping rage overtook his every muscle as he thrashed against the chains. The edges cut into his wrists.

Bill put the revolver away and placed a hand on his son's shoulder. "This is for your own good, Junior. One day, you'll thank me."

CHAPTER 34
RANGER

Ranger didn't have a lot of options to get around Donny's powerful scope and rifle. Only a crazy idea would do the trick, and one stood out high above the rest. The gambit he had in mind would take time to execute. And considering Donny was keeping him pinned down, he would have to move fast.

With his back against the rear wall of Rosie's house, Ranger slid down to the hard ground. It was dark outside, but not dark enough. Every source of light felt like a death sentence to Ranger. Only the shadows brought him any comfort, but it was a false economy.

With a deep breath in and out, Ranger inched away from the house and did what he could to keep the building between him and where he estimated Donny might be. The sniper could have rushed around to Ranger's flank in the time he'd taken to come up with a plan, but it was a variable that would need to be forcefully ignored.

Crouched down, Ranger moved along the wall as far as he deemed safe before his head would start poking out from cover. Donny wouldn't need to see much of his exposed skull to end his life. He'd shown Ranger what he was still capable of doing.

Ranger paused at an invisible threshold to take another breath in before he progressed with the plan. He took an extra second to see if a better solution would come to him, but his burned-out mind was running on fumes as it was. It wasn't too late to turn back and hide inside to work out a smarter play. But he'd be playing into Bill's hands, giving him the opportunity to send more people to their location. Time was his greatest enemy.

"Okay," Ranger muttered, exhaling. "Here goes nothing." He pulled out Rosie's cell phone. The device was locked and neither Ranger nor Laura knew the pin code, but that wouldn't be a problem. He pressed and held down the power and volume buttons until the phone automatically dialed 911, bypassing its own security. Ranger got through to a 911 dispatcher and asked for the fire department. He told them he'd spotted a fire two streets over and gave out an approximate address. In a few minutes, Donny would be swarmed with emergency vehicles and would be forced to run, losing sight of his target. And with any hope, Ranger would see him.

Ranger drummed his fingers against his thigh as he waited at the back of the property for the fire department to respond. He checked the Beretta and Glock in the back of his jeans and opted to keep the Beretta out and ready.

In just under six minutes, two fire trucks came blazing into the area two streets over. Once the engines swarmed the location where Ranger believed the shot had come from, he made his move.

Accepting that Donny might still have eyes on him, Ranger stayed low and charged. He sprang over a fence into the neighbor's yard and rushed from one makeshift cover to the next as he snaked his way toward Donny's location. A large pickup came rushing down the street with bright head-lights, forcing Ranger to duck at the last second behind a parked car. He held his breath and prayed the driver hadn't seen him creeping around looking suspicious as hell. The truck sped by without stopping.

A few residents appeared in the street to see what the commotion with the fire department was about. None of them noticed Ranger in the shadows. Their eyes and ears were trained on the distraction he'd made.

While the fire trucks blared their sirens, Ranger moved between parked vehicles, then cut his way through the yards of the houses on Rosie's street until he found himself in the next road over. He was getting closer to where he figured Donny would be and hoped to witness him fleeing the emer-gency vehicles. So far, he hadn't seen anyone running around with something resembling a large-caliber rifle slung over their shoulder.

Ranger cut through a person's yard and bounded over a low fence into the road where he'd directed the fire depart-ment to go. Doing his best to ignore anyone in the street, he rushed up to a house that was one lot over from where he estimated Donny had set up his rifle. With his body pressed tight to the building, he edged his way around the backyard and tried to avoid the growing number of curious onlookers who were filling the streets.

The next house over appeared to be an empty home in poor condition. It would have been the perfect location for Donny to use. Ranger glanced back toward Rosie's home and saw the exact angle Donny might have taken to kill the woman who never deserved to die. Her greatest crime had been trying to help Laura and James out of the situation Ranger had instigated.

As Ranger stared at the building with seeds of guilt flooding his mind, he spotted a man moving toward Rosie's place with a hurried determination. This person had a suppressed pistol in his hand but no rifle.

"Donny," Ranger whispered as he saw the familiar outline and followed.

The plan had worked and flushed Donny out from his vantage point. But Ranger hadn't expected the son of a bitch to run headfirst toward Rosie's house.

He steadied his grip on the Beretta and bolted through a fenceless yard toward Donny. He had to stop him before he reached Laura and James. Laura might have been armed with Rosie's shotgun, but she would be up against a man who had killed many people. What if she hesitated to pull the trigger when Donny broke into the house?

There was no time to be subtle. Ranger took the same rushed pathway as Donny and risked being spotted by a local or a member of the fire department as he found his way across to Rosie's street again. He gazed ahead and watched Donny reach the front of the house with his pistol leveled in both hands. He must have ditched his rifle in a hurry when the emergency vehicles came into the street.

Donny stepped up to the front door and paid no attention to the CSR Ranger hadn't dared to go near. Instead of worrying about the rifle, he seemed to be staring at the front door, which had Rosie's blood splattered all over it. Did he regret what he had done?

It didn't matter. Ranger knew what had to be done and wouldn't hesitate when the time came.

He was about to get the drop on Donny when he spotted two other men appear to Donny's right flank. They were dressed in dark clothing and were also carrying suppressed pistols as they approached Rosie's home. They seemed to pop up from nowhere and must have been inside the large pickup Ranger had seen rushing down the street.

The two men spoke to Donny with frantic motions like

they were making a plan on the fly to raid the house. "Shit," Ranger muttered. Donny had backup. Two of Bill Wilkins' people, no doubt. Ranger ducked down behind the closest parked car for cover to observe the three men. With Donny in the lead, they made their way down the side path of the property and had to be heading for the back door.

"Don't do it," Ranger whispered as he imagined Laura and James meeting their ends thanks to his reckless idea to flush Donny out with the fire department.

With no time to chastise himself, Ranger ran as fast and as quietly as he could, following the three armed criminals. Donny checked his surroundings multiple times as he moved, constantly glancing over his shoulder. It was a smart thing to do, all things considered. This was Ranger's wheelhouse. Donny had the advantage when it came to wide-open spaces and long distances, but not in urban tactics.

Ranger would do whatever it took to stop them. There was no way in hell he was going to let another innocent person die.

CHAPTER 35

DONNY - FIFTEEN MINUTES AGO

After Bill ended their call, Donny sat up from his prone rifle and stared out into the night. He couldn't believe what he'd done to Rosie. The image of her head snapping back played on a loop in his mind again and again and didn't seem real. It wasn't like he hadn't killed someone before. Donny had lost count of the number of deaths he'd witnessed through the scope of a rifle held in his hands. This, though, was the first time he'd ended the life of a person he'd known. And a woman at that.

All of Bill's targets had been men. Killing a woman had been a line Donny thought he'd never cross. But the old man had pushed him into a corner and had twisted his every thought until Donny had made the worst mistake of his life and squeezed the trigger.

How was he supposed to accept that he'd shot and killed a woman who had brought him coffee and burgers more than a dozen times? A kind person who had smiled at him and looked him in the eye as she'd asked him how his day was going?

"What have I done?" he muttered. There was no coming back from it.

More time passed by with Donny staring into the abyss. He wasn't keeping an eye on the house like he was supposed to, giving Ranger an opportunity to take Laura and her kid out the back and run. If that happened, Bill would never give him another chance. Rosie's death would have all been for nothing. He couldn't let that happen.

Donny forced himself to get behind the rifle again. That was what he wanted, wasn't it? The chance to keep on fighting, to keep doing what he did best? But what did that even mean? He couldn't continue to justify the murder of US citizens whom Bill Wilkins deemed to be his enemies.

Donny let go of the rifle and closed his eyes. He fished out his flask from his hip pocket and took a hefty swig with a shaking hand. The alcohol barely took off the edge. There wasn't enough of the liquid in the world to make things better. He would never forgive himself for this.

Emergency lights flashed in the distance and were accompanied by sirens. Donny used the scope of his APR Custom .338 Lapua and spotted two fire trucks headed his way. "What?" he asked out loud. He pulled his head back and swept the area without the scope. There were no flames leaping into the air that he could see. There was no smoke bellowing and twisting into the night. All he could smell was the sharp tang of burnt gunpowder as it lingered, reminding him of what he'd done.

Donny watched as the fire trucks came closer and closer to the house. They turned one corner, then the next, seeming to be on a path to his location. It didn't make any sense, unless…

"Frank," he let out, figuring Ranger must have called the fire department on him. If that was what'd happened, it meant Ranger was up to something. Most likely, he was attempting to disrupt the fire superiority Donny currently held.

If he was spotted by a firefighter on the roof of the decaying home, sporting a large rifle, an army of police officers would be called out to deal with him. Maybe it would be for the best. They could surround him and open fire. They could put an end to Hatchet, the US Marine who had disgraced his name and everything else he had fought to protect.

He was ready to give up, to let his path of destruction come to an end. But then he saw something. A pickup with bright headlamps came tearing into Rosie's street. It was rushing toward her home. And there was no doubt in Donny's mind who was driving in such a way. Bill's men had arrived as promised.

Donny thought about running. It seemed like the best move. His location was compromised, and Ranger was most likely in the wind with Laura and the kid by now. Donny had failed Bill and senselessly murdered Rosie as a result. The enforcers Bill had sent would soon find the house empty and report back to Bill how much Donny had screwed things up. Maybe if he helped them find Ranger, there was a chance Bill would let him live.

Donny dropped off the single-level roof at the back of the home and landed with a heavy thud. "Dammit," he muttered as pain shot through one of his ankles. He brushed it off as best he could and got moving, rushing toward Rosie's place. As he did, his suspicions about the pickup were confirmed when two men dressed in dark clothing emerged from the vehicle. Each was armed and on edge. He wasn't familiar with either one of them. Then again, Bill had a lot of guys he could call upon.

Both men made their approach to the house and turned on tactical flashlights on their pistols as they went. They were each carrying customized Glock 19s with red-dot sights. It made Donny wonder if he was dealing with a couple of former Navy SEALs, given their choice of sidearm. Or maybe they were nothing but enthusiastic wannabes.

Donny drew his suppressed Sig Sauer P320 and stopped at the front door, waiting for Bill's guys to meet him.

CHAPTER 36
RANGER

Ranger kept Donny and his friends in view at the end of Rosie's home. Once they were close enough to the back door, he rushed down the opposite side of the house, keeping his footsteps as light as possible. When he reached the end of the building, he listened as they inspected the locked door to the laundry.

Laura and James were deeper inside the house, hiding in the bathroom. Laura would have the shotgun leveled at the bathroom door as instructed. If Donny or one of his co-workers disturbed her, they'd receive a face full of buckshot for their trouble. A blast at such a close range would take down one of the three at the very least. But Ranger would then need to deal with the remaining two attackers as quickly as possible, even if that meant killing Donny.

A loud crunch sounded as one of the men kicked in the lightweight door to the laundry, granting them all access.

Once Ranger was certain the trio had gone into the house, he doubled back to gain entry via the rear bedroom. The window he'd unlocked could slide open from the outside. One of the three might have been watching the back entrance if they had half a brain. They wouldn't expect him to drop in from the side of the house instead.

Ranger was ever aware he was taking on three dangerous men, one of whom had already killed an innocent woman in cold blood. A man he thought he knew well. But Donny had changed. The soldier he knew had only ever resorted to violence when they were at war. But that was a different time in a different world.

Ranger hadn't heard Laura's shotgun go off yet, so he slid the window open and leaped inside as fast and as quietly as his exhaustion allowed. He slid the window shut and ducked down under the bed inside, figuring the room would be searched any minute. He settled into place and kept his head close to the door, aiming the Beretta at the entrance.

Less than thirty seconds later, the bedroom door opened. Donny's associates filled the dark with their flashlights and did a rudimentary check of the room. They seemed to be in a rush and declared the area to be clear without looking under the bed or in the closets. They'd been lucky, Ranger thought. If either man had done his job right, they would have met their end.

Once the two enforcers with bright lights left the bedroom, Ranger crawled out from under the mattress and edged up to the open doorway, keeping himself clear from view. He listened as the pair checked the second bedroom. Once that room was cleared, they stomped to the bathroom, making the floor creak. All the while, Donny was with them, backing their play. The thought made him want to be sick. Ranger needed to stop the three before they kicked in the bathroom door.

He took a breath and flicked the safety off on the Beretta. Then he aimed down the corridor at the three guns for hire. They didn't see Ranger in the dark as he pointed Donny's pistol at them. He fixed his aim at his friend's skull and was ready to shoot.

Donny deserved worse than death, but Ranger had bigger problems than his own rage to deal with. He had to drop Donny with a single shot, then take out the other two home invaders before they could make sense of what was happening.

As Ranger's finger curled around the trigger of the Beretta, he felt a pang of guilt form in his chest. He was about to kill his friend. A man he had bled alongside. It went against his every instinct, but the once respected sniper had left him with little choice.

Ranger depressed the trigger a few millimeters more with the Beretta's sights lined up on Donny's temple. It would be a clean shot. One Donny would never see coming.

The blast from Rosie's shotgun thundered out, splintering a hole in the bathroom door. Laura had realized what was happening and defended herself. Unfortunately, her shot missed.

Bill's two men jumped sideways from the door on one side while Donny dove to the floor away from the blast on the other, closer to Ranger. There was a moment of shock as the three shared a look. Then one of Bill's guys spotted Ranger.

"Oh, shit," the man said. With Donny on the ground, he fired his pistol three times over Donny's head in Ranger's direction. The suppressed thud of each bullet cracked into the bedroom wall behind him, pulling Ranger back and out of sight.

"Kill him," the second one of Bill's thugs yelled. More shots rang out and drilled the wall in the bedroom. From the way Donny had dropped to the ground, the two morons must have still been firing over his head. It was a dangerous tactic that strongly suggested they weren't well trained.

Ranger kept his Beretta ready as his every sense went into

overdrive. He needed to return fire and get in the fight. If he didn't, the invaders might storm the bathroom instead. He edged up to the corner as much as he could while the door-frame splintered to pieces from being shot. Bullets were passing through the edges of the thin wall of the cheap home, inching closer to Ranger. Donny was less than ten feet from him around the corner, but Ranger was pinned down in the narrow space.

"Come on," he said, chiding himself. He had to kill Donny and his two trigger-happy morons. Even if it meant he got shot in the process and bled out afterward. As long as he kept the mother and son alive, everything would be okay. They could escape in the pickup outside if need be.

The firing stopped. "Go, Donny," one of the enforcers called out. "Get up. Take him out."

Ranger's brow furrowed. Why were they pushing Donny to charge into the bedroom? It would be suicide. He got an answer a few seconds later when he heard the sound of the bathroom door being kicked in.

"Drop it," someone yelled to Laura.

"Okay, okay," she said as the shotgun clattered to the tiled floor.

"Don't move," the other goon added. Footsteps stamped into the bathroom. Ranger listened as Laura and James screamed. Soon enough, they were bound with zip ties and were told to be quiet. There was nothing he could do to stop it. Not with Donny blocking his path.

He inched closer to the corner and heard breathing. "Stay put, Frank," Donny called out. "Don't do anything stupid."

"What the hell are they doing to Laura and James?" Ranger yelled back.

"None of your concern. If you've got any brains left in that thick skull of yours, you'll get out of here while you still can."

"Not a chance. You think I'm gonna walk away after what you've done?"

Donny fell silent. Ranger waited for a response, but one never came. "What? Got nothing to say?"

"I warned you about Bill Wilkins," Donny said, his voice low.

"Don't blame him for this. Bill didn't pull the trigger. That was you."

James let out a cry as more commotion came from the bathroom. Laura yelled at the men and sounded like she was fighting back. "Donny," one of the two men called out.

Ranger couldn't see what was happening, but he sensed something was being communicated in silence between the trio. He steadied himself and prepared for more gunfire.

"What are you doing?" Laura screamed. "Let me go." Her feet scuffed at the floor and kicked the walls. She was being dragged from the bathroom. Ranger was certain of it.

"What do we do with the kid?" one of the men asked.

"Bring him along just in case she gets any ideas. Bill can decide what to do with him."

Ranger gritted his teeth, then shouted, "You leave them right there."

The two men laughed. One of the pair called back, "You're in no position to tell us what to do, asshole."

"I'll kill you," Ranger yelled.

"Stop it, Frank," Donny scolded, his voice closer. "It's over. We have them both. Just come on out and get this over with."

"No," Ranger whispered. Then he backed up to the window, keeping his pistol trained on the bedroom doorway. He didn't know if it would work, but he thought about climbing back out of the house and rushing to the back door to cut off any escape. With Laura and James in their possession, it would be risky as hell.

Ranger placed one hand on the window as James and Laura's blaring objections continued. They were about to be carted away while Donny kept him trapped in the bedroom. How could Donny take part in this?

"Don't think about going out that window," Donny said.

"Was it worth it?" Ranger called out to his friend. "Is this what you want?"

"No, goddamnit," Donny said, his voice breaking. "You forced this on me. You showed up at the quarry and stuck your head where it didn't belong. Look what I had to do to square things with Bill. Do you honestly think I wanted to kill her?"

Ranger let the air free from his lungs. "I can't answer that, Donny. I thought I knew you."

A silence overcame the conversation as Laura and James continued to struggle. They were still close to the bathroom. If Ranger didn't know any better, it sounded like Bill's goons were waiting for Donny to rush in after Ranger.

"For fuck's sake," one of the thugs shouted. "Kill him already. Otherwise, the deal is off."

Ranger dropped low after hearing the unwanted encouragement and returned both hands to his pistol. If Donny charged in now, it would be the last thing he ever did.

The creaky floor near Donny didn't make a sound, though. He stayed where he was.

One of the men groaned. "Jesus Christ, Donny. Take the girl and get out of the way."

Ranger listened as footsteps shuffled about near the bedroom door. He kept the Beretta's sights on the doorway and ignored the pounding in his chest.

"Take the kid to my ride," the clear leader of the three ordered.

"Got it," said his counterpart. James began to moan and scream as he was pulled away from his mother in a hurry.

Laura responded with her own yelling, adding more disorder to the house. Panic filled Ranger as he heard James being taken through the house.

"Come on out, shithead," the remaining goon yelled from a few steps back from the doorway. "Or I'll flush you out the hard way."

Ranger dropped low and moved sideways from the window to a wall, giving himself as much cover as possible. He was running out of time and options. The man continued to creep toward the room, making the floor creak with each step. Ranger squared his aim as an object poked through the opening.

"See this, asshole? It's an M84. I'm sure you're familiar with it."

"Shit," Ranger whispered. The guy had a stun grenade. If he tossed it into the room, the situation would be over in seconds. Even if he shielded his eyes from the blinding white flash it produced, the bang would deafen and disorient him long enough for the prick to storm in and unload a full magazine into Ranger's body.

"You got five seconds."

Ranger flicked his eyes back to the window. There was still time to dive through it. He could go after the thug taking James. But he couldn't stand the thought of leaving Laura behind.

"Five, four…"

"Come on, Ranger," Donny shouted. "It doesn't have to end like this."

"Three, two—"

"Okay," Ranger said. "I'm coming out."

"Smart move, my friend," the man said. "Throw your piece on the ground in front of the door and drop to your knees. Slap your hands on your head and don't try anything, got it?"

Ranger sighed. He knew what would happen if he surrendered. He'd be executed, and Laura and James would still be dragged back to the farm, kicking and screaming. Fortunately, he had one trick left up his sleeve.

"I'm throwing my gun down," Ranger said as he tossed Liam's Glock 21 to the front of the bedroom door. Then Ranger dropped to his knees and hid the Beretta under his shin. He placed his hands on his head to lure the man into the room and prayed Donny was far enough away not to notice.

"Good boy," said Donny's comrade as he crept into the room with his gun drawn. He found Ranger and aimed the suppressed pistol at his face.

Ranger stared up at the man dressed in black and avoided glancing down at the Beretta.

"Get the girl in here," the man said to Donny. "I want her to see this."

Ranger didn't let his gaze falter as he watched Donny pull Laura into the room with his pistol pressed to her body. Ranger stared into Donny's eyes with as much disappointment as he could find.

"Take a good look, darlin'," the man said to Laura. "Let me show you what happens when you fuck around with the Wilkinses." He tensed his aim, ready to shoot. Ranger snapped his hands down for the Beretta and rolled sideways as he scooped it up, but it was too late.

A single round spat out of a suppressed pistol and into the man's skull. He fell sideways into a heap on the ground. Donny moved away from Laura and put two more rounds into Bill's guy and stood over the corpse.

Not wasting the opportunity, Ranger raised the Beretta from under his leg and jumped to his feet with a step back. He aimed the gun at Donny's face and shouted, "Don't move!"

CHAPTER 37

Donny lowered his pistol but didn't look at Ranger. Instead, he stared down at the man he'd just killed.

Ranger kept his Beretta aimed at Donny as Laura took a step back with wide eyes and an open jaw. "What the fuck?" she asked out loud. Ranger had the same question running through his head but couldn't find the strength to ask it.

Donny let out a sigh and held his arms out wide, allowing the pistol in his hand to dangle free from a single finger as he clutched the trigger guard. Slowly, he faced Ranger, keeping his movement steady.

"I said don't move," Ranger grumbled.

"It's okay, Frank. I'm not going to hurt her. Or you." Donny tossed his pistol to the floor and kicked it out of reach. He took out his combat knife and did the same.

"Bullshit," Ranger said. "That's why you're here. You cut a deal with Bill Wilkins, didn't you?"

Donny sighed. "I did…but I guess something changed."

"Something changed? What the hell is that supposed to mean?"

Donny shook his head with closed eyes. "I don't know."

Laura pushed farther into the room with both arms still zip-tied behind her back. "Where's James?"

"Oh, shit," Donny let out. He caught Ranger's attention and said, "That other prick is still out there with him. We need to go."

"You're not going anywhere," Ranger said as he flicked his eyes between Donny and the floor. Along with a dead body, there were three pistols and a combat knife on the ground. Donny could grab any of them and do God knows what.

Ranger knelt down, keeping his pistol aimed at Donny as he grabbed the combat knife to cut Laura's restraints free. He beckoned her toward him and sliced the zip ties free from her wrists.

"I know you don't trust me, Frank—"

"Trust you?" Ranger asked as he slid the knife into his belt. "You're a killer who butchers innocent women for Bill Wilkins. I don't know why you shot this guy, but I don't give a damn. Get on your knees and put your hands on your head."

Donny's brows raised. "Ranger, I—"

"Where the fuck is James?" Laura yelled, cutting him off. "You both need to save him. Please."

Ranger squinted at Laura and gritted his teeth. "We can't trust him."

"I know that, but that animal out there is taking my son. Please just save him, Frank."

"Okay," Ranger said, absorbing the desperation in her voice. He steadied his aim on Donny and flicked the Beretta. "You heard her. Let's go. Through the window." Ranger grabbed Donny and shoved him hard toward the bedroom window. He then glanced down at the Glock on the floor and back up at Laura. "You see that gun? There's already a round in the chamber, and it doesn't have a safety. All you have to do is point and squeeze. If anyone other than me comes back here, you shoot, got it?"

Laura nodded and retrieved Liam's Glock. The weapon had been passed around a lot in one day.

Donny slid the bedroom window open and leaped out before Ranger had time to think. If he wanted to run, now was the time. Ranger rushed over to the window to find Donny standing outside, waiting for him.

"Come on, Frank," Donny said, offering him a hand.

"Stay the fuck back," Ranger ordered.

Donny held up his hands and stepped several paces away.

As Ranger climbed through the window, he waited for Donny to switch sides again and make his move. But nothing happened. He stood still, waiting.

"Over there," Donny whispered as Ranger dropped low. "The black pickup. Bill's guy has the kid in there."

Ranger kept his focus on Donny. The piece of crap had killed Rosie like she was nothing. He didn't care why he'd had a sudden change of heart. As far as Ranger was concerned, the man was a snake that needed its head cut off.

"Frank, please," Donny said, urging Ranger to look at the pickup. "We don't have much time."

Ranger held his gaze for a moment longer, then gritted his teeth to look at the vehicle. He couldn't see James, but he knew the boy had to be somewhere inside it, being held against his will. His captor was sitting behind the wheel, with the engine running and the lights on.

"What's his name?" Ranger asked with bitterness in his voice.

"Who? The kid?"

"No, the jackass in the truck."

"No idea. He's one of Bill's guys. We gotta take him out. Come on." Donny gestured for Ranger to follow.

"Don't you move."

"What is it?"

Ranger jammed the pistol up into Donny's throat. "You can't seriously think I'm buying any of this, right? You're going to kill me the second my back's turned."

Donny shook his head. "I just want a chance to make things right."

"Make things right? That's impossible. You can't fix the dead." Ranger found himself seething and ready to riddle Donny with every round he had in the magazine of the Beretta.

"Just let me help you. Kill me after."

Ranger held his glare for more time than he could spare. "You'd better not be lying. I swear to God, I will drop you before you take one look at me."

Donny smiled out of the corner of his mouth. "I know you will, Frank."

Ranger waved him forward with the Beretta, not wanting to take point. "What's the play?"

"We keep it simple. I'll distract him while you move down the passenger side of the pickup. You should be able to take a clean shot once we coax him away from the kid."

"Okay," Ranger replied. "Sounds risky, but it'll have to do. We can't let this guy take James."

"James?"

"The kid," Ranger snapped.

"Oh, yeah. Got it. You ready?"

"As I'll ever be."

"That's the spirit," Donny muttered.

Ranger resisted the urge to shoot Donny in the leg and use his wailing pain as a distraction. He stifled his anger and focused on what was important for now: getting James back in one piece. He could decide what to do with Donny once Laura's boy was safe.

Ranger stayed low while Donny picked up his pace,

moving toward the black pickup like he wasn't a threat. The vehicle was pointing in the opposite direction to them, but the man inside must have seen Donny coming in the mirror. He opened his door and got out in a hurry. He still had the same pistol in hand as before.

"Where's Cole?" he asked in a hushed voice as Donny approached.

"Cole?" Donny replied. "Oh, your buddy? He needs help with the girl. I can watch the kid." Donny leaned toward the rear passenger seats to look for James.

The man stepped in Donny's way and raised his gun. "How dumb do you think I am? Where the fuck is Cole?"

Donny backed up a step with his palms out wide. "Hey, don't shoot the messenger here. Cole sent me out to ask you for help."

The man narrowed his gaze at Donny and placed both hands on the pistol. "What about Frank Ranger? Is he dead?"

Donny nodded. "Took care of him myself."

Ranger reached the back of the pickup and made his way down the passenger side of the vehicle. As Donny and the man continued their conversation, Ranger popped up and checked inside the truck for James. He spotted him on the floor by the back seat with his arms and legs bound. He also had a piece of cloth stuffed into his mouth to keep him quiet. The kid was wriggling about with a look of pure terror on his face. He was past breaking point. The sight sent a flood of rage through Ranger as he squeezed the Beretta tight.

"I'm calling him," said the second gun for hire as Ranger ducked back down. He inched his way along the truck, using the distraction to his advantage.

"He's not picking up," the man said. "Why the hell isn't he picking up, Donny?"

"Hey, I know as much as you. When I left the house, Ranger was dead, and Cole had Laura. Trouble is, she's a fighter. I can see why Bill wants us to bring her in alive, you know?" Donny chuckled, but the man didn't reciprocate. It was clear that this operative of Bill's trusted Donny about as much as Ranger did. He was about to snap.

Ranger made his way around to the front of the pickup and got a better angle on the man, but he needed to get closer so he could take a single shot. He hadn't thought to take one of the suppressed pistols inside the house and only had the loud Beretta. There were people everywhere who might have already heard the shotgun go off inside. A pistol firing in the night would draw unwanted attention from the firefighters and the police.

"Step the fuck back, Donny," the man said, raising his pistol higher.

"Whoa, hey. We're on the same side here. What gives?"

The man chuckled. "You dumb fuck. Bill told us to waste you the second we were done here. Did you seriously think he'd let you back in after the fuck-up at the quarry?"

Donny's face dropped. "What?"

Ranger felt like spitting in the dirt. Donny had murdered Rosie just to save himself. And up until a few minutes ago, he was going to swap Ranger, Laura and James for a chance to get back in with the Wilkins crew. As it turned out, the deal had been sour from the start.

"That's right," Bill's man continued. "And now you're going to join that bitch from the diner." He lifted his pistol in line with Donny's face as Ranger watched. He wanted to let it happen. A bullet to the face was exactly what Donny had earned. Why get in the way of justice?

James cried out in the truck, loud enough to be heard through his gag, reminding Ranger what was at stake. He moved out from behind cover and aimed his Beretta at Bill's man. "Put it down."

"What the hell?" the goon said. Then he glanced at Donny.

"You lying fuck. I knew it. What did you do to Cole?" His eyes darted in every direction as he kept Donny's head in his sights.

"He's dead," Ranger said. "You'll be next if you don't do as I say."

That was when Donny made his move. With a yell, he charged at the prick who'd taken James.

"Dammit," Ranger yelled as Donny crossed his sights. Donny and the man got tangled up in a brawl as they each wrestled for control of the pistol. The only way to stop the goon would be to shoot them both dead.

Deciding to prioritize James over Donny, Ranger ran back to the passenger side of the truck and tried to open the door to the back seat. The door didn't budge. The contractor had been smart enough to keep the rest of the truck locked.

Multiple shots rang out of a suppressed pistol and thudded into the dirt. Donny let out a yell, prompting Ranger to drop back behind the safety of the pickup with his pistol ready.

"Donny?" he called out. "Talk to me."

No one answered, so Ranger half stood, peeking with the Beretta through the door window. He saw the man yank the pickup's door open and climb back into the idling truck. He crunched it into gear as Ranger sprinted to reach the other side of the truck. The thug hit the gas before Ranger got far and did a careening U-turn. The tires on the pickup spun as the engine roared. Ranger followed the movement and lined up his Beretta on the driver. He had a kill shot.

Right as he squeezed to fire, a rock from the gravel being kicked up hit him in the face.

"Shit," he yelled with both eyes shut. He tried to blink and wipe away the debris to find a better angle, but it was too late. All Ranger could do was watch as the vehicle sped off down the street, no doubt headed to Wilkins Farms.

Ranger yelled as he kicked at the gravel road. He'd had the man dead to rights, but a single rock and Donny's ego had saved the driver. How was he going to explain it all to Laura?

"Son of a bitch, that hurts," Donny moaned.

Ranger faced Donny with a lowered pistol. He knelt down to find the moron clutching his arm. Blood seeped through his fingers. Ranger made a quick inspection. A bullet had grazed Donny and had torn a shallow, jagged groove across the skin of his bicep. He was lucky that was all that'd happened.

"Help me up, Frank." Donny winced.

"Why? I should shoot you right now."

Donny groaned as he climbed to his feet on his own, still bleeding. "I suppose that's fair."

Ranger sighed and glanced back down the street. "Why the hell did you charge at him? I had it under control."

Donny sighed. "I thought it would help the kid. I thought at the very least if he was busy shooting me, you could save James."

Ranger stared at Donny and drummed his trigger finger on the guard, imagining himself finishing the job Bill's guy started. It would be justified. "Come on," he grunted. "Let's go deliver the bad news. After you."

"Sure thing, boss," Donny said, taking the lead again. Ranger still didn't trust him. Donny could have failed to take down the guy in the pickup on purpose. There was no telling what the man was capable of after the end he'd given Rosie. Wherever the truth lay, Ranger would have to tell Laura how badly they'd screwed up.

CHAPTER 38

Ranger and Donny walked in silence back to Rosie's house. Ranger allowed him to keep breathing for the time being and hoped he wouldn't later regret it.

They went down the side path to the back door and moved into the dark home. Ranger flicked on the lights as he went and got a shock when Laura came out from nowhere.

"Where is he? Is he okay? I heard that truck leave."

Ranger tucked his pistol away and held out both hands. "I'm sorry, but the guy got away with James tied up in the back seat."

"He what?" she yelled. "You can't be serious? I thought you two were soldiers. You couldn't stop one man?"

Ranger shook his head and replayed the failure again in his mind. "I thought I had it under control. I had the shot, but the truck flicked a piece of gravel into my eye." He left out the key detail of Donny charging at the guy in the first place. And he wasn't sure why, either.

Laura paced Rosie's living room, staring past Ranger to Donny. She stabbed a finger toward him. "You trusted this asshole. That's where you screwed up."

Ranger ignored her warranted anger. In a moment of desperation, she had told him to trust Donny in a roundabout way. This was simply her venting the fear that would be running through her every thought. Her son had just been kidnapped.

"It's okay," Ranger said. "I'll get James back. I promise." He had no idea how he would achieve something so impossible, but he didn't care. Laura needed to hear the words, even if she doubted them deep down.

Donny stepped farther inside the living room and ran a hand through his hair. "What a day, huh?"

"What a day?" she asked as she pulled the Glock from the back of her pants. With two hands, she aimed the weapon at Donny's face. Donny saw the threat and didn't budge. He held his arms out wide.

"What are you doing?" Ranger asked her.

"Stay out of it." She kept her eyes on Donny. "Did you kill Rosie?"

Donny held her gaze. "I did."

Laura gritted her teeth. "You're not going to deny it?"

Donny shrugged. "What's the point?"

Laura let out an almighty roar and lunged at Donny. He didn't move or try to defend himself as she held the Glock in one hand and slapped him as hard as possible. Ranger stayed back and let her unload but tried to stay close enough to intervene if needed. She hit him over and over with unfocused swings, then jammed the pistol into Donny's forehead. "On your knees," she yelled. Donny did as he was told.

"Laura," Ranger said calmly, "don't do this." He was only eight feet away from them both, but Laura had plenty of time to pull the trigger. She couldn't miss.

"He has to die," Laura muttered.

"I know. Trust me, I do. But this isn't something you want on your conscience."

"Let her do it, Frank," Donny said. "I killed Rosie. I deserve this."

"Shut up," Ranger spat at Donny.

Laura seethed a breath in and out. "You don't get to decide if he lives or not. He killed a woman I've known for years. Do you know how many times she's helped me out in the past? She was like a mother to me."

Ranger felt his shoulders slump. "I know you're angry, but—"

"But what? My only child has been taken to Bill Wilkins, and this asshole killed my closest friend. There's nothing you can say to make things right again."

Ranger held up a palm, hoping to simmer her down a notch. "I get it. But hear me out. You don't want to do this."

Laura scoffed. "Oh, come on. If the man who killed your wife was here right now, we both know what you'd do to him."

Ranger tried to respond, but he had nothing to say that wasn't a lie. She was right.

Donny cleared his throat and said, "Just let her do it, Frank. She'd be doing me a favor. I've spent the last eight months working for Bill, killing people who, for all I know, could have been as innocent as Rosie. And for what? Some money? The chance to feel useful again? I deserve this, Frank. Just let her do it."

Ranger stared into Donny's eyes and found genuine remorse. Laura had the Glock pressed hard into his skull. At such a close range, Donny could snatch the gun from her grasp before she knew it. Instead, he remained on his knees, waiting for the end.

Ranger shook his head and glanced at Laura, then back to Donny. The man's life was resting on his shoulders, and he didn't know what to say. Donny had killed countless people in his own country and had murdered an innocent woman, all to please Bill Wilkins. The right thing to do was to put him down. But at the same time, they had been through so much together. How could Ranger be the one to decide Donny's fate?

"I'm going to do it," Laura said. Ranger wasn't sure whom she was even talking to. He stared into her bitter eyes as she bared her teeth. Her rage had taken over so much that she couldn't see the wood for the trees.

"I have a better idea."

Donny and Laura both looked at Ranger with crinkled brows. With their attention on him, he shared his thoughts. "Instead of killing Donny, why don't we put him to work?"

"Huh?" Donny asked.

Ranger crossed his arms over his chest. "You wanna make things right? Then, for starters, you're going to help me rescue James."

CHAPTER 39

BILL

Bill paced the strip in front of his home on Wilkins Farms as he watched the black pickup rush toward him. Its lights bounced along the road as the driver sped with an urgency that almost gave Bill chest pains. A minute ago, the men who were watching the gate had reported the return of Cole and Archer. They'd been given the job of killing Ranger and collecting Laura from Rosie's home, but something had gone wrong. Only Archer had returned.

The pickup came to a hurried stop with screeching tires. A sweat-coated Archer emerged from the driver's seat and charged around to the rear passenger door. He opened it and retrieved Laura's kid. The boy was bound and gagged, but there was no sign of Laura.

"Where should I take him?" Archer asked.

"Why is he here? I only wanted the girl."

"Sorry, boss. It's a bit of a long story."

Bill stared into Archer's eyes with a sneer on his lips. "Put him inside my house. Lock him in a spare room. And take off the ties and gag."

"On it, boss."

"Then report back to me. Understood?"

"Yes, sir."

Bill stepped up to the pickup and knew the mission had gone to hell in a handbasket. The wrong person had been extracted, and Bill had to presume Cole was dead. No doubt at the hands of Ranger, or possibly Donny. Whatever had transpired, Bill was going to find out.

Several of Bill's men gathered around the pickup to see what all the commotion was about. They were armed and ready for a fight. Bill had called them all in not long after Donny had screwed things up at the quarry. Just to be safe. They'd all been standing around, waiting for something to happen.

Archer returned to Bill and came to a stop. He was short of breath but stood at attention like he was still in the military. Both Cole and Archer had served in Iraq as privates. But each man had been dishonorably discharged for killing civilians. That had made them efficient at doing Bill's dirty work, but not this time.

"At ease," Bill mocked. "Tell me what happened. Where the hell is Cole?"

Archer told Bill everything. About the house, the shotgun blast Cole almost caught. About how he'd nabbed James and had been ordered by Cole to take the kid and go. He hadn't seen Cole go down, but he was positive the man was dead. "Donny and Ranger were working together. They attacked me, but I got away. They must have killed Cole. Nothing else makes sense."

"I see," Bill said, keeping his eyes on the ground. "So what you're saying is that you and Cole fucked up royally."

"No, boss, we—"

"Bullshit." Bill kicked the side of the pickup as hard as he could, leaving a solid dent in one door.

"I swear it's not like that. Donny screwed us over."

Bill let the rage flow out of his lungs as he composed himself. Apparently, Donny had switched sides. Oddly enough, not before killing Rosie. Whatever the man's reasoning no longer mattered. Bill was going to do everything within his power to have Donny's and Ranger's lifeless bodies presented to him.

"I'm sorry, boss," Archer said.

Bill spun on his heel and approached Archer with a sardonic smile. Once he reached him, he dusted the dirt from the man's black jacket. "You're sorry, huh?"

"Just tell me what to do to make this right."

"Well, that's easy, son." Bill grabbed hold of Archer's collar and headbutted him with a solid crunch. Archer slipped over and landed on one knee only to receive a kick to the face. He crashed into the dirt and groaned. Bill drew his .357 Colt Python and pointed it straight at Archer's face. His breath heaved in and out. "No more fuck-ups," Bill roared. "You understand me? If Donny and Ranger are alive, that means we have two former soldiers coming to this farm to rescue that boy in there. One is a goddamn sniper, and the other is a pain-in-the-ass thorn in your side." Bill faced the men who were all watching. "Call in every available brawler you know who can hold a gun. A million dollars to the man who takes down either Frank Ranger or Donny Brown. A bonus if you kill 'em both. You got me?"

Nods and sneers filled the faces of the men. Some even got out their cell phones and started dialing.

"I said, do you understand?"

An array of yeses came from the crowd.

"Then get to work."

Bill's people scattered in all directions. Archer scrambled to his feet and followed the others. Bill glared at the man as he left and made a note to himself to deal with Archer once everything was back to normal. Until then, he needed every available man who had a pulse to protect the farm.

Bill holstered his .357 Colt Python and spat in the dirt. As if things weren't bad enough, he still needed to work out what to do with Junior. He'd left the boy to stew in the container with his dead pals. It was a situation he would need to deal with sooner than later, but not before he handled the two pests in town who were threatening his entire operation.

Before the night was over, he swore to himself that Frank and Donny would no longer be a problem.

CHAPTER 40

DONNY

An hour after James had been taken, Donny stared down into the valley that held Wilkins Farms. It was a dark night as he switched between his night-vision-enabled spotting scope and the long-range scope he had on his Ruger RPR Magnum. The long-range rifle was chambered in .300 Winchester Magnum and was more than capable of hitting targets at two thousand yards away. And Donny was roughly two thousand yards from the farm, give or take thirty feet, but he planned to be a lot closer when the time came for him and Ranger to rescue James.

Back at Rosie's house, Laura had taken a good lot of convincing not to kill him. She'd aimed the Glock 21 at his face for five minutes before Ranger talked her into letting him live.

"At least for the time being," Ranger had said. "Let him help me bring James back to you. Then you can decide his fate."

Donny took a hefty swig of bourbon from his flask and thought about death. There he was, about to fight and possibly kill some of Bill's men, all to rescue James and give

Laura another opportunity to end his life. He wouldn't stop her if she tried again. The shot he'd placed on Rosie was still playing on a loop in his head. Laura would be doing him a favor if she went through with it.

While James was in Bill's possession, there was still time for Donny to make things right again. Not everything. He could never make up for the loss he'd inflicted on Laura or anyone else who knew Rosie. But helping to rescue James was a decent start.

Rosie's death had forced him to think about the lives he'd taken for Bill Wilkins. How many of them had actually deserved the end he gave them? How many had been guilty of anything other than pissing off Bill? He couldn't answer the questions, and another sip from his flask failed to stop the words from forming in his head.

Ranger had trusted Donny with the task of running reconnaissance on the farm. At any moment, Donny could run. He had the means and stores of cash squirreled away to keep him going for months. Not to mention millions in offshore bank accounts. Along with fake passports and fake IDs, Donny could take his pickup to the border and disappear into South America with ease.

So far, he'd stayed on task. He didn't know if it was Ranger's damn presence making him feel guilty for the life he'd been living, but Donny realized he had to make a change before it was too late. He'd spent too long thinking he could find solace at the end of a rifle.

As Donny left Rosie's to observe the farm, Ranger had a quiet word with him. The plan was to set fire to Rosie's home after removing any guns from the place. Rosie and the unknown man's body would be burned up and destroyed in the blaze. Only dental records would identify them. It wasn't very graceful, but Ranger figured it would help to cover their tracks in case the police came knocking and launched a town-wide operation to find out what the hell had been going on.

"What happened?" Ranger had asked Donny right as he was about to leave.

"What do you mean?" Donny fired back.

Ranger glanced over his shoulder as if he was making sure no one could hear him. "What changed your mind? You were hell-bent on squaring things with Bill. So much so that you killed Rosie. You owe me an explanation. What happened?"

It was a loaded question. One that Donny tried his best to answer. "I don't know. I guess it all hit me."

"What did?" Ranger asked, squinting.

Donny sighed and scratched the mustache on his face. "The monster I'd become."

Donny left before Ranger could respond. Five minutes later, Ranger would be setting fire to Rosie's home, keeping the fire department in the area. Then he and Laura would take Donny's truck, the one Ranger had stolen, and head to one of his safe houses outside of town. Specifically, to one he believed no one else knew about. Donny felt sick handing Ranger the address, but there was nowhere else for them to go in the meantime.

The farm was abuzz with activity. One car after the other arrived from the only road to the property and got cleared for entry by the security team at the gate. Bill had an army at his disposal. Wild Bill didn't seem to mind offloading a small fortune to guarantee that his home stayed well protected.

As Donny swept the area for the tenth time, he noticed something. There was no sign of Liam Wilkins. Donny had met the kid once or twice in passing but didn't know him all that well. Still, he'd heard all about Liam's exploits around town. Most people said that Liam Wilkins was nothing but a rich, entitled brat who thought it was fun to play gangster with his old man's money. But despite all that, Bill loved his only son and would do anything to protect him. Liam was no doubt holed up beneath the farm to stay safe from the fight to come.

After Donny had done enough recon work, he headed back to the safe house. His most secure safe house was the one he lived in. It existed in a region of Namrena that was a blend of residential and open land. The area was typical of what most people would find on the outskirts of town, with a mix of undeveloped land and scattered homes. The place was quiet and somewhat secluded, offering Donny the two things he cherished the most: privacy and space. The area's natural desert landscape also provided a peaceful environment to exist in without being too far away from the town's amenities. It was a shame he'd had to tell Ranger about it.

The safe house was on an unsealed road that was barely wide enough to fit a single vehicle. Rocks and dirt kicked up as Donny drove down the road toward his place. It was next door to a fenced-off power substation that occasionally saw a worker or two come by to perform maintenance. Donny had an array of security cameras pointed toward the substation, but not one worker had ever paid any attention to his home. They always did their job and left.

Donny pulled into his property. On the outside, it looked like nothing more than a tall shed with an oversize roller door. But inside, Donny had fitted out rooms to his liking, building the spaces using the skills he'd learned back when he was working construction. He'd dropped out of school at sixteen to work for his uncle, building houses, and didn't join the military until he turned twenty-two.

Donny had spent a lot of his childhood behind a rifle with his old man. They were at the range most weekends and would head out once a month on hunting trips to the White Mountains. When Donny quit his job after an argument with his uncle about pay, he saw an advert for the US Marines. He'd only ever worked for his uncle as a laborer and had never completed any official training. If he went to another construction company, he'd have to start over. The idea of signing up for the military sounded like a far more exciting opportunity. He met with a Marine Corps recruiter and signed up.

Donny had always gone into the Marine Corps with the aim of becoming a sniper. He had a natural skill with rifles and had hunted elks, black bears, turkeys, and even mountain lions. He figured he could handle whatever the Corps might throw at him.

He was wrong.

It was ten times harder than anything he'd expected, but in three years, he'd gone through recruitment training, infantry training, served in the Fleet Marine Force, got accepted into the Scout Sniper course, and was deployed to Afghanistan as a certified Marine Scout Sniper.

The war had been eye-opening for Donny. Never had he seen such carnage. Never had he witnessed how bad things could get when war ravaged the world. He lost count of the number of kills he'd made on-mission. Many never made the official record. There didn't seem to be an end to the number of fighters who would throw away their lives for the Taliban. People he'd seen the week prior in a village who had waved at the US soldiers with welcoming smiles would charge at an outpost or a patrol, knowing that they were on a one-way mission. And now Donny and Ranger were facing the same prospect.

Donny gained access to the property via a side door. He was met by an armed Ranger, who pointed Donny's own Beretta at his face the second he came inside. Donny had told Ranger to hold on to the pistol. He had more than enough guns stored in the safe house to share around.

Ranger lowered the Beretta and returned the pistol to the thigh holster Donny had provided him with. "I thought you were going to call first," Ranger said. Donny had also given him and Laura a burner phone each to reach him on.

"Sorry, guess I'm not used to needing to call anyone before I come here."

"Fair enough," Ranger said. "How'd it go?"

Donny looked at Laura, who was sitting on a sofa he had put in the living area of the home. The twelve-foot ceilings gave the space a loft kind of vibe that Donny enjoyed. Laura had her arms wrapped tight around her body and kept her jittery eyes focused on the floor as she ever so slightly rocked back and forth.

"Well?" Ranger said, stepping closer.

"In a word, bad. Bill's got fifteen guys on the surface with long rifles. God knows how many are below. From what I could see, none of the workers' cars were there. I think he's sent them all home."

"He's preparing for an attack," Ranger said.

"Pretty much. He's called in every gun in town. They were barricading the main gate as I left. I also saw them nailing particleboard to the windows of the house. He's hunkering down."

Ranger ran a hand through his beard. It was still strange to see him without a shaved face and a neat haircut. "What's the play?" he asked.

"The same as I said before. You get in close while I cover the area. I'll direct you where to go, and take out as many of the bastards as I can. Then we draw them out from their hidey-holes so you can extract James."

Ranger shook his head. "What could go wrong?"

"You got a better idea?"

Ranger said nothing and walked away.

Donny followed. "That's what I thought. Look, I know

this all sounds like a suicide run, but I can't see any other way."

Ranger stopped. "I just want to bring James home to his mother. I don't care what we have to do."

Donny held his hands out wide. "Hey, I get it. I want to bring the kid home, too, but I still think we can pull this off and live to tell the tale. We just have to focus."

Ranger sighed and left the room. He headed into the kitchen space and grabbed a bottle of water from the counter, undoing the lid a moment later. Donny followed him again. He was pushing the soldier, but that was what Ranger needed if they were going to succeed.

"Think about it like this, Frank. It'll be just like old times. How many crazy missions did we pull off in the sandbox, huh?"

"This is different. We're not going into some village in Afghanistan to deal with the Taliban. We're trying to save a kid from a psychopath. What do you think will happen if we don't make it in time?"

Donny placed his hands in his pockets. He didn't need to say it. He knew James would meet his end if he and Ranger didn't rescue him.

"So now you know what my problem is," Ranger said. He took a swig of the bottled water and replaced the lid. He stepped up to Donny and kept his voice low. "I can't be the reason that kid dies. I just can't. If he does, it will all be my fault. I caused this entire mess from start to finish. If I had just stayed out of it at the diner…"

Donny saw Rosie in his mind again. Her head snapped back as the round from his rifle struck. His shaking hand reached for the flask in his pocket. He closed his eyes and stopped himself from taking a drink in front of Ranger.

Donny exhaled and placed a hand on Ranger's shoulder. "What's done is done. All we can do is offer that girl our best.

Nothing more. If that means we die in our boots, so be it. What do you say, Frank? One last mission? One last journey into hell?"

A sigh escaped Ranger's mouth. He placed the water bottle down and offered Donny his hand to shake. "Promise me you'll do everything you can to save James. I mean it. If I die, you don't run. You save him and then get the girl the hell out of here."

"I promise," Donny said. He grabbed Ranger's forearm and squeezed, shaking in agreement like old times.

Ranger grabbed the water and took another swig.

"All right," Donny said. "Let's get this shitshow on the road."

CHAPTER 41

With a dark night on their side, Donny and Ranger were ready to leave the safe house at around midnight. They were as prepared as they would ever be to launch an assault on Wilkins Farms. Laura had been asked to stay behind, but she refused to do so and wanted to be nearby to help James once the two soldiers rescued her son.

"It's too dangerous," Ranger had said.

"I don't care. I'm coming."

"But, Laura—"

"I'm coming. Got it? You can't stop me. I'll raid the farm myself if I have to."

Donny chimed in, "Let her come, Frank. She can help us with extraction. We might need her if we get hit."

With his arms folded over his chest, Ranger stared at the concerned mother. "I don't like it, but I guess I can't stop you."

"You can't. That boy is my world. Without him, I have nothing. Do you understand?"

"I do," Ranger said with a shadow across his brow.

"Oh," Laura replied. "Sorry."

Donny took a second to realize what Ranger meant. When Donny had first heard about Kaitlyn's death, he couldn't believe Frank had lost his mind and killed his wife. It wasn't like that kind of thing didn't happen. Soldiers came back from the hell that was war and were different people. But after seeing the extremes Ranger had gone to in his attempts to keep Laura and James safe, it was clear he'd had nothing to do with his wife's untimely end.

Ranger walked over to the kitchen counter, which had been cleared for an assortment of pistols, rifles, and grenades Donny had retrieved from storage. The expensive hardware would be needed for the mission. Ranger grabbed the Glock 21 Laura had aimed at Donny's face only a few hours ago and handed it back to her. "Keep this on you at all times. If one of Bill's people gets anywhere near the car, you shoot them and get the hell out of there."

"Not without James."

"Still, you shoot first. We are outnumbered here. There's a good chance we won't make it."

"Not with that attitude," Donny said. But Ranger didn't seem to appreciate the humor. Donny didn't know how else to act, given what they were about to do. Their chances of survival were low. He'd been the same when he served. Right before a dangerous op, joking around was the only thing that had kept him sane.

Ranger planted his hands on the counter and stared at the arsenal below him. Donny had laid out a Ruger AR-556 rifle chambered in 5.56 NATO. Next to the rifle were eight magazines, each preloaded with thirty 62-grain M855 Green Tip cartridges. The ammunition would do the trick against light body armor at range while also allowing Ranger the flexibility of a lower recoiling weapon. He could opt to charge in with something like a .308 battle rifle, but speed was going to be their best asset.

Beside the AR-556, Donny had given Ranger a suppressed 9mm Beretta 92 Elite LTT with a red dot optical slide and enough magazines to shoot his way out of trouble. He could swap it for the one he'd been running around with all night.

Donny had also gifted Ranger some night-vision goggles, a long-range walkie, three M84 stun grenades, five M67 frag grenades, and a tactical plate carrier with front and back Level IV ceramic body armor plates. To complete the look, he'd also laid out a surplus US Army Advanced Combat Helmet. Ranger would be rolling in with full battle-rattle. Well, as close to it as Donny could provide. Ranger had field-stripped each gun and made sure they were cleaned, oiled, and in working order.

"You good, Sergeant?" Donny asked Ranger as he watched him take a long breath and let it out.

"Yeah. Just getting my head in the game."

"Good. One last gift for the table." Donny took out a sheath for the combat knife Ranger had placed on the bench. The one he'd stolen from Donny at the quarry. "I know you've got that little hidden blade on your belt, but I'm sure this would do a better job." Donny collected the sharp knife and sheathed it for him.

Ranger gave him a nod as a smile popped up at the corner of Donny's mouth. He knew the look Ranger was sporting. He'd seen it a hundred times before. Bill Wilkins might have had them outnumbered with a home-court advantage, but the moron had no idea what was coming.

"Let's do this."

The trio left the safe house in two of Donny's pickups. Donny drove alone while Ranger and Laura rode together. Donny needed to take a different route to reach high ground and find the perfect location that would give him a full view of the farm. He was going to drive as far as he deemed safe, then proceed on foot with his equipment and rifle. While that was happening, Ranger and Laura would take the back roads to Wilkins Farms and cut across the desert with no headlights on so Ranger could find himself a concealed path to effectively approach the mission area.

Donny and Ranger both knew Bill would have several of his men watching the roads and scanning the horizon for threats. They would need to take their time if they had any chance of hitting the farm without dying in the first five minutes.

While Ranger seemed determined to meet his end in a blaze of glory, Donny wouldn't be so reckless. And not because he was afraid to die, but for the simple fact he had a few tricks up his sleeve no one in town was aware of. Not even Bill Wilkins. Donny had shown off his skills as a marksman when he was under Bill's employment, but he'd never given the man the complete picture. It was the one thing his uncle had taught him back when he was still working construction. "Never reveal your full hand. Not until the time is right."

Donny chuckled at the memory and glanced over his shoulder at the bed of the pickup. Inside the bed of the truck, he had more hardware than his sniper rifle. And when the time came, he wasn't going to hold back. Wilkins Farms was going to be put on the map and turned into a tourist destination once the night was through.

CHAPTER 42

LIAM

Liam stirred himself awake after falling asleep for the third time. The drug that had been forced into his body when he was hauled into the farm was still working its way through his system and had made him drift in and out of consciousness more times than he cared to admit. Despite a flow of rage coursing through his veins, he couldn't fight off the chemical reaction.

Each time Liam woke up, part of him still believed he would be waking up in his bed at home after having a bad dream. But reality came knocking for him the second he tried to stand up or raise his hands higher than his chest in the chair he had been restrained in. Thick chains and cuffs rattled in the darkness of the converted shipping container, prompting Liam to yank on them harder and harder every time he remembered they were there. Despite his fatigue, his anger was still as present as always.

His father had left him there to rot. Roll's and Mack's bodies had at least been removed, but he could still smell the metallic sting of their blood sprayed against the surface of the container.

"Ah, the prodigal child has awoken," said a man's voice from the other end of the shipping container.

Liam stared into the void and could make out a figure. The single bulb that lit the space had been extinguished when his father left him to stew in the dark. His eyes were still adapting to the lack of light, so he couldn't see a face. It wasn't until the man brought a cigarette up to his lips and drew in a breath that he could make out any distinguishing features. Liam didn't know who he was staring at in the nicotine glow, but he knew it was one of his father's men.

"Who the fuck are you?" Liam snarled, his voice full of gravel.

The man sucked in another breath of smoke and blew it out as he ran a gloved hand over the stubble of his chin. He reached up a hand and clicked on a hanging light. The sudden brightness overloaded Liam's eyes, forcing him to ram his lids shut. He couldn't bring his hands to his face to block out the light. The hanging utility flashlight was pointed right at Liam's face. He tried to turn away from it, but there was nowhere to go.

"Let me get that for you," the man said as he adjusted the flashlight's intensity down, enough so Liam didn't have to squint anymore.

"Who are you?" Liam asked.

The man took a few slow, calculated steps toward him with both hands behind his back. He looked to be in his forties and was wearing dusty jeans and a plaid shirt with the sleeves rolled up. No doubt, Liam's father had instructed the man to dress like that to look like a farmhand. Not all of his men took the suggestion seriously, but the ones who did seemed to stay around longer.

The man's boots clicked along the floor of the container as he moved closer to Liam. The whole while he wore a smug grin, like he knew something Liam didn't.

"I'm gonna ask you one more time, fuckhead. Who are you?"

The man stopped his approach, keeping his hands around his back. "That's a fair question, Junior. The name's Cade. Pleasure to officially meet you." Cade offered Liam a hand to shake, but Liam didn't entertain the idea for a second.

"Don't call me Junior. No one calls me fucking Junior, okay?"

"Noted. I meant no disrespect."

"Whatever. So why are you here? Why are you watching me in the dark like a freak?"

"Another fair question. Short answer: Bill gave me an order to keep an eye on you."

"And the long one?"

Cade flashed Liam a wide, telling smile and produced a menacing combat knife from behind his back. "Let's just say I'm here to do more than watch."

Liam tried to stand but was stopped once again by the cluster of chains. "What the fuck, man? Are you going to kill me?"

Cade stepped closer. His fingers drummed on the handle of the knife as he tightened his grip on the weapon. "Now why would a loyal member of the Wilkins Farms crew want to harm a hair on your body?"

Liam attempted to scuttle backward as Cade got closer. "I don't know. Fucking jealousy or some shit."

Cade stood tall and chuckled. "Me jealous? Of you? You got to be shitting me. Ain't no one here on this goddamn farm who's jealous of you, boy."

"Then what is this?"

Cade lowered himself down to a squat and placed a hand on Liam's knee. His other hand readjusted the knife into a reverse grip as if he was preparing to stab Liam in the thigh. Cade stared into Liam's eyes with a hardened expression.

He turned his empty hand into a fist and tapped it against Liam's leg. "Do you know how long I've been working for your old man, huh? Doubt it. You just float around this farm like your shit don't stink and act like we're all nothing but worms."

"You are a fucking worm," Liam spat. "All of you."

Cade punched Liam square in the face with his knife hand. The point of the blade caught Liam's eyebrow, cutting him. Blood seeped out and over his eye.

Liam laughed. "Oh, you fucked up now. The second I get out of here—"

"You're not getting out of here. At least not in one piece."

"Really? That's the play you're going to make? Kill the boss' son right on his own farm?"

"I don't give a flying fuck about Bill or this patch of dirt. I'm done serving you pricks. All Bill does is keep us down enough so we never rise up. Sure, he's paid me somewhat decent over the years, but it's not enough anymore. I got big debts and too many mouths to feed."

"What's that got to do with me?"

Cade chuckled, flashing his teeth. "You don't know, do you? Oh, this is perfect."

"What?"

"Dallas Jaramillo Chapa. Ever heard of him?"

"Yeah, what about him?"

"That fine gentleman from Tucson put a price on you and the old man about two hours ago. One million, dead. Or two mil alive. For either one of you. Apparently, he got spooked after a meeting with Bill earlier today. The buzz around the farm is palpable."

Liam sighed. "Jesus Christ. You're just here for the payday, huh?"

Another strike came for Liam and cracked him on the

bridge of his nose. He closed his eyes and turned his head away, bracing for a follow-up hit, but one never came.

"You're lucky Dallas is offering double for alive," Cade said.

Liam rolled his head around and let another stream of blood flow and drip all over his clothing. "Just kill me now. You don't wanna drag my ass to Tucson. Trust me."

Cade stood tall again. The knife stayed in his grip at his side. "Oh, I've thought about it. Don't worry. But like I said, I have debts and five mouths to feed. Two million dollars would sure take care of that."

Liam chuckled. "Good luck getting me out of here, asshole. I won't come easy."

"I figured as much. Good thing I came prepared." Cade stepped to the other end of the container and sheathed his knife. He then dropped down and pulled a rag and some duct tape from a small backpack that had been sitting against the container's wall.

"Come on," Liam muttered. "How many times am I getting tied up today?"

It was Cade's turn to laugh now. "Don't pout, Junior. It's not a good look."

Liam bared his teeth at Cade. "I said don't call me Junior."

"What you gonna do about it, Junior?" Cade put extra emphasis on the last word.

"Come here and find out."

Cade's jaw clenched. He stared at Liam for a beat, then tossed the rag and duct tape to the floor. He drew his knife again and placed it in a hammer grip. "Fuck it. A million will do."

Cade charged for Liam with a haughty look of death in his eyes. Just as Liam had hoped. Right as the man reached him, he lunged his boot and cracked Cade on the knee. He buckled forward and fell into Liam's lap. As he fell, Liam used his limited reach to seize the wrist of Cade's knife hand with both hands. The blade came within an inch of stabbing his thigh. Before Cade could climb to his feet, Liam used every piece of energy he had left and twisted the blade up and into the man's throat. Cade gurgled for air as Liam dragged the knife sideways through his neck and hosed the walls of the container with arterial spray.

Cade collapsed into a heap on the dusty floor, clutching fruitlessly at the gaping hole in his throat. He was dead within thirty seconds and was now lying in a pool of his own blood.

"Next time, bring a gun," Liam said with a wild grin. As adrenaline flowed through his veins, he held the combat knife steady in his hands. He took a moment to lean back and close his eyes. Once he calmed himself down, he got to work, jamming the point of the knife into the ratchet of the handcuff on his left wrist.

CHAPTER 43
BILL

The hit Dallas had laid out on Bill and his son wasn't making things any easier. The looks his own men were giving him had put the bygone farmer on edge and were sending his blood pressure to an all-time high.

Xaver had given him the news in person, pulling Bill aside with a warning to watch his back. As if the hell he'd faced all day and night hadn't been enough, he now had to deal with the strong possibility that one of his own people would betray him for the reward money. And given how much cash was on offer, not a single one of them could be trusted. Not even his most loyal crew members.

The bounty Bill had promised his men for the deaths of Donny and Ranger seemed to have been forgotten in the chaos. When Bill was closer by and a far easier target by comparison, his impulsive proposition became redundant. For all they knew, Donny and Ranger wouldn't hit the farm for a few days. Maybe not at all. By then, any number of eager contractors might have taken up Dallas' offer and killed him.

The police Bill had on the take wouldn't be much help.

They couldn't exactly look the other way if the farm got turned into a micro war zone. If a firefight broke out in the valley, people would hear it. Calls would be made. Not even Namrena's police chief, whom Bill paid off monthly, could keep things under wraps. Bill would need to handle his problems on his own while not encouraging the authorities to come knocking.

Bill was concerned for Junior. He, too, had a kill or capture order on his head. Dallas wanted the Wilkins bloodline eradicated. Most would consider Bill to be the primary target. Even so, he needed to treat the threat against Junior just as seriously. He'd sent a man down to watch over him. One who had worked for the business for eight years and had never once made a mistake or given Bill a reason to doubt his loyalty. Still, the price Dallas was offering was going to test the roughest people on the farm.

Bill didn't have time to worry about Junior. Not with the number of problems he now had circling over him like vultures in the desert, waiting for a carcass. Most of the people Bill had called in to defend the farm didn't know where Junior was or what had happened to his two sidekicks. If things stayed that way until morning, Bill could grab Junior from the shipping container and get them both the hell away from the farm. Then he could arrange a negotiation with Dallas. Short of leaving the state, Bill had no other choice but to get things back on track with his cartel connection.

"Where's my mommy?" James asked, cutting into Bill's thoughts. Bill had decided to watch over Laura's boy himself and had moved the kid to his room for the time being. James was sitting on a chair in the corner of Bill's room. He'd been given food, water, and some old toys to play with, but the boy had touched none of them. He just sat there and asked where his mother was every so often.

Bill ignored the question and continued pacing the floor.

His .357 Colt Python stirred at his waist, loaded and ready to put down the first man who was crazy enough to come knocking without declaring who they were. Bill had also laid out his father's old .308 Winchester Model 70 on his bed. It was loaded up with a five-round detachable magazine and was sitting beside a bandoleer pouch with another six spare magazines. Bill had gotten the hunting rifle out, intending to take on Donny should the need arise, but the idea now seemed futile given the way things had developed. Thoughts of Donny made him think of Carl.

"Would be nice to have you here," Bill muttered to himself. Without his right-hand man by his side, Bill felt vulnerable and isolated. Xaver was a good lieutenant, but there had been something about Carl that no one else in the operation could match.

The way Bill had disposed of Carl's body was now filling him with a crushing guilt he couldn't silence. He wished things could have been different for the man. He'd been ten times more worthy of taking over the operations at the farm than his own son, but the rough business that was meth-amphetamine had done away with that possibility.

A knock came at Bill's door. "Boss, it's Rico." Rico had been on the payroll for four years and helped keep the farm's hidden armory supplied with everything it needed to function. Tonight, Rico's skills would be put to the test.

"Why aren't you using the walkie?"

"Sorry, boss. Just thought it would be easier to talk in person."

Bill ripped his .357 out and aimed it at the door. He inched up to the lock and twisted the bolt open. He then stepped to the side in a hurry, giving himself as much of an advantage as possible. "Come in. Door's open."

With two hands, Bill leveled his aim. When Rico came into

the room, he had him lined up with a shot to the face. One false move, and the man would be dead on his feet.

"Whoa, boss. No need for that. I come in peace." Rico held both hands up. He was visibly armed with a pistol strapped to his waist. But the gun was in its holster. He was also wearing tactical magazine holsters and thick body armor. Bill hated vests and had opted not to bother. If one of his people went for the reward money, an uncomfortable Kevlar vest wouldn't save him.

"What do you want?" Bill asked, not lowering his revolver.

Rico glanced at James for a moment, then back to Bill. "I just thought you'd want an update on things."

Bill sighed. Rico's body language didn't have a hint of deception in it, but that meant little when there was a big payday on the line. "Well, go on. Update me."

"Okay. I will. Any chance you could lower the Python? Or at least aim it away from my face?"

Bill grunted and lowered the revolver. But he didn't holster it. Instead, he kept it handy. Bill might have been older than Rico, but he was still a fast draw and would put any man down who tried to get the drop on him.

"Thanks, boss," Rico said.

"Out with it, then."

"Okay. The perimeter is secure. We've had no cell phone activity show up on the scanners, and none of our spotters have seen movement in the distance."

"Are they using those night-vision optics?"

"Of course. I've also got several jammers scattered around the farm to interrupt any comms our attackers might have on hand. And not to mention two guys on the roof with Barrett M82s covering a wide area around the main house. If anyone takes a step into the valley, they'll be cut down with .50 BMG before they know it."

Bill nodded. He'd heard the commotion on the roof earlier and had figured it was Rico's doing. There was no way for anyone to come in via the roof. Not without breaching the asphalt shingles and roof decking with a lot of noise.

"What about the gate?" Bill asked.

"What about it?"

"Did you rig it up like I asked?"

"Yes and no," Rico said as his eyes stared at the floor.

"What do you mean? We've got more than enough C-4."

"I know, but I thought about it. If the police came knocking for any reason and spotted explosives on the gate, things could go from bad to worse."

"Are you saying it's got nothing?"

"Not at all. It's been reinforced, and I've laid down some spike strips in front and behind. Should disable any vehicle that tries to rush in."

Bill let out a groan. "I suppose that's something. Anything else to report?"

"No. Well, at least nothing to do with my job."

Bill knew there was something else Rico wanted to say. He exhaled and finally holstered his revolver. "What is it?"

"It might be nothing, but I noticed that some of the extra guys we called in are talking."

"Talking?"

"Yeah. They are breaking away from the rest of us for private chats. Two or three of them, at least. I think they might be planning to move against you."

Bill pinched the bridge of his nose. "Of course they are. Fucking Dallas."

"I'm sorry, boss."

"Don't be, son. He's made them all a substantial offer. Plus, these guys you're talking about, they aren't our usual people. They're just hired guns doing what hired guns do best."

"What should we do about them?"

Bill scratched at his gray beard and closed his eyes. Was it time to grab Junior and throw him into the back of his 300C and hit the road? He had a rucksack filled with cash and supplies hidden in his room. More than enough for them to leave the country and never look back. But there'd be a steep price to pay. The farm had been in the Wilkins name for generations. It might have evolved to be more than a simple patch of agriculture, but at its core, it was still a red-blooded Wilkins farm.

Bill gave Rico a smile. "Let them scheme. But note down who they are. When push comes to shove, I'll have a special mission for them to complete."

"On it, boss," Rico said. He rushed to leave the room.

"And, Rico."

"Yeah, boss?"

"I'm sorry for pointing my gun at you. Please understand, I meant no disrespect."

Rico stared at Bill with an open mouth like he'd just announced to the world he had cancer. Bill wasn't surprised. He never apologized for anything. That's not what the boss man was supposed to do. Even if he was in the wrong, Bill knew it would come across as weak. What he'd said to Rico was in hopes that a loyal member of his crew would stay that way. If it meant he had to stoop to a bit of groveling, then so be it.

"Don't sweat it, boss," Rico said. He gave Bill a firm nod and left, closing the door behind him. Bill moved up to the door and twisted the lock. His hand fell onto his revolver again as he let out a long breath. The last day had taken its toll, all starting when he'd found the drifter scuffing along on the outskirts of Namrena. Thoughts of Frank Ranger made Bill realize something vital. A piece of information he'd forgotten about that would change everything.

"Son of a bitch," Bill muttered as a smile formed. He pulled out his cell phone and got to work. There was still time to save the farm, but it was going to require a play most men in his position would never consider.

"Where's my mommy?" James asked again. His question remained unanswered. Bill had bigger fish to fry.

CHAPTER 44

RANGER

Ranger and Laura were about four clicks out from Wilkins Farms when Donny called on the burner phone.

"Pull over. Stop the car and kill the lights," Donny said when Ranger answered. There was an excitement in Donny's voice Ranger couldn't quite place. It could have been bad or good. Whatever it was, Donny was desperate to speak.

"The game has changed."

"How do you mean?" Ranger asked on the burner's crappy speakerphone so Laura could hear the conversation.

"I got a call from a contact—a guy who's got nothing to do with Bill or Liam Wilkins—but let's just say he knows all about the business that goes down on the farm."

Ranger's brow twisted. "Slow down. You're not making any sense. You got a call?"

Donny chuckled. "Listen, forget how I know what I'm about to say. It doesn't matter. What does matter is that the farm's cartel connection in Tucson has put a hit out on Bill and Liam Wilkins. One mil each dead, two mil each alive."

"Holy shit," was all Ranger thought to say.

"What does this mean?" Laura asked.

Donny answered, "It means things at the farm are going to shit. We can use this to our advantage."

"How?" Ranger asked.

Donny cleared his throat. "I'm glad you asked."

"Oh, no," Ranger let out, knowing something insane was coming.

"The people at the farm all know who I am," Donny started. "They understand what Bill hired me for and how well he paid me. I still have the contact details of some of Bill's people. Maybe I could put out the word that I'll add to the bounty. I can tell them to spread around that I'll match the offer from Dallas, essentially doubling the reward money. Bill's own people will tear him to pieces before the night is through. We won't have to lift a finger."

Ranger shook his head. "You can't be serious."

"Why not? It's not like I have to actually pay anyone if it happens."

"That's not the problem. Think about it. Who do you think will be keeping a close eye on James right now?"

The line went silent for a moment. Then Donny realized what Ranger was trying to tell him. "Bill."

"Oh, God," Laura let out. She also seemed to understand.

Ranger placed a hand on her shoulder. "This hit might seem like useful news, but it only puts James in more danger than he already is."

"Dammit," Donny muttered. "I thought we were onto something."

The sound of the pickup's diesel motor idling rumbled peacefully in the background as Ranger stared out into the night. Just to be safe, Ranger hadn't killed the engine like Donny had asked.

All their problems seemed to have solved themselves for a

second. But reality came crashing back down. Things had gone from bad to worse.

Then a thought came to Ranger. One that was a gamble to speak aloud, but he knew he had to try. "Do you still have Bill's number?"

"Yeah, why?"

"Maybe we can still use this bounty thing to our advantage. We could contact Bill and offer to protect him and Liam in exchange for James. If he's got bigger problems to worry about than us, then maybe he'll go for it."

Donny didn't respond.

"Did you hear me?" Ranger asked.

"I heard you. I'm just running through the scenario in my head."

"And?"

"It might work. But he wouldn't trust us. He'd assume we were just after the bounty money as well."

"He doesn't have to trust us."

"What do you mean?" Donny asked.

"Mutually assured destruction."

"Huh?" Laura asked.

Ranger gave her a smile. "It's simple. We won't go for the bounty on Bill and Liam if he doesn't harm James." Laura's eyes lit up with a smile.

"I don't know about this," Donny said.

"It's our best play. We contact Bill and offer to extract him and Liam so they can leave the farm safely. But only if they bring James along."

"How do we then get James?"

"Once we're far enough away from the farm, I think Bill will see reason and hand James over. We'll each go our own ways without a drop of blood being shed."

"Provided the extraction goes well," Donny added.

"Of course. But if we have to drop a few of Bill's men on the way out, so be it."

Donny fell silent and didn't give Ranger a yes or no.

Ranger turned to Laura and signaled for her to say something. He hoped his vague gesture would give her the hint to add to the argument.

Laura shuffled closer to the phone. "Donny."

"Yeah."

"If you help bring James home to me…let's just say that I might forgive you for what you did to Rosie."

"Okay," Donny said.

Ranger and Laura sat in silence for a moment. The night was as clear as they came, and the moon was three-quarters full. Ranger could see in either direction for miles and miles. The thought of assaulting the farm in such conditions against people who no doubt would be equipped with expensive rifles and high-end optics sent a pang of futility down his spine. But an extraction was a much smaller can of worms. One they had half a chance of achieving if Bill and Liam cooperated.

"All right," Donny said. "Give me a few minutes, and I'll meet up with you both. We'll contact Bill together."

Donny ended the call, leaving Ranger and Laura staring at one another. Ranger spoke first. "This might work."

"I hope so," she replied with a thickness of doubt in her words.

"What is it?"

She shook her head. "I don't know. I guess I'm just thinking about this idea some more. What if Bill and Liam don't hand James over?"

"They're backed into a corner with their own people. What other choice do they have?"

Laura shrugged and turned her attention to the window.

"People do all kinds of crazy things when they're out of options."

Ranger wanted to disagree and tell her she was wrong, but he knew firsthand what she was saying. He'd lived the last year of his life backed into a corner. The question was, what would Bill and Liam Wilkins do when they ran out of options?

CHAPTER 45

Donny took almost fifteen minutes to arrive at Ranger's location. Ranger wanted to ask him why it had taken him so long, but he figured the man might have been grappling with a hard decision in the process and needed the extra time to come to a conclusion. For better or worse, Donny was there and on board with the plan.

"Do you think this will work?" Ranger asked him, desperate for an answer.

"Maybe. He might already have his own way out, to run off with Liam and live out the rest of his days on a tropical beach somewhere, sipping margaritas."

Ranger nodded and wondered whom Donny was really talking about. He tried to picture the soldier reclining on a beach lounger in the Bahamas, wearing a Hawaiian shirt while he had daiquiris and sangria served to him. Ranger shook off the laughable thought.

"How do we handle this?" Ranger asked. The two men were standing at the back of the pickup Ranger had been driving. Laura was close by, leaning against the tailgate with her arms folded over her chest. Her eyes seemed to be fixated on the road beneath her like she was lost in thought or stuck in limbo. Her mind was focused on her son and nothing else.

Donny took a moment to pace around before he spoke. "I've been thinking. We have to tread lightly. We want to give Bill the feeling he's in control while also proving that we can get to him if he declines the offer."

"How do we do that?"

Donny took a gander at the horizon. "I could take out one of his guys. I'll pick a random jackass and pop him from, say, fifteen hundred yards. Enough to make return fire a difficult prospect."

Ranger hated killing people, no matter who they were. But dropping only a handful of Bill's people at the most was better than needing to take out a dozen of them or more.

"What do you think?" Donny asked.

"If it comes to a demonstration of force, then that's probably our strongest play. Who should do the talking when we call?"

"Not you. You'll send Bill into a spin if he hears your voice. I'll have the best chance of getting through to him."

"What do you want me to do while you're talking to him?"

Donny shrugged. "Keep an eye out, I guess. The second we call, he'll know we're close by. That might tempt him to rush a few cars our way to smoke us out."

"That's what I'm afraid of. What if this makes him hunker down more or go on the offensive?"

Donny let out a breath. "Well, I have another idea, but you won't like it."

Ranger groaned. "What now?"

Donny smiled, adding more turmoil to Ranger's brain. "If my single shot against one of Bill's guys isn't enough to say we mean business, we'll need to hit them again."

Ranger's brow narrowed as he tried to interpret what

Donny meant. "What are you saying? You'll take out another guy?"

"No. Follow me," Donny said, gesturing at Ranger. The two men left Laura where she was standing. Ranger walked along behind Donny with caution in his step. He knew whatever Donny had in mind wouldn't be good for anyone.

Donny stopped at the tailgate of his pickup and pulled out a set of keys. He pressed a button on a remote and opened the truck's hard lid that covered the bed. When the cover lifted enough, Ranger got a good look at what Donny was hinting at. Ranger stared down at an Mk 153 SMAW. The long tube was a shoulder-launched multipurpose assault weapon. In simple terms, it was a rocket launcher.

"Where the hell did you find that?" Ranger asked.

Donny laughed. "Never you mind."

Ranger shook his head as he ran both hands through his hair. He'd fired the weapon in training before he was deployed to Afghanistan. Or at least a modified version of the one Donny had sitting in the bed of his pickup.

"I've got three rounds. I figure if Bill doesn't take us seriously, we hit him with this."

Ranger blew out a long breath as he stared at the rocket launcher. "I don't know where to start."

"Hey, my idea's not that bad, is it?"

Ranger gave him a sardonic chuckle as he stepped away from the pickup. "Well, first off, that thing has an effective range of about five hundred yards. And second, we're trying to save a kid, not blow him the hell up."

"I hear you," Donny said, "but check this out. We both know you have the skills to sneak in close enough to use this bad boy without getting killed. You forget, I've seen you work. And as for the kid, we won't fire a single round anywhere near him. We'll hit one of the cars on the farm. Something away from the main house. That's where

James will most likely be. Hell, I can make sure the vehicles are empty if it means so much to you. James will be fine."

Laura came over from where she'd been standing and poked her head around the open lid of the bed on Donny's pickup. Her eyes went wide the second she spotted the rocket launcher.

"What the hell is that? I thought you said you were going to help rescue James, not blow him up."

Donny backed away with his arms out wide. "Would everyone please just calm the hell down? You're both acting like I want to send a rocket through the front door or something. This is just a show of force, remember? Something to remind Bill that we're dangerous."

Laura muttered to herself, then faced Ranger. "Frank, please tell me you're not listening to this bag of crazy."

Ranger stared into her desperate eyes, then glanced at Donny. The sniper was also watching Ranger like a hawk, waiting for his opinion on the plan.

"Please, Frank. There has to be another way," Laura begged.

Ranger sighed. "While I don't agree with Donny's methods, this would force Bill to take us seriously."

"Okay. Apparently, you're just as insane as he is."

"Laura, I—"

"You both think you've got it all worked out," she said, cutting Ranger off, "but you don't know the Wilkinses like I do." Her breath heaved in and out as she stared at Donny and Ranger with a concern in her eyes only a mother could possess.

Donny stepped closer to her. "Laura, I know this day has been a bit rough."

"A bit rough? Are you serious?" She looked ready to take a swing at Donny.

Donny continued, "I get that you want me to die and all that, but you need to trust me."

"Trust you? You killed my friend and left her body to burn in her own home. Do you think I will ever forget that?"

"Not in my lifetime," Donny said without blinking an eye.

Laura looked ready to pull out the Glock again, so Ranger stepped in and walked her away from Donny. "It's okay," he said. "All we're trying to do here is bring James home in one piece."

"With a rocket launcher?"

"Maybe. I don't know yet. But whatever way this all goes down, it won't be pretty. The important thing is we're not giving up. Not until they put us down. If that means we have to get a little creative with our approach, I guess that's what's going to happen."

Laura stared at Ranger as her eyes watered. "I just want him back," she sobbed.

He pulled her in tight and held her. "It's okay," Ranger whispered. "We'll get him back."

Laura nodded as she sniffed, then pulled away from Ranger's embrace. She walked back to the second pickup in a hurry and climbed into the passenger seat.

"So that went well," Donny said as he closed the lid on the bed.

Ranger sighed, wishing he could take a hot shower and a long nap. But anything that came close to such a luxury was going to have to wait. He had a rocket launcher to drag across the desert toward Bill Wilkins.

CHAPTER 46

BILL

Bill finished making several phone calls and felt rather pleased with himself. He stood from the bed in his room and moved around the open space with a renewed sense of purpose. The calls he'd made would require a strict change in strategy when it came time to defend the farm, but ultimately, it was the smartest action to take. The only thing against him was time. He needed to implement the changes right away to pull off what he had planned.

James glanced up at Bill from his seat in the corner as Bill headed toward the bedroom door. "Where's my mommy?" the kid asked again.

Bill answered for a change. "She'll be here soon, son. I guarantee it."

Bill left his room and locked the door on his way out. He needed James to stay right where he was, at least for the time being. As he walked down the corridor, he dialed a number on his cell phone. One he'd received only a few hours ago. One he prayed was still in use. Donny answered the call after seven rings.

"Bill?" Donny asked, surprise filling his voice.

"Don't hang up. I know you're working with Frank. And I'll bet my last dollar Laura is with you both as well."

Donny took a second to answer. "Who says I'm not halfway to Mexico City by now?"

"You could be, but I doubt it."

"Is there a point to this conversation?" Donny said.

"Of course. I'm not one to mince words or waste time. I've got a proposition for you."

Donny sighed into the phone. "Okay. I'm listening."

"How about a trade? You give me Laura. In return, I'll hand over the boy."

"Fuck off," Donny said. "Talk to me when you've got something real to say." The call ended.

Bill let a chuckle rumble in his gut. The trade idea was a little something to rattle Donny's chain. What Bill really needed to happen would be a lot more achievable. He dialed the same number again.

"I told you to—"

"Fuck off?" Bill asked, finishing Donny's sentence for him.

"Yeah, so how about it?"

"Not just yet. My offer before, it was a little steep. I'll admit that. How about we talk money for the boy instead of a trade?"

"Money?" Donny asked.

"Five hundred large for the kid. Then y'all leave town. You, Laura, the boy, and the goddamn drifter vanish from Namrena. How does that sound?"

Donny paused again. He was either mulling the offer over in his mind or stalling for time. Bill didn't care. He only needed him to consider it.

"Call me back if you'd like to think about it," Bill said.

"No, no. That won't be necessary. I got a better idea."

"You do?"

"Yeah. Forget money. We've got something far more valuable to trade with you for James."

"This should be good," Bill said with a wide grin.

"It is. How about we extract you and Liam from the farm."

Bill let out a groan. "I take it you heard about the hit."

"I did. Was tempted to give it a shot myself, but killing you won't get James back to his mother, will it?"

Bill thought about the boy. "I've got some contingencies in place."

"I'm sure you do, but what happens when one of your guys wises up and forgets his loyalty to the operation?"

"You let me worry about the farm."

"The farm? Do you honestly think things will go back to normal after tonight? Who are you going to sell your meth to? The only guy you had outside of Namrena put a price on your head."

Bill shifted his cell phone from one hand to the other. "Tell me about this extraction idea of yours."

"It's simple. We rush in to pull you and Liam out and get you both to safety. You can make it a bit easier for us by standing down any of your men who are still taking orders. We'll protect you from any of them who might follow."

"What's to say you won't kill us for the reward money?"

"You'll have James with you, of course. We won't harm you if you don't harm him."

Bill took a moment to think. His money plan wasn't going to stick, but it didn't matter. Donny's "extraction" proposal could still work in his favor.

"What do you say?" Donny asked.

"We got a deal."

"All right then. Get yourself ready and call me back with an extraction point. Make sure it's somewhere we can get in and out of easy enough."

"Fine. I'll be in touch," Bill said.

"Don't dawdle. Wouldn't want one of your men taking you down before we can pull you out. That'd be a real shame."

Bill wanted to let Donny have it, but he held his tongue. The time would come when Donny, Frank, and Laura would all get what they deserved. Bill just needed to play it cool for a short while longer. It was a shame he couldn't impart the valuable lesson to his own son. Maybe someday when Junior saw the light and understood why Bill had to rid him of his two useless sidekicks.

"I have an extraction point in mind," Bill said.

"Already?"

"Yeah. There's a place on the edge of the farm. I'll text you the coordinates now. It's a quiet little spot, away from everything, including my men."

"How are you going to get there?" Donny asked. Bill could hear the suspicion in his voice.

"You leave that to me. I'm sure I'll be followed, so be ready to do your part of things. Once we're far enough away from it all, we can sort out what comes next."

"You mean James."

"Who else?"

"How long?" Donny grunted, ignoring the question.

"One hour. And don't pull any of this sniper crap on me. I know you've got the skills to hit me from a mile away, but I promise you, my death won't give you what you want."

"Wouldn't dream of it."

"I'm sure," Bill said. "I'll see y'all at the spot in one hour."

Bill ended the call this time and let out a deep-throated laugh. Whatever way Donny and his war buddy played things at the extraction point wouldn't matter. Before the night was through, Bill would have everything he needed to put the farm back on track.

A few minutes later, Bill met with Rico downstairs in the main house, but away from anyone else who might be listening in.

"I've a job for you, Rico. An important one."

"Okay, boss. What is it?"

Bill smiled from ear to ear. "Come with me."

CHAPTER 47

RANGER

"We can't go to this location he's sent me," Donny said with his arms out wide.

"I know it sounds like a trap, but we can be careful," Ranger replied.

"Careful? We're talking about waiting for Bill at a location on his own land. And all the while, he'll be holding James hostage while we supposedly escort the old man and Liam to safety. You think he'll just come along without a bunch of guys to ambush us? It's a damn trap."

"I'm not leaving here without James," Laura said, jumping into the conversation. The trio were still on the side of the quiet road. Not a single car had passed them by since Donny had made Ranger pull over.

Bill had sent Donny a set of coordinates. In less than an hour, they were supposed to meet with him to help extract the father and son from the farm while James sat in their company. The location wasn't far away, but the issue was access. The only roads to the extraction point came from within Wilkins Farms. No doubt Bill had chosen the location for that very reason.

When Donny had looked up the spot on his GPS, he said what they were all probably thinking. "I guarantee Bill has half a dozen of his guys out there waiting for us to arrive. And to make matters worse, there's no fast way for us to exfil if the shit hits the fan."

"We're not leaving without James," Ranger said to reassure Laura. The look on her face doubted his every word, but he meant them. He was going to get James back, no matter what it took.

"What's the plan, then, Frank?" Donny snapped. "Because it sounds like you've got it all figured out."

"I don't know. But we're going to that location. We have what it takes to beat Bill. You ask me, I'd rather fight him out there than at the farm."

Donny got right up close to Ranger and flared his chest. "Am I hearing you right? The farm sits inside a valley. That means I could find a cozy little vantage point and have an optimal range on the high ground. From there, I could rain shit down on any dipshit that has it coming without them ever knowing it. This extraction point is on flat terrain. The nearest piece of high ground is over three thousand yards away. Bill knows that's a hard shot to make without a lot of time and luck on your side. Understand?"

"Yes," Ranger said, letting Donny ease back after a few seconds. "I get it. It's a screwed-up mission. Most likely a trap in enemy territory with no high ground to work with. We've been through worse."

Donny grumbled and kicked the dirt on the side of the road. "Jesus, Frank. You're talking like we can call in an air strike if things don't go our way. God, you don't know when to quit, do you?"

"It's not an option."

Donny stared at Ranger, then glanced at Laura for a moment before he stepped away. Ranger understood what was going through his head. He wanted to bail on the whole thing and run. If he did, if he took a step in the wrong direction, it would spell the end for James. Ranger couldn't let that happen. Even if it meant he had to drag Donny kicking and screaming to the extraction point, he would.

"We could run some recon on the area first," Ranger offered. "There's time."

Donny refused to look in Ranger's direction. He continued to scuff at the dirt with his boot and started muttering to himself. Ranger studied his demeanor and doubted if Donny was going to come through for James like he'd promised.

Ranger slowly lowered a hand down toward the grip of the Beretta he had holstered on the side of his thigh. He kept his eyes on Donny's hands at all times in case the situation went sideways. He still wasn't sure how trustworthy his old friend truly was. Only a short time ago, he had murdered a woman to save his own hide. If Donny decided to run, Ranger would finally put him down.

"All right," Donny said, whipping his attention toward his pickup. "Let's get this shit over with."

"You're on board?"

"Apparently. Goes against my every instinct, but what the hell, right? Gotta die sometime."

"We're not dying. We can still handle this the smart way. We'll go in and sweep the area as we move and minimize the risk. Besides, James won't make it out of here if we're all dead."

Donny chortled and gave Ranger a wide grin. "Don't fuck with me, Frank. We both know you're destined to go out in a blaze of glory one day. It's only a matter of time."

"Donny—"

"No. I don't want to hear any more of your reassuring bullshit. Just grab your gear, and let's go."

Ranger resisted the urge to say anything else. He needed Donny's head in the game if they were going to have half a chance of saving James. Bill Wilkins wasn't a man to underestimate. Ranger had seen that firsthand. Whatever reason he had for agreeing to the extraction couldn't be good.

Ranger and Donny checked over everything they'd need for a fight. Ranger was ready and slapped Donny on the shoulder. "Thank you. This might be the biggest mistake of our lives, but it's the right thing to do."

"The right thing to do, huh? Now there's some famous last words."

"Maybe. Guess we'll find out soon enough." Ranger moved toward his pickup. The trip would be mostly off-road.

"Oh, and Frank," Donny said before Ranger reached the driver's side door.

"Yeah?"

"Don't forget my baby."

Ranger stared back to where Donny was pointing. "You can't be serious?"

"As sure as shit, my friend. Load it up in your bed. If things go crazy, you'll know what to do."

Ranger sighed. "Okay." He trudged over to the Mk 153 SMAW and gazed down at the weapon as a wave of regret washed over him.

CHAPTER 48

Ranger and Donny crawled their pickups along uneven terrain toward the extraction point Bill Wilkins had arranged for himself and his son. There was no road or path to take that wasn't riddled with ruts and shrubs. To remain as hidden as possible, they drove with their lights off while wearing night-vision goggles that were folded down from an attachment on their helmets. The journey was taking far longer than Ranger had expected, and the one-hour deadline was drawing near.

Laura held on tight as best she could as the pickup rocked side to side and up and down. "Are we almost there?" she asked, desperation in her voice. She was on edge more so than before.

"Not far to—"

The front side of the pickup dropped into a three-foot-deep hole Ranger never saw coming and landed with a thud. Both he and Laura lifted from their seats and crashed down hard, almost smashing their faces into the dash of the vehicle. No airbags deployed, but their seat belts stopped them from taking any serious damage.

"Are you okay?" Ranger asked Laura in a hurry.

"Fine. Just get us moving again."

Ranger nodded and tapped on the gas, but the pickup wouldn't budge. He pressed the accelerator a little harder until he realized the back wheels were spinning in the air.

"Oh God, we're stuck," Laura said.

Without panic, Ranger put the pickup into neutral, then engaged the four-wheel drive so the front wheels could gain traction. He realized he should have had the four-wheel drive activated the entire time they'd been off-road, but his mind had been too focused on the mission and how they were going to take James back.

With more gentle pressure, Ranger tapped the gas and felt the front wheels produce torque. The truck lurched forward but soon rocked back into the hole. He tried to move forward again with a lot more acceleration but ended up in the same position.

"Crap," Ranger let out.

"What do we do?" she asked, almost begging.

Donny buzzed on Ranger's burner. Ranger wanted to ignore the call and handle the problem on his own, but he had no idea what to do. He wasn't much of a driver these days and had spent little time behind the wheel when he'd been off-road in Afghanistan. Not as a sergeant.

"Donny," Ranger answered.

"You're stuck, aren't you?"

"Looks that way."

"Tell me you're not in two-wheel drive."

"I was. But it's not making a difference. I can't get enough traction to force the rear wheels far enough down. Can you help me?"

"I can, but there's not enough time. We might as well continue in my truck. Take what you can from the gear and load up with me."

"Got it," Ranger said, turning to Laura. "Let's go." He climbed out of the pickup and rushed to the bed. He pulled out the Ruger AR-556 Donny had provided for him, along with a few rucksacks of gear. Laura stood beside him as he handed her the bags and grabbed the damned Mk 153 SMAW. Ranger knew Donny would have a meltdown if it got left behind.

A few minutes later, they reached Donny's pickup and dumped off their gear and the Mk 153 SMAW. Laura sat up front with Donny while Ranger stayed in the open bed. Donny had raised the lid and left it that way. The two-seater couldn't fit the three of them comfortably. Plus, Ranger wanted to be armed and ready for a fight now that they were within firing range of the extraction point.

With night-vision goggles on, Ranger scanned the area in a 360-degree sweep. The goggles had a zoom function Ranger used to dial in close to anything that looked out of the ordinary. He didn't locate any of Bill's people moving around or another vehicle apart from the one he'd abandoned in a ditch. There were some mountains in the distance, but the thickness of the shrubs along the flat ground made it hard to see much beyond a few hundred yards. Just like Donny said, Bill had chosen the spot for a reason.

"We're clear for now," Ranger said over the comms he'd now activated. Both Donny and Laura had the same gear and could hear him from inside the pickup.

"Copy," Donny pinged back. "Won't be long now. We're only three hundred yards out."

"Where's James?" Laura asked over the comms. She'd been shown how to use it with the briefest of tutorials.

"He'll be here soon," Ranger said. "I'm sure Bill is just keeping him back from the spot for the time being."

"What if he's already killed him? What if this is all a big lie to lure us in?"

"James is alive," Ranger said without a single piece of evidence to back up his claim. "And we're going to get him back."

"How can you be so sure?"

Ranger closed his eyes and thought of the lies he'd told himself since James had been taken. They were like the ones he'd once believed when he swore he would find the man who'd killed his wife and separated him from his daughter. Was he going to give up on saving James the way he had on returning to Cindy?

"Let's stay off the comms unless we need them," Donny said, coming to Ranger's rescue.

Ranger didn't respond and got back to the job at hand before he let his memories take control. It wasn't the time or place to lose his concentration.

A few minutes passed by as the slow crawl continued. Then Ranger spotted a lone man in the distance. The figure appeared from a thicket of shrubs like he'd been hiding behind them. Ranger zoomed in and found Bill Wilkins, but he couldn't find James.

"I got Bill Wilkins at nine o'clock. No James. No Liam."

"I see him," Donny said.

"Where is James? Why isn't he with him?" Laura asked in a frantic voice.

"Unclear," Ranger replied.

Donny brought the pickup to a stop and left the engine running. Both he and Laura climbed out and rushed to the bed as Ranger dropped to the ground with his Ruger AR-556 at the ready.

Donny prepped his Ruger RPR Magnum and adjusted the scope according to the conditions. He raised his night-vision goggles and held up the rifle. He stared down the scope he had aimed in Bill's direction. "I can pop him right here," Donny said. "Surely he knows that."

Ranger stared at Bill and wondered the same thing. The answer came to him a few seconds later. "When you had him on speaker before, he said something like no good will come from his death. If you shoot him, we have no idea what will happen to James."

"Son of a bitch," Donny muttered. "The old man knows a thing or two."

Laura paced the spot. "Let's just take him hostage. You can force him to tell us where James is."

Ranger and Donny exchanged a look. "He wouldn't make it this easy," Ranger said.

Donny shrugged. "What else are we supposed to do?"

Laura started walking toward Bill. Donny sighed and followed.

"Wait," Ranger said. "This is what he wants. We can't do this."

"I don't care," Laura called back. "That son of a bitch is going to tell us where he's got James."

Ranger didn't budge as he tapped his index finger on the trigger guard of his rifle. He knew what Laura was doing was being spurred on by emotion. Donny was probably going along with it so she didn't rush up to Bill and do something that couldn't be undone.

"You coming, Ranger?" Donny called.

Ranger took a moment to think. He wanted to find James in one piece and would do whatever it took to achieve the goal. But what they were doing wasn't going to end without a price being paid.

Ranger wanted to stop Donny and Laura and pull them back. But there was no time to come up with a plan B. Ranger did what he could to ignore the bad feeling in his gut and exhaled. He pulled his focus toward Bill and said, "Coming."

CHAPTER 49

Ranger, Donny, and Laura reached the extraction point and came within twenty yards of Bill Wilkins. Bill had activated an LED lantern and had set it down at his feet. The light gave off enough of a glow that Ranger caught a look of confidence in Bill's eyes. Enough to send more pangs of alarm to his every instinct.

Donny and Ranger had each raised their night-vision goggles on their helmets but held on tight to their rifles. Even Laura had her Glock out but had been instructed by Ranger and Donny not to fire on Bill unless everything went to shit, and she had no other choice. Laura had reluctantly agreed to the command, but Ranger saw the twitch in her eye that told him she was going to empty the Glock's magazine into Bill's gut the first chance she got.

Bill was smoking a cigarette and sporting an old hunting rifle over his shoulder. He had his revolver on his hip. The same one Ranger had spotted on him in his truck where it all began. He wasn't wearing body armor and seemed to be relaxed for a man who was outnumbered in the middle of nowhere at night. He was standing on his own land, but none of his people were around, and there were no vehicles in sight beyond Donny's two pickups. Ranger, Donny, or even Laura could kill him before he spoke a word. But then they'd have no idea where to find James. Bill's game was already underway.

"Beautiful night," Bill said, staring up at the sky. "Reminds me of the hunting trips my old man used to take me on as a boy. Whenever he found time to get away from the farm, we'd camp out under the stars on a night like this and take it all in. Then, in the early morning, we'd go hunting with this here rifle. He was a straight shot, the old man. Taught me everything I know. But of course, in those days, the son of a bitch worked his ass off, dawn till dusk, seven days a week. Meant these trips only happened a few times a year at most. Even though I knew he couldn't spare the energy, I'd ask him again and again to take me. He'd say no every time until one day, I'd get lucky, and he'd agree." Bill exhaled with a slight chuckle. "I didn't know it then, but in those moments, right after he said 'yes,' that was the happiest I'd ever be in my entire life."

Donny yawned. "Jesus. Is this story going somewhere, Bill?"

"Oh, don't mind me. I'm just an old man reflecting on his life."

"That's great and all, but we didn't drag our asses out here to listen to your pathetic life story. Where's James?"

Bill chuckled and sneered as his focus fell to the dirt. "James is fine. He's in a safe place."

"He should be here," Laura said through gritted teeth. Ranger held her back as she lurched toward Bill. "Easy," he whispered to her.

"Calm yourself, sweetheart," Bill said. "Your boy is okay. He's just not with me right now."

"He's with Liam, isn't he?" Donny asked, stabbing a finger at Bill.

"Now come on, Donald. Do you take me for a fool? If James were here right now, you'd have killed me already. You or that rabid dog of yours." Bill glowered at Ranger, then pointed a finger of his own. "I should have dealt with you when I saw you sniffing around this town."

Ranger stared right back at Bill. He'd left Donny's Mk 153 SMAW back in his truck. But if he had the chance to send a rocket straight into Bill's loud mouth, he wouldn't hesitate to do so.

"Forget about Ranger," Donny said, grabbing Bill's focus. "We're here to negotiate. Now, I don't see Liam or any of your people around for miles. The farm is a long enough distance away that they wouldn't be able to reach you in time if this little meeting of ours fell apart. So tell me, what are we doing here? How do we resolve this?"

Ranger was impressed with Donny's ability to speak. Despite being a killer for hire, the man had a way with words.

"I suppose we can get down to business," Bill said. "I have something you want. You have something I want."

"What is it you want?" Ranger asked, taking point.

Bill gave him a twisted smile. "You."

"What?" Donny spat out.

"You heard me. Your boy is a wanted man. He's being hunted by the US Marshals Service for the murder of his wife."

"That's all bullshit. He didn't do it."

"Not what I heard," Bill continued. "Story is, he came back from Afghanistan and lost his fucking marbles. Slaughtered his own wife in cold blood. Left his daughter without her mamma."

"Shut the hell up, Bill," Donny roared.

"How'd it feel, killer? Did you watch the life fade from her eyes when it happened, or did you walk away and put the game on? Cops said they found you unconscious by the body with the murder weapon in hand. They said you tried to blow your brains out but missed. Did you try to take the easy way out and screw it up? Get a bit sleepy after that?"

Ranger said nothing and held his gaze. The way he saw it, Bill was either stalling for time or was trying to rattle their cages. His muscles tensed as he held the Ruger AR-556, ready to fire on anyone who came charging toward the extraction point Bill had arranged.

"Strike a chord, did I?" Bill asked Donny.

Donny seethed and muttered to himself.

"What's it gonna be? Is Ranger coming with me?"

"We're not stupid," Donny said.

"Stupid? No. Desperate? Yes."

Donny gritted his teeth. "Either you take this thing seriously, or—"

"Or what?" Bill asked, cutting Donny off. "You'll kill me? You do that, then I can't check in with my long-range walkie here in five minutes. If I don't check in, my men have strict orders to send Laura's boy back in a dozen pieces, one at a time. Understand?"

Laura's breath raged in and out of her lungs next to Ranger. She gripped the handle of the Glock so tight, her knuckles went white.

"All right," Donny said, continuing the negotiating. "We're not here to kill you. Just say what it is you want to happen, and we can talk about it."

Bill stared at Donny with scorn in his eyes and said, "This is the way things are gonna play out. You lay down your weapons. All of 'em."

"Okay." Donny laughed. "Then what?"

"Then Ranger is coming with me."

"So you can kill him?"

"No. So I can hand him over to Dallas, along with a few million in cash. See, I've explained to my associate what you told me happened at the quarry. But I may have changed the story a little. I sold him a lie that a rival hired Ranger to take me out at that meeting. But Ranger here missed. He killed my number two guy instead. So now, I'm handing him over to my friends in Tucson so they can do whatever the hell they want to him and make us square."

Donny's voice almost broke. "They'll kill him."

"Probably worse than that. I'd imagine there'll be some torture first. These guys are affiliated with the cartels down south. They won't mess around."

Donny shook his head. "Dallas won't believe you. And even if he does, he'll still want you dead. Just like you sent those two assholes to Rosie's house. They were gonna put me in the dirt after I helped them finish the job. Isn't that right?"

Bill gave Donny a sideways grin and held his hands out wide. "You got me. Guilty as charged. But you're forgetting one great big thing, Donny. I'm fucking Bill Wilkins. I produce more meth than this state has ever seen. I'm fucking God around here. Not some dirt-eating, washed-up hack of a sniper who can't handle killing some third-rate waitress."

"Don't," Ranger said, gripping Donny's forearm with a steely clasp. He could feel the tension in his arm as Donny fought hard not to let Bill get under his skin. The man seemed to be an expert at it.

Ranger stepped forward and faced Donny, giving him a look that he hopefully understood. With a long breath out, he tossed his Beretta into the dirt. He did the same with the AR-556, combat knife, spare magazines, and grenades. He even went as far as removing his helmet, leaving only his body armor on.

"Take me," Ranger said. "I'm yours." He took a few steps toward Bill with his arms raised.

"Frank, no," Donny said. "This isn't what I meant. You're not going with Bill."

"You can't," Laura muttered. "There has to be another way."

"He's coming with me," Bill said. "Now turn around, Ranger. Hands on your head. Do a spin for me so I can make sure you're unarmed."

Ranger did as instructed and made a slow sweeping turn. When he was facing Donny, he flicked his eyes toward his belt, toward the small knife he had hidden away in it. Without giving anything up, Donny showed Ranger that he understood.

"Looks good to me," Bill said as Ranger reached Bill. "On your knees." Ranger complied.

"This is crazy, Frank. Please," Donny said to the back of Ranger's head, hopefully playing along. "We can still find James."

"Not possible," Bill said. He pulled out his long-range walkie and checked in with someone named Rico. Apparently, if Bill didn't do so again in five minutes, then Rico had orders to harm James exactly as Bill had described. Five minutes wasn't enough time to kill the old man and reach the farm. Plus, they didn't know where James was being kept. Bill seemed committed to his plan. He had that glint in his eye that told the world he'd rather die than give up.

"What about James?" Laura asked. "How do we get him back?"

Bill chuckled. "Nothing gets by this one. The next time I radio in, I'll give Rico the green light to drive James out here. Then we can do the swap like the civil people that we are and be on our way. You two take James and leave while I take Ranger to Dallas. Everybody gets what they want. Well, except poor Frank here, but I think we'd all be doing him a favor. The man's been living the life of a ghost for the last year."

Ranger absorbed Bill's words and let them swirl around in his head. He wasn't going down without a fight, but part of him wanted to believe that maybe Bill was right. What sort of life had he been living?

"I'll kill you," Donny said to Bill. "The second you step off the farm, I'll put you down."

"Donny," Ranger called out, still unsure how much of what he was saying was an act, "you'll do no such thing. Take the deal. Laura gets her boy back, and I'll finally be out of your hair."

Donny went to say something, but he stayed silent. Whether the words had been real or not, Ranger appreciated what Donny had promised. He needed to do his part and protect Laura and James. He needed to let Ranger complete this mission on his own.

Bill made the call. Rico would soon be on his way for the exchange.

CHAPTER 50
RICO

Rico Casias guided the kid out of the farmhouse and was on his way to a spare pickup he had parked down by the back entrance to the home. All the extra muscle Bill had requested to defend the farm had been paid for their time and dismissed. Bill had come up with an alternative way to protect the farm without the need to spark an all-out war.

Rico was relieved, to say the least. Sure, he'd equipped the farm with enough firepower to push back an attack from a dozen well-armed men, but the idea of open combat scared the hell out of him. He hadn't served in the military and had never been in a shoot-out. Rico was just a guy who had connections to decent military surplus and a whole host of illegal firearms and ammunition. He'd gotten involved in Bill's operation by chance and soon realized that once you were in, there was no way out.

How Bill had dreamed up his plan to appease the people in Tucson while stopping the attack on the farm was nothing short of genius. At least to Rico. It was clear why Bill was in charge. It was a shame his son lacked the same abilities.

Rico had heard the whispers around the farm about Bill's

son and his constant screw-ups. If William Wilkins ever took control of the operation, most of the guys would either walk away or attempt to take over the farm.

"Where's my mommy?" the boy asked for the third time.

"You'll see her soon, okay? Just come with me," Rico said as they continued to the pickup. He placed the boy into the back seat of the four-door vehicle.

It had been a long night, but Rico felt like he could finally breathe again. He didn't like the whispers that had passed around the farm. There had been plans to rush Bill and hog-tie him for delivery to the unhinged gangs in Tucson. But that all went away once Bill made his plans and phone calls. He'd found out all about the man named Frank Ranger and the fact that he was a wanted man. There had also been a thought to call in the US Marshals to pick Ranger up, but the farm didn't need that kind of heat. Instead, Bill had arranged what he'd arranged. Rico only hoped the people in Tucson didn't go back on the deal. It was in their best interest not to. Without Bill Wilkins and the farm, they'd lose a major supplier of methamphetamine. It left Rico to wonder if they had even been serious about the original hit or if it was a tactic to shake Bill's tree and see what fell out. Dallas did have a melodramatic reputation.

Once Rico had climbed into the driver's seat of the pickup, he checked the magazine on his Sig Sauer P320 and made sure the rounds were seated well. He peeked at the round in the chamber by racking the slide partway back and was satisfied with his inspection. He engaged the safety and reholstered the gun in his concealed-carry holster. The exchange Bill had planned could go south at any moment, and Rico wanted to be prepared for anything.

"Ready, kid?" Rico said to the rearview mirror.

The boy avoided his eyes and stared out the window, no doubt searching for his mamma.

"I get it," Rico said as he turned the ignition over. He entered the coordinates Bill had given him into the truck's GPS. "I'd rather be home with my family as well, but here we are." Rico got the journey underway as Bill radioed him again, checking in as agreed. Rico was also glad that he wouldn't be forced to go through with the messier side of Bill's contingency plan. He didn't have the stomach for killing on a good day and especially didn't want to murder some terrified kid. If push came to shove, he would have needed the help of one of Bill's hired psychos to do the deed. Even then, Rico wouldn't have taken part.

As the pickup moved away from the main area of the farm and onto a dirt track, a large bump in the road jostled the vehicle. "Damn potholes," Rico muttered. He hadn't been along the route Bill had ordered him to take. It led to a part of Bill's land that wasn't in use. The track was hard to make out and had several shrubs growing on it.

Rico followed the rise and fall of the path and checked in with Bill several times as he went. If Bill had done the impossible, then it meant he had Frank Ranger in his possession. Anyone else who was with him would be made to wait for the exchange to take place. Little did they know Bill was going to betray them the second Rico arrived. Rico had been ordered to shoot Donny Brown dead the instant he was distracted. Laura was to be left alive. She would be reunited with her boy, but what Bill had in store for her afterward would be far worse than a bullet in the head.

Rico let out his breath to steady his nerves. The things he'd heard about Donny Brown didn't fill him with confidence. The man had been a sniper in Afghanistan and then had killed countless people for Bill in the States. If Rico missed or screwed up the shot, he was certain Donny would return fire and drop him in a heartbeat. It left Rico wondering why Bill had chosen him, of all people, for this task.

Maybe it came down to loyalty. Bill was a good judge of character. He knew Rico wasn't the kind of man who would go against his employer. Especially one with a reputation like Bill's.

"I can do this," Rico said as he gripped the steering wheel tight.

A thump in the back of the pickup made Rico slow up. "What are you doing back there?" he asked the boy. The kid didn't answer and continued his mindless staring out the window. He was fidgeting with an empty bottle someone had left behind in the truck. He seemed to squeeze it for comfort. Rico figured he must have dropped it or knocked the glass against something solid.

Rico shook his head and sped back up. The noise was nothing worth stopping for. Not when Bill was relying on him to deliver. But a minute later, the same thump came again, only this time Rico was able to pinpoint it a lot easier. He swore it originated from the back. And it couldn't have been caused by the kid.

Rico brought the pickup to a stop and left the engine idling. "Why me?" he muttered as he exited the driver's seat and drew his pistol. He held the P320 with both hands as he approached the bed. That was where he'd noticed the commotion. He didn't expect anyone to be back there, given the truck had been stored away in the fleet by the shipping containers, but it wouldn't hurt to check.

He removed his support hand from the pistol and used it to lean on the bed so he could have a decent look. It was dark and hard to see into the space without a flashlight, but there was nothing there apart from some old rope and a fixed toolbox.

"Screw this," Rico said, giving up on the search. Whatever the disturbance had been was long gone or never there to begin with. Rico shoved his handgun away and turned to go back to the driver's seat. He heard the scuff of feet behind him and knew in that split second that he'd made a mistake. As Rico reached for his pistol again, whoever had been lurking around the back of the pickup buried a thick knife into his shoulder. He let out an almighty yell as the blade got pulled out of his body and stabbed back into him again.

Rico tried to run away, but his legs gave out from underneath him. He collapsed into a heap on the ground and felt a warm gush of blood flow from his body.

The coldness of the night air set in as Rico felt the world around him fade away. The last thing he saw before he died was the haze of his killer as they reached down and stole his P320. Once his vision had failed him, he listened as footsteps crunched over the dirt road, away from him. When he died, his attacker sped away in the pickup.

CHAPTER 51
BILL

When Bill checked in with Rico on his walkie, he got no response. At first, he wasn't worried, but after the third hail with no reply, a grumble of concern etched its way from the back of his mind. Without trying to draw too much attention to the problem, Bill drew his .357 Colt Python and leveled it at Ranger.

"Something wrong, Bill?" Donny asked with a wry smile as he reached a hand down to his sidearm. Bill kept his revolver trained on Ranger as he stared at Donny. "Nothing that concerns you. Just keep your hand off that pistol and stay where you are. We'll get this matter resolved."

Donny kept his hand open where it was, ready to draw on Bill.

Three feet in front of him sat the arsenal of weapons he and Ranger had brought along with them to the meet-up, including his ridiculous sniper rifle. Bill had permitted Donny to keep his sidearm on him as agreed but had insisted Laura be relieved of any weapons.

If Rico didn't answer his walkie soon, Bill was going to take action. Getting into a shoot-out with a couple of ex-military vets wouldn't go well. Even though Bill held the advantage, these men were fast and capable. Bill didn't dare move his aim away from Ranger, who was still kneeling in the dirt, facing Bill, with his hands on his head. He could take him out easily enough, but Donny would draw on him in a flash if that happened.

"Come in, Rico," Bill said over the walkie again. "Goddammit."

"Sounds like you got problems," Donny said.

"Shut your mouth," Bill groaned as he wrapped a finger around the trigger of his revolver. "Unless you want to see Ranger's brains splattered all over the desert."

"Take it easy. There's no need for this to turn ugly. We can still sort out this mess without killing each other."

Bill narrowed his gaze at Donny. He knew the man was trying to sell him a line. If Donny was given the slightest opportunity to attack, he would. Bill didn't enjoy the idea of dying on his own land at a meeting that had gone belly up, so he steadied his resolve and tried to think of a way out of the situation. "Lose the sidearm, or else."

"Not a chance. I do that, you'll kill me."

"Where's James?" Laura asked.

"He'll be here," Bill replied as Donny steadied her with some hushed words. Her Glock was sitting in the dirt a few feet in front of her. She kept eyeing it every couple of seconds.

Bill scanned the horizon for a beat to see if he could work out what was wrong. Rico would have been halfway to him the last time he checked in. He'd said he had the kid, so there was no way for Bill to give an order to any of his other people to go through with the grisly hell he'd promised Laura. He didn't want to see the boy slaughtered for no good reason, but if Bill was going to die, he wouldn't go quietly. James would suffer the consequences of his mother's actions. She was half the reason Junior was such a useless mess. Bill recog-

nized he should have done something about their relationship a long time ago.

"He's not coming," Ranger said from the dirt.

Bill glared down at him. "How would you know,
George?" Bill put extra emphasis on the last word, high-
lighting the fact that Ranger had lied to him about his name
when they first met.

"Something's gone wrong. We know it. You know it."

"Nothing's gone wrong. Any second now, a pickup is
going to arrive at this location."

"If you say so."

Bill resisted the urge he had to flip the revolver around
and smash Ranger in the skull with it the way he had done to
Junior. He sucked in the cool night air through gritted teeth
and blew out some of his rage. Ranger would get what was
coming to him soon enough. Bill just had to hold on until
Rico got his shit together and arrived. There had to be a
logical explanation for the delay.

Bill had chosen the man to deliver the kid for a reason. He
had proved his loyalty to the farm and to Bill and didn't seem
capable of betrayal. When Bill got one of his other men to
drop him off out at the supposed extraction point earlier, he'd
sat in the back seat with his pistol handy. It was the best way
to insulate himself from Dallas' offer.

A set of headlights appeared on the beaten track, coming
from the direction of the farm. "Ah. Here he is," Bill said.
"Right on schedule." With the distraction of Rico arriving, Bill
pointed his .357 at Donny. "Take out your sidearm and drop it
with the rest of your hardware."

"Not happening."

"Do you really want to test me?" Bill asked. He shifted his
aim to Laura's face. At that short distance, it would be impossible to miss, and Donny knew it.

"Do what he says," Ranger added.

Donny gave Bill a hardened stare with flared nostrils. "Fine. We'll do this your way." He gently took out his sidearm and tossed it into the dirt.

"Good lad. Now take ten steps back. Both of you."

Donny grabbed Laura by the elbow and guided her back. She seemed reluctant but did as instructed. She was still eyeballing the Glock.

Bill turned to the approaching pickup and was ready to tear Rico apart the second he got out of the vehicle. He'd need a damned fine reason for the screw-up. The man had almost caused the meeting to turn prematurely deadly.

The pickup came to a stop, but Rico didn't kill the engine or the lights. In fact, he had the high beams on and was half blinding Bill. Even Ranger was forced to squint.

"Shut off those lights, dammit," Bill called out as he left Ranger where he was and approached the pickup. Rico was asking for an ass-kicking now. Bill thought he was more of a professional than this and started to lose faith in him. Before Bill reached the driver's side door, the engine shut off, and the door opened in a hurry.

A blood-soaked figure emerged from the pickup with a handgun drawn. "Don't you fucking move," a familiar yet gravelly voice yelled.

Bill stopped in his tracks and squinted, keeping his Colt Python at his side. Within a second, he realized whom he was staring at. "Junior?"

"I told you not to call me that," William yelled. He paced toward Bill with fire in his eyes and what looked like Rico's Sig Sauer in his hands.

"Where's Rico?" Bill asked, keeping his voice stern.

"Dead. So is the asshole you sent to watch over me. But I did you a favor there, Pops. He was planning on dragging me down to Tucson for a nice payday. You've got some disloyal people in your crew."

"You're right," Bill said. "And you were right to kill Cade. He was an asshole. I shouldn't have trusted him to—"

"To what? Keep me prisoner?"

"I'm sorry," Bill said. There was nothing else he could say. He needed to tread lightly after putting his son through hell. He was never going to kill his son. He just wanted to break him down and rebuild him into a real man. That involved some pain and sacrifice.

"You're sorry?" William said with a frenzied chuckle. He released the pistol from one hand and held it sideways. "You're fucking sorry, are you? You killed my friends, old man."

"Son, I can explain." The .357 was still in Bill's hand.

William cackled to himself. "Oh, this should be good. Go on, tell me. What fucking reason did you have for murdering Roll and Mack in front of me?"

Bill closed his eyes and exhaled. He'd been so close to making things right again on the farm. And he was going to sort Junior out once he'd solved all his other setbacks. But his son had taken matters into his own hands and had obviously escaped the container. How he had killed Cade and Rico then arrived at the meeting was anyone's guess.

"James," Laura yelled as she approached the pickup.

"Not another step, bitch," William said to Laura, pointing the Sig Sauer at her. She came to a stop, but her eyes went on searching for her kid. She was providing a decent enough distraction. If she continued to piss off his son, Bill could do what needed doing. Something he should have done a long time ago.

He'd tried to get Junior involved in the operation at the farm, but the boy had no knack for the business. He was more focused on looking the part than doing the work. The boy wanted to take shortcuts wherever possible and thought the world owed him something. Bill knew it was time to put an end to his son's life. It was the only way forward.

"What have you done to him?" Laura yelled at William, her voice pitching high.

"Not a damn thing. He's in the back seat, silent as always."

"Give him to me."

William laughed again. "Not a fucking chance. No, you and I have some catching up to do. But I'll deal with you in a minute." He shifted his aim back to Bill, but then Ranger caught his eye. He was still kneeling in the dirt, taking it all in.

Junior sneered with glee. "What do we have here? If it isn't the piece of shit who started this whole mess. Looks like your luck's run out, huh?"

"We were about to make an exchange," Bill said. "James for the drifter. We can still do that and walk away."

"We're not going anywhere," William said. He swept his eyes over the scene and spotted Donny. "Shit. Even your sniper's in on it. The gang's all here."

Bill took a step forward. "I know the day has been difficult, son, but if you can work with me, we can pull through this in one piece and then talk about everything that's happened."

Junior closed his eyes for a second. When he opened them, they were boring down on his father like a diamond drill. "I will never forgive you for today. You slaughtered my friends while I sat there, helpless to stop it. Nothing you can say will ever make that right again."

Bill sighed. "I was afraid you'd say that. I'm sorry it's come to this."

"I'm not. This farm is mine. It was always going to be. You just didn't know it. Your time is up, old man."

It was Bill's turn to chuckle. "That's your problem right

there, Junior. You think just because we're family that I owe you the world."

"Don't call me that."

Bill ignored him. "The only thing I owe you is a bullet to the fucking head." Bill lunged forward with his .357 and squeezed the trigger.

CHAPTER 52

RANGER

Right as Bill went to squeeze the trigger and fire at his own son, Ranger decided he'd had enough of playing prisoner. He stood to run away from the exchange of bullets that was about to explode between the Wilkins men.

Ranger was used to the sound of gunfire, but when Bill fired his Colt Python at Liam, the eruption from the revolver was almost deafening. Ranger had been as close as any person could be to the conflict. He barely made it to his feet as Bill pulled the trigger, stopping him in his place.

Bill's shot went wide and struck the pickup Liam had arrived in. Liam squeezed his eyes shut from the sudden noise, but when he opened them, they were filled with indignation. Bill lowered his revolver for a moment as if he was overcome with guilt for the attempted murder of his own flesh and blood. A raw moment of silence filled the night air as the father and son stared at each other in shock.

Ranger stayed still but vigilant. He knew any sudden movement would make him a target for either Wilkins, and he was caught between them.

"You shot at me?" Liam asked as his features crumpled.

"Son, I didn't mean to—"

A blood-soaked Liam raised his pistol at his father and fired. Bill tried to shoot again, but he was too late. Liam got off three rounds. Two struck Bill in the chest, and the third went straight through his neck. Blood gurgled from his throat while two red circles grew in size on his chest and darkened. Bill collapsed backward into the dirt and dropped the Python to clutch at his neck with weakening arms. The old man would be dead within a minute.

Liam shifted his gaze to Ranger, who was already ducked down and bolting toward Liam. Ranger figured it was better to die charging at death than to cower away from it. Liam adjusted his aim away from his dying father to Ranger, using the space that existed between them. He fired three rounds and hit Ranger twice in the chest and once in his left arm, causing him to misstep and trip over. Ranger roiled around on the rough ground and sucked in hard for air. The vest had caught the two rounds to his chest, but the punch of the 9mm rounds and the shot to his arm took the wind out of his lungs.

"How does it feel, asshole?" Liam yelled to Ranger as he scampered in the dirt to get back up. Ranger didn't say a word. He was still fighting to regain control of his breathing, remembering his training. He held on tight to his bleeding wound. The round had gone clean through his bicep.

Liam stared around at Donny, who had charged at the weapons pile. "Back up, asshole. Unless you want some of this."

Donny stopped three feet from a rifle and held up his hands. "Okay," he said, backing away.

Liam's eyes shifted to Laura. "Looks like I found you, girl."

Laura didn't reply, and neither Ranger nor Donny said a word as Liam stepped between the three and leveled his pistol at each person, one after the other.

Behind Ranger, Bill Wilkins took his last bubbled gasp and died. Ranger knew the man was gone. He'd heard that sound before when someone caught a round in the neck. In those situations, there was nothing that could be done but apply pressure to the wound and watch as the person died.

"Why'd you do it, huh?" Liam asked Laura. "Back in the diner. Why did you side with this piece of crap?"

"Because you're a monster," Laura yelled. "Where is James?"

Liam threw a thumb over his shoulder. "Like I said, he's in the goddamn truck. Which is where you're going once I'm through killing these fucks. They can join the old man in the desert. Seems like as good a place as any for them to rot."

"Screw you," Laura yelled. Then she made things a lot more complicated and rushed toward the pickup.

Liam let out a roaring cackle as he cut Laura off and grabbed her with a spare arm. He took her by the hair and yanked hard. "Settle down, bitch."

Ranger tried to stand as a white fiery rage filled his insides.

"Uh-uh," Liam said, pointing the Sig Sauer at him. "Don't think I've forgotten about you. Stay there, friend."

Ranger continued to clutch at his bleeding arm and stared at Liam with flared nostrils. The first chance he got, he would kill Liam. He should have done so at the diner. Ranger had known back then that Liam Wilkins wasn't the kind of person who deserved to exist. The asshole thought it was okay to treat a woman like crap in front of the people she knew. Laura was nothing to Liam but property.

In the corner of Ranger's eye, Donny inched closer to the pile of guns. Ranger made sure not to draw attention to the fact. Donny was the only person not entirely in Liam's control.

"All right. Time for you to be reunited with your kid,"

Liam said to Laura. He dragged her toward the pickup, keeping his back away from Ranger and Donny. Laura kicked and yelled as Liam controlled her with the grip he had on the chunk of hair. He laughed and seemed to be enjoying himself.

"Fuck you," Laura screamed.

"That's it. Let it all out. Shout as loud as you want. No one's going to hear it."

Laura snarled her teeth and heaved her breath in and out. Her eyes were wide and only focused on Liam's smug face as he forced her backward toward the pickup. With an almighty yell, she drove her elbow into Liam's gut and was released from his grip. She spun around and kicked him in the groin, sending him to his knees. Before he responded, she bolted to the truck.

At the sight of Liam dropping to the dirt, both Ranger and Donny seized the only opportunity they'd get. Ranger rushed to his feet, then charged at Liam while Donny went for a gun. But both men weren't quick enough.

A single shot rang out, splashing the desert.

"Don't move," Liam shouted from the ground at Donny and Ranger as he darted the Sig Sauer between them. The two soldiers were still too far away to avoid getting shot, so they stopped. Ranger couldn't afford to take another hit. "What did I say? Away from the guns," Liam said to Donny. Donny grumbled and did what Liam wanted, taking three large paces back.

At any point in time, Liam could have shot and killed Ranger and Donny. Then he'd have Laura all to himself. Instead, he was letting his ego take control and was screwing around like a lion playing with its meal.

Laura had reached the truck on the driver's side and tried to open the rear passenger door, but it wouldn't budge.

"It's locked, bitch," Liam said, short on breath as he got to his feet again. "You can't be too careful these days." He kept the handgun trained on Ranger and Donny as he stepped backward toward Laura again, speaking to her over his shoulder. "Turn around."

"Fuck you," Laura replied.

Liam chuckled to himself. "Wrong answer." He fired the pistol next to her head, hitting the pickup.

"James," Laura yelled as she shuddered. James' muffled screams were audible inside the truck.

"He's fine. I shot nowhere near him. Now turn around. I can easily put the next one through the kid's face if you'd like."

Ranger and Donny took steps closer as Laura gave in and spun around. Liam didn't seem to notice this time as he fished out the pickup's keys from his pocket. He hit a button on the fob and unlocked the vehicle. He leered at the girl and moved closer to her. "Now, get in the fucking truck before I get mad."

She nodded. This time without a hint of disrespect. Ranger figured she just wanted to be with her son and would do whatever it took to reach him.

Laura opened the now unlocked door and climbed inside. She soothed James the second she could. "Shh, shh. It's okay. Mamma's here. I got you, baby."

"So touching," Liam said, feigning happiness as he faced Ranger and Donny. There were at least fifteen feet between them. And the weapons Bill had made them discard were out of reach. Liam aimed the Sig Sauer at the pair. "So, who wants it first? I got enough bullets for you both."

Ranger stepped forward, knowing what he needed to do. It wasn't a choice he took lightly, but it was the only thing he could think to do given how dire the situation had become. "Take me," he said. "Let everyone else go. I'm the one you want, right? I'm the asshole from the diner who embarrassed you."

"Shut the hell up. You don't give out the orders here. I'm in charge. You're on my fucking land on my fucking farm. You hear me?" Liam threw his arms out wide. "Everything you can see is mine, including the girl and her damn kid."

"Is that how that works?" Donny asked. "You kill the old man and what? It all just goes to you? You might wanna check the will first."

"Fuck you, Donny the sniper. The soldier who fought in the war. Well, I don't see what the fuss is all about. You're not so tough without a rifle in your hands."

Donny chuckled as he took a step closer. "You got me all worked out, pal."

Ranger realized Donny was trying to keep Liam talking. They just needed him to make a mistake. One last slip-up and they'd take their chance.

"You know what? I think Donny just volunteered to be first. Why don't you come here and—"

Liam never saw Laura coming as she charged at him with nothing but a glass bottle in her hands. She let out a loud yell as she swung the bottle at Liam's head. Unfortunately, her yelling gave Liam a split second to react. He twisted enough that the bottle only grazed him and didn't even break.

The second the bottle clipped Liam's head, Donny and Ranger charged. Ranger was closer and reached down to his concealed belt-buckle knife. He yanked out the blade in a hurry with his right hand and looped the buckle over his middle finger, making a bladed fist. He roared at Liam and threw a punch toward his chest when he was within range. Liam twisted again and caught the knife in his shoulder.

"Fuck," Liam yelped. As the blade came back out of him, he started blindly firing the Sig Sauer. Ranger rolled out of the way and dropped behind the front of the pickup, still clutching the knife, while Donny scattered and ran out into the darkness of the desert.

Liam stopped firing and clutched his shoulder, regaining control of himself. He grabbed a stunned Laura before she attempted to follow up on her attack, seizing her again by the hair. Before Ranger and Donny could return to the fight, Liam shoved Laura back toward the truck and threw her inside the open door. He slammed it shut and rushed to jump in behind the wheel of the vehicle.

Liam started the truck and revved the engine hard. Ranger got out of the way as Liam sped away and did a sweeping U-turn, almost running Donny over off the beaten path.

"Donny!" Ranger yelled as he recovered. "Get to your truck."

Donny understood and made a run for his pickup. Ranger then bolted after Liam.

"Faster," Ranger huffed to himself as he ran after Liam's vehicle as fast as his legs would carry him. The pickup got caught out in the ruts and divots that plagued the land where no track existed. Liam probably didn't know this part of the farm very well and had no doubt spent his whole life staying close to the house.

Ranger dug deep and ignored the throbbing pain in his arm and chest. He bolted after the pickup and came within five feet of the open bed as Liam gained traction. Laura and James both screamed inside the truck as Liam waved the gun around. Then the psycho started firing on Ranger through the back window.

Safety glass and bullets whizzed by Ranger as he continued to run. He leaped onto the bed and landed rough. The belt-buckle knife on his finger slipped free and skidded out of his control somewhere in the bed.

Liam twisted toward Ranger and shot wildly in his direction. His attempts went high, low, and wide, damaging the pickup more than anything else. But at the same time, he was endangering Laura's and James' lives.

Ranger scampered along the bed of the pickup and flashed a glance back at Donny. He could just make out the sight of him rushing out in the dark toward his truck. With any hope, the paranoid bastard would have a backup sniper rifle stored away he could use to take out Liam. Otherwise, it was down to a wounded Ranger to prevent Liam from killing someone else.

Liam continued to fire and shot around Ranger as the pickup bounced over another hole. The madman wasn't driving in any particular direction now that Ranger was on board. Instead, he was driving in circles, as if he wanted to shake Ranger free.

"Fuck you," Liam shouted as he continued to gun the engine. He straightened the wheel for a moment, then lined up a shot on Ranger. One that would be hard to miss. He squeezed the trigger, but all that came out was a click. He hadn't realized that the slide was locked back and that the magazine was empty.

Liam yelled and threw the empty pistol at Ranger. It dropped short and bounced around in the bed while Ranger grabbed James with his good arm and hauled him through the destroyed back window to the bed. Laura climbed through on her own as Liam continued to moan and shout absurdities at anyone who was listening.

"No, you don't," Liam yelled as he snatched Laura's foot in one hand while trying to keep the truck straight on the rough surface.

Ranger pulled James to the side and tried to fit through the gap to claw Laura's leg free, but there wasn't enough space. It didn't matter in the end. She pushed herself into the air with both hands and kicked Liam with her spare foot. He shouted in pain, letting go. Ranger dragged her the rest of the way through as Liam yanked the wheel hard to the right.

Ranger scooped up James and made sure the frightened child saw his face. "Are you ready to be brave?"

James didn't say a word, but he nodded. Ranger wasn't sure if he understood what was about to happen, but it didn't matter. He held James tight as he and Laura rolled out of the pickup and landed hard in the dirt and gravel. Ranger spiraled a few times but protected James with everything he had left in him. Laura flattened out by their side and recovered a lot faster.

Liam continued to shout and protest, but he didn't stop the truck. He had to have known the fight was lost. Ranger or Donny would soon recover their weapons and end his life if he stuck around.

"Let's go," Ranger muttered as he hobbled with James toward Donny's pickup. But behind them, Liam took a sweeping turn and came to a stop. He lined up Ranger, Laura, and James with his headlamps and revved the engine.

"Shit," Ranger let out. "Run."

The stupid son of a bitch was going to mow them down before anyone had time to stop him. Ranger realized he should have gone for his rifle before charging after Liam, but he had been too worried about shooting Laura and James by accident. All he could do now was to push them out of the way when Liam got close enough and pray they'd find a way to stop him.

Ranger heard the loud engine whining in the dark and was ready to meet his end, but a few seconds later, the sky lit up with a bright blaze. He fell over with James in his grasp and Laura by his side. When he turned around, he saw Liam's pickup turn into a flaming wreck.

When Ranger scanned the area, he spotted Donny standing on the roof of his pickup. He'd fired a rocket from the Mk 153 SMAW. Ranger didn't see where it landed but had heard and felt the explosion. The round must have hit the truck's gas tank given how big the fireball had grown. There was no way the spoiled psycho son of a dead narcotics distributor would have survived.

"Holy shit," Laura said as she stared at the flames. Donny reloaded the weapon and followed up his shot with a second hit, causing them all to flinch as another explosion rocked the open land. James held his mother tight but didn't look away.

"Is the bad man dead, Mamma?" James asked. Ranger had hardly heard two words from the kid.

"Yeah, baby. He's gone."

Ranger stood on shaky feet and clutched his wound while the pickup's fire raged on. Only the frame of the vehicle was visible in the raging flame. He stared into the light and felt mesmerized by it. It wasn't until Donny grabbed him by his good arm and guided him away that he closed his eyes.

"Come on, Ranger. We have to go. Those explosions would have carried loud booms across the whole town. The police will be here soon enough. You don't wanna be around when that happens."

Ranger nodded as Donny carted him along to their ride with Laura and James at their side. He collapsed into the bed and watched as Donny made sure everyone was okay. He rushed to collect as much of their dropped weapons and gear as he could carry. Provided none of it was left behind, the police would have fewer chances to work out who had been there, causing all the chaos.

"All right," Donny said as he got behind the wheel and put the truck into gear. He started the long process of getting them the hell away from the carnage. Ranger closed his eyes as he was rocked side to side on the bumpy land and couldn't resist falling asleep.

CHAPTER 53

When Ranger woke up, he was back at Donny's safe house, resting on a sofa. It was the clean safe house, the one with the high ceilings that had been built inside a large shed. He had no memory of how he'd gotten there, and when he glanced down at his wounded arm, he realized it had been treated and wrapped in gauze.

"You're awake," Donny said when he walked into the open room.

"Apparently. How long was I out?"

Donny glanced at the watch on his wrist. "About twelve hours."

Ranger's eyes went wide. "Twelve hours? What the hell? Where are Laura and James?"

"It's okay. Everything's fine. They're in my room, resting. The kid was also pretty exhausted from the night, so he's been sleeping. He's probably awake by now, but I'm guessing he and Laura need some space."

Ranger pushed himself upright and stared at Donny. This was the man he knew. The one who cared about other people.

Ranger only wished he had found him sooner. At least before Bill Wilkins had gotten his talons into him.

"How do you feel?" Donny asked.

Ranger cleared his throat and rubbed at the pounding headache he had. There was a bottle of water beside the sofa. He snatched it up and twisted open the lid, taking a hefty gulp of the liquid the second he could. "Thirsty. Have the cops come knocking?"

"No. But it's only a matter of time before they find us. The Wilkins boys are dead, and word travels fast. That means a bunch of cops just lost their monthly bribes and will have to do their jobs for a change. There's no way people around town didn't hear those explosions. It wouldn't surprise me if the farm got raided."

Ranger shuffled forward to the edge of the sofa and gazed down at his feet. His boots were off, but he was still wearing his dusty jeans. He'd only been in Namrena for one day, but it had been an intense time. So much had happened in the space of twenty-four hours. People had died. Fortunately, most of the body count consisted of folks who didn't deserve to live in the first place, but there had been an innocent death among the chaos. Rosie's undeserved murder would stay with him for a long time. Donny might have pulled the trigger, but Ranger had put her in an impossible situation to begin with. When Ranger looked at Donny, he knew his friend was suffering from the same guilt.

"What's the plan?" Ranger asked.

Donny shrugged. "There's nothing for me here, so I'm gonna hit the road. See where it takes me. How about you?"

Ranger stood on heavy legs and took a moment to stretch. "Well, normally, I would say it's time for me to keep moving, and my instinct would be to head south."

"But now?"

"Now, I need to do something I should have done the second I escaped prison."

Donny moved farther into the room and stood closer to Ranger. "You're heading home?"

"I think so. But I can't just go back to Montana and hope for the best. I need to investigate Kaitlyn's murder from a distance and build up a case to prove to the police that it wasn't me. It's the only chance I've got to find my way home back to Cindy before it's too late."

Donny smiled. "You never did know when to quit."

"I've heard I can be a real pain in the ass."

The two men chuckled as Laura came into the room. She had her arms folded over her chest and looked like she could take a long nap. No doubt she had been stressing out over her son for the entire twelve hours Ranger had been unconscious, and hadn't slept.

"Sorry if we disturbed you," Ranger said.

She waved him off. "James is out like a light. I think he will be for another few hours at least."

"He deserves a good rest," Donny said. "You guys can stay here as long as you like."

"Thank you," Laura said, avoiding Donny's eyes. There was still a hatred present that wasn't going away anytime soon, if ever. Ranger understood. Donny had done something that no amount of hospitality could ever undo.

"Now, Ranger," Donny continued, "I wouldn't recommend you hang around here. Unfortunately, I've heard through the grapevine that your name is spreading around town. It won't be long before it reaches the police."

Ranger exhaled. He knew as much. He had a bit of cash in his rucksack, but it had been lost in the chaos. It would be too risky to go looking for it, so Ranger decided he would be better off starting fresh and finding some work along the way.

"I'd best be off, then," Ranger said.

"Just like that?" Laura asked.

"I'm sorry, but Donny's right. I can't stay here. After the hell we raised saving James last night, the authorities will sniff around. My name is on several lists. Plus, there are people out there who I'm sure would give anything to find me."

Laura stepped farther into the room and moved up to Ranger while avoiding his eyes. She opened her arms and gave him a hug. "Thank you. For everything. You may have kicked the hornets' nest ten times over while you were here, but you freed me from Liam and Bill. I only wish that…"

Laura trailed off, and Ranger knew why. "She was a good friend," he said. "I'm sorry that…I'm sorry."

Donny scratched the back of his head and stared at the ground. There was a look of remorse in his eyes that Ranger knew he would never be free from again.

Laura stepped back from the hug and sniffed. She wiped away a tear with her sleeve and folded her arms back over her chest.

"What will you and James do?" Ranger asked.

She also shrugged. "I don't know. With Rosie gone, I don't have a job to go to. This all happened so fast."

"I have a solution for you," Donny said. "Give me a second." He left the room, leaving Ranger and Laura confused. When he came back, he had a brown paper bag with him that was full to the brim with something. He handed the bag to Laura. "Here. Take it."

"What is it?"

"Just take it."

Laura let out a hesitant arm and took the package. She opened the bag to peek, and Ranger saw what was inside: thick wads of cash.

"No, I can't take this," she said, handing it back.

"Yes, you can. You and James can go anywhere with this money. Maybe even leave this state and start over somewhere new."

"I don't want to take your dirty blood money."

"It's not blood money. It's ten grand in cash from my Marines pension. It's clean."

"Okay," Laura said, pulling the money back. She rifled through the notes again. "This doesn't make us square, though. No amount of money will ever make up for what you did to Rosie."

"I know. Believe me, I do. You may not believe me, but I'll never forget what I did to Rosie. Ever. But I'll sleep easier tonight knowing you and your boy have the means to get out of this place. God knows it's taken enough from you."

Laura didn't respond and continued to stare at the money as if lost in thought. After a long while, her eyes watered. When she glanced up at Donny, she delivered her words in a calm, even tone. "After we leave, if I ever see you again, I'll kill you." She vanished from the room with the money in hand and didn't look back.

"Wow," was all Ranger could say.

"Yep. She's a firecracker, that one," Donny said.

"No kidding. You think she'll do it?"

"What? Kill me? Without a doubt."

The two men shared a chuckle until a quiet settled over the room.

"Now for you, Frank," Donny said. He left the room again and returned with a similarly sized brown paper bag. "Here," he said, tossing the package to Ranger. "Ten grand. Clean money, blah, blah, blah. Not enough to take you back home, but it's a start."

Ranger inspected the bag and found more money than he'd had in his possession for a long time. "Thank you, Donny. This will go a long way."

"I hope it does. I have something else for you." Donny held up a cell phone. A cheap-looking one. He tossed it to Ranger.

"A phone?"

"A burner. Don't use it for your day-to-day activity. Keep it aside. It's got one number programmed into it. One that will get to me if you ever need help with something. Day or night, I'll answer."

Ranger took the phone and put it in his pocket. "I'll remember that next time I need a sniper who doesn't mind shooting rockets at trucks in the desert."

"Hey, I knew you guys were clear. Well, clear enough. Besides, I had to take that son of a bitch out somehow. If he ran you down, he would have then gone after Laura and the kid."

"James."

Donny chuckled and gave Ranger a light punch on his good arm. "I know his name, you jackass."

Ranger smiled. "Just yanking your chain. Well, I'd better get moving. There's something like thirteen hundred miles between here and home. Not to mention a lot of law."

"About that. I got a guy up in Phoenix who can help you out with something."

Ranger shook his head. "This should be good."

"It is. He specializes in fake IDs. Specifically, passports. For about half of your money, he can help make the journey a little easier. All you need to do is keep your head down and the cops won't find you. Here are his details. He runs a legit business in Phoenix alongside the passport operation."

Donny handed him a business card. Ranger took it and checked it over. It was for a photography supply store. "You sure know some shady people," Ranger said.

"Ain't that the truth." Donny chuckled, tapping Ranger

again on the arm. "Come on, I'll get you some food and water for the road. Maybe a new rucksack."

Ranger followed Donny as he showed him to the rucksack and supplies. Donny had known Ranger would need to move out of town in a hurry, so he'd helped in every way possible.

Once Ranger was packed, he took a shower and shaved his beard. He also used the same electric clippers and gave himself a buzz cut. As the hair all fell away, he saw his old self in the mirror. Behind his broken eyes, he found the man who would do what it took to go back home and make things right.

Ranger got dressed in some fresh clothing Donny had given him and said his goodbyes to Laura and James. He even offered a hand for James to shake. The kid accepted with a gentle grip and gave Ranger a smile. All Ranger could think about when he stared into the kid's eyes was the daughter he had lost precious time with. He vowed then and there he would do whatever it took to be reunited with Cindy. He owed her that much.

"Are you sure I can't give you a lift, Frank?" Donny asked.

"No, it's okay. I'll find my way."

"See that you do. Maybe we'll cross paths again someday."

Ranger thought over their shared past. The battles they'd fought in, the men they'd lost, and now the mayhem they'd experienced in Namrena and the devastation caused. It was a lot to take in. A piece of Ranger wanted to never come across Donny Brown ever again. But for the most part, Ranger had enjoyed fighting alongside his old friend again. "If we cross paths," Ranger said, "I hope it's to meet up for a beer and nothing else."

"That would be nice." Donny chuckled.

The two men shook hands and then pulled each other in

for a hug. They slapped backs and laughed. Donny walked Ranger to the door to show him out.

"Take care, Frank. And stay out of trouble. I mean it."

"I'll try. No promises, though."

Donny expelled a heavy breath and smiled. "I don't know why I bother."

Ranger gave Donny a nod and faced the right direction. He found his way to the dusty road and continued. He pulled an old map from his pocket and studied the roads. This time, he wasn't headed south and away from his problems. He was starting the journey to Montana. What would happen to him along the way was anyone's guess.

Clipped to Ranger's map was the worn photo of Kaitlyn and Cindy. The last day had crinkled it more than the previous year alone, but Ranger would no longer cling to this last dying connection he had to his family. He was going to take the long way home and solve his wife's murder. Then it would be safe for him to see Cindy again and pick up where he'd left off. He didn't know how he would make up for all the lost time, but he'd do his best.

Ranger thought about the four guys from his squad who were still alive and the possibility that they had a connection to the man in the suit or what the bastard had done to his family. They say revenge is a fool's game, but if Ranger ever found them or that slimy killer again, he would take his time and rip apart those responsible for the death of his wife, piece by piece.

With only a rough idea of what roads to take, Ranger tucked the map away and put his head down. He was heading north, and soon, Namrena would all be behind him, gone from his eyes, but not forgotten.

CHAPTER 54
THREE DAYS LATER

Deputy US Marshal Dane Briggs rolled into the dusty town of Namrena in his unmarked Ford Taurus Interceptor after spending twenty hours on the road from Billings, Montana. As soon as he arrived, he didn't head to the local diner or stop off at a gas station to stretch his legs. He went straight to his intended destination: Wilkins Farms.

Dane had received word from the US Marshals' office in Tucson about a ruckus going on down on the farm. There had been several explosions and gunfire that had reached the ears of the locals. Police were dispatched and had discovered the bodies of Bill and William Wilkins, along with several others. Consequently, the police also found what was being deemed as one of the biggest drug busts in Arizona in the last twenty years. According to the reports Dane had read, the farm was nothing but a front for an underground methamphetamine lab that had been supplying a large chunk of narcotics to Tucson and the surrounding areas. The farm was now crawling with Drug Enforcement Administration agents, who were scouring every inch of the farm to better understand the operation that had been in full swing until a few nights ago.

Dane didn't care about any of that. He was only after one thing. In the search at the farm, one name continued to spring up from those who had been arrested at the site: Frank Ranger.

Dane had spent a year chasing down the ghost who was his sister's husband. The man he believed to be responsible for her death. Dane had alerted every US Marshals' office in the country to contact him if the name Frank Ranger ever came up in any investigation or local jurisdiction. He'd been given the activity of people named Frank Ranger many times before, but they had always been false leads. They weren't the Frank he so desperately wanted to bring to justice.

Dane had opted to drive from the offices in Billings, Montana, all the way down to Arizona to give himself some time to think. He knew Frank would be in the wind by the time he arrived, but he wanted to get into the headspace of a desperate man who had somehow gotten himself involved in the world of illegal narcotics and a shoot-out between scumbags in Arizona.

"What were you doing here, Frank?" Dane asked himself as he reached the gate to the farm. He ran a hand through his graying stubble and thought about the man he had known for years. The one who would have never been associated with anyone working in a meth lab. Dane had respected the hell out of Frank. But then the man had lost his mind and murdered Kaitlyn. The experience left Dane questioning every person he'd ever known. He came to the conclusion that you truly didn't know what anyone was capable of.

Ranger's own daughter, an innocent angel in all the chaos, had been living with Kaitlyn's and Dane's mother, Victoria, for the past fifteen months. But only three months ago, Victoria had passed unexpectedly in her sleep, leaving young Cindy in the care of Dane and his wife. The poor girl had already had her life uprooted the day Kaitlyn had been butchered by her own father. Now she'd had to move from Helena down to Billings. Fortunately, Dane's two daughters were a similar age and had done a fine job of welcoming her into the Briggs household.

Armed DEA agents were covering the gate at Wilkins Farm and immediately stopped Dane's vehicle as he approached. He held his badge out a rolled-down window to identify himself.

"Deputy US Marshal Dane Briggs. I'd like to take a look around the area." Dane raised the brim of his cattleman crease cowboy hat so the agents could stare into his eyes and know he was on the level.

One agent stepped forward. He was holding a Remington 870 shotgun loosely in hand, leaning the barrel against his shoulder, almost as a show of force.

"What business does the Marshals' Office have with a drug bust? There are no fugitives here. All the arrested assholes have been sent down to Tucson."

"I'm not after any of them. I'm looking for a man who was here before the bust was made."

The agents shared a look. Dane had seen it before. They were weighing up how much information they would share with this outsider. There was some fierce competition between the different agencies, especially when it came time to make a major bust.

The shotgun-wielding agent spoke again. "We can't let you in here to 'look around.' Our boss wants to see some heavy sentences carried down from this operation. We can't risk letting in some yahoo to compromise everything."

Dane pursed his lips. "I get it, fellas. You think I'm an outsider trying to muscle in on your bust? Tell me something, though. Are you boys from around here?"

"Yeah. Tucson. What of it?"

"Oh, it's probably nothing. But I'd be willing to bet my

last dollar y'all were aware of this farm long before the explosions. Hell, I'd say it was on your radar."

The agent with the Remington 870 lowered the shotgun down to both of his hands. "What the hell are you saying?"

"Nothing. Not a thing. Only, it'd be real interesting to see who knew what and when about old Wilkins Farms. Maybe I should ask around town. Get the lowdown from the locals who've had to put up with this shit for God knows how long."

Dane slid the Ford Taurus into reverse and wrapped an arm over the back of the front passenger seat, making a show of his exit.

"Wait, wait," the agent said. "There's no need for that. You'll spook our CIs. Word around town is that this bust is just the beginning. It could lead us to some serious players down south."

"Sounds about right. I take it you don't want someone like me sniffing around town asking the wrong questions?"

"No."

"Then I suppose we're at an impasse. Unless, of course, you can give me a few hours to look around the farm. I won't touch anything. I swear. What I'm after is information. Pure and simple. You see, I'm hunting down a man who butchered his own wife in cold blood. Can you imagine that? Bastard even tried to take his own life after the fact. Then, when he was handed down a life sentence, he escaped police custody. He's not the kind of man who's safe to be in public."

The agent nodded with a narrowed gaze. "This guy got a name?"

Dane chuckled and stared forward. "You bet your ass he does. Frank Ranger. Disgraced ex-sergeant of the US Marines." Dane emphasized the word "ex," knowing the ramifications it held.

"Jesus," the agent said as if the name held some significance. "All right. You can go in. But you've got one hour. We'll be watching your every step, so don't pull any shit. Got it?"

Dane held his dead stare ahead into the farm. He tipped the brim of his cattleman crease and said, "Thank you kindly." The gate was opened, and Dane was given passage into Wilkins Farms.

He parked his Ford Taurus Interceptor and got to work. It was only a matter of time before he found the breadcrumb he'd need to pick up the trail on Frank Ranger. In his experience, the police always missed something vital. And Ranger would be considered a low priority with the DEA kicking around. The details he needed would only be noticed by someone in the US Marshals office.

"I'm coming for you, Frank," Dane said. And when he found Ranger, he wasn't going to haul him in just so the man could escape custody again. He was going to put the man he once loved like a brother in the ground where he belonged.

<<<<>>>>

ABOUT THE AUTHOR

Did you enjoy *Bullet Proof*? Please consider leaving a review on Amazon to help other readers discover the book.

Joshua Harkin is an action thriller author based in a town just outside Melbourne, Australia. With twelve years of writing experience, he has previously had psychological thrillers published under a pen name. A lifelong fan of action thrillers, Joshua channels his passion for the genre into crafting gripping stories filled with suspense and intensity. When he's not writing or devouring the latest thrillers, he enjoys quality time with his wife and kids. He also has a background in animation and IT, adding both a creative and technical edge to his storytelling.

https://joshuaharkin.com/

ALSO BY JOSHUA HARKIN